I0563214

Hung Over with Grandma
Awarded First Place Best Women's Fiction
2017 Feather Quill Book Awards

Tales of Stella and Jonas
Second of Series

Hung *Over* with *Grandma*, the second novel by West Virginian Becky Hatcher Crabtree, continues the story of an independent spirit, Stella, and Jonas, her Inupiaq man.

"Wow! Becky Crabtree has done it again with *Hungover with Grandma!* Yes, Stella and Jonas got married, but the end of the ceremony is just the beginning of a huge surprise as the newlyweds honeymoon in the cold, dark winter of Barrow, Alaska. Meet Mary Jo, Stella's new mother-in-law, and her sister Phoebe, two irresistible Inupiat elders who will delight you as they take on the wicked Timmy Lee who is out for revenge.

"This is a fast-paced book that takes the reader from West Virginia to Alaska and back again. *Hung Over with Grandma* is a thriller read and a love story on many levels. The reader will get a glimpse into life in the Arctic and the bumps and triumphs of a new family bonding. Crabtree continues to write with insight, clarity, and satisfying humor."

Jay St. Vincent, Associate Professor (Retired)
Ilisagvik College, Barrow, Alaska

"Another page-turner, *Hung Over with Grandma* introduces two delightful new characters who will find their way into your hearts, much like the main character Stella and her soon-to-be husband Jonas. This story elicits a wide variety of emotions, but will keep you chuckling and shaking your head throughout."

Vanni Prichard,Director of Assessment and Accountability (Retired), North Slope
Borough School District, Barrow, Alaska

Hung Over with Grandma

Becky Hatcher Crabtree

Library of Congress Control Number: 2016957467

ISBN 978-1-888215-63-2 (Paperback)
eBook ISBN 978-1-888215-61-8 (Kindle edition)
eBook ISBN 978-1-888215-62-5 (ePub edition)

Book design: Connie Taylor, Fathom Publishing Company

Thanks to the State of West Virginia and the WV Department of Transportation for the highway map used for the cover background.

While the places in this work of fiction may be real or based on real locations, the persons and activities depicted are entirely fictional, are based solely on the author's wild, free-ranging imagination and any resemblance to persons living or dead is purely coincidental. In other words, the author has spun a yarn based on a pack of lies. There's not a word of truth in it.

Fathom Publishing Company
PO Box 200448
Anchorage, AK 99520
www.beckycrabtree.com

Dedication

This book is dedicated to

those who suffer from forms of dementia

such as Alzheimer's Disease

and to those who love them.

In memory of my mother

Rachel Illene Brooks Hatcher.

Table of Contents

Acknowledgments

As Stella and Jonas probably know, the Beatles song lyric reads, "I get by with a little help from my friends." In this case, I got by with a lot of help from lots of friends.

First, I thank readers who have shared their thoughts on my preceding book, *Drunk on Peace and Quiet.* Their kind words have sustained me through some long nights.

My brother's dog Roxie had pups. Evan Beasley got a pup and named her Riley. She's a good dog and you'll meet her in this story. Thank you, Evan, for suggesting she join the characters.

Many have shared stories of their loved one and the situations caused by dementia and Alzheimer's disease, most notably Donna Musick.

Sandro Jankovic provided information about evidence of lug nut tampering along with other law enforcement procedures. Greg Gordon shared conditions at Pelican State Prison in California, where he was employed (not incarcerated!). It was fun to hear his stories of inmate behavior. Jeff Greer and Phillip Wickline, real-life Monroe County deputies, answered my questions about police protocol at the scene of a wreck. Jesse Beasley shared the first hand sights and sounds of driving with loosened lug nuts.

Samantha Sizemore edited the manuscript (fast!). So did Vanni Prichard. Vanni also contributed photographs of Barrow, Alaska, and her opinion in a blurb. Thank you both for being the detail-oriented women that you are.

Ethel Burke messaged correct Inupiat spellings and meanings regularly across the miles between Atqasuk, Alaska and West Virginia, and Steve Culbertson proofread and corrected the Inupiat-Appalachian glossary.

Friends on the North Slope offered up their personal shots of Arctic scenery: Molly and Jack Ahkivgak, Bridgette Ahgivgak, Nasuk Ahyakak, Linda Akootchook, Doug Armstrong, Daisy Edwardson, Yvonne Fonua, Jessica Itta, Megan Kalayauk, Frederick Joseph Kanayurak, Selene Leavitt, Olive Nungasuk, Linda Stanford, Phoebe Kippi, and Donald Zanoff. The photos made me a little homesick for the North Slope, then your sweet generosity made me a lot more homesick.

Special thanks are extended to my dear friends and colleagues, Aimee Romeijn and Gary Boen. They were kind enough to walk around in Barrow's cold temperatures to take beautiful photos on request to help tell this story. I owe you!

Connie Taylor of Fathom Publishing amazes me with her never-ending patience, energy, and supply of professional advice. She has given me opportunities to share my books beyond even my daydreams and solves technical problems that rattle my mind. When I see "Keep Calm" posters, I think of her.

My friendship with Merri Hess has survived three decades and shows no signs of fading. She brings out the best in me and saves me thousands of dollars that a therapist could have earned by listening to all my drama. She encourages me to write when I lose my way and helps me say "no" to things that take me away from writing and other important things. Thank you, Ms. Hess.

My teacher and my friend, Jay St. Vincent, shares her love of words with me even though I don't get the punctuation rules quite yet. She fixes mistakes in my manuscripts and steers me to better writing and clearer thinking. I would have never written a book, much less three, without her guidance.

Finally, Roger Crabtree deserves great praise. He does all the things that I forget to do when I'm writing. It's a long list. Thank you, sweet baby!

Becky Hatcher Crabtree
November 2016

Inupiat Glossary

Aaka – Mother/Grandmother

Aarigaa – Good! Oh, how nice!

AC bag – Grocery bag, poke

Alappaa – It's cold

Aluuttaġaaq – Caribou meat with gravy and rice

Anaq – Poop/feces

Any much – Unlimited

Araa/Azaa – Oh, my!

Aqpik – Yellow berry that grows close to the ground,
    salmon berry, cloudberry

Atchu – I don't know

Inupiat – Plural of Inupiaq, members of the group of northern
    Eskimo people, also refers to their language

Ii – Yes (pronounced ee)

Mukluks – Boots

Nanuuq – Bear

Qanitchat – Foyer, entranceway

Quyanaqpak – Big thank you

Sigaaq – Cigarette

Siksrik – Ground squirrel

Suaktuq – He or she scolds

Tiipak – Prissy/flirty

Tunik – Slang for Caucasian person

Tuttu – Caribou

Utqiagvik – Place of the snowy owls (Barrow, Alaska)

Uutukuu – Little bitty

Uvlaalluataq – Good morning

Chapter 1

I'm Gettin' Hitched!

Stella

"Shoo, y'all get on out of here." Even if I am a 57-year-old bride, I need a moment of peace and quiet before the wedding, I laughingly realized as the Sunday School classroom door was pushed shut by the last giggling bridesmaid. I could hear the songs from the iTunes mix that Jonas and I had chosen for the pre-wedding and knew it was nearing the end of music and time to start my walk down the aisle.

I needed just a minute more to talk to my best friend Anna, dead since last summer. Both her daughters were bridesmaids and I hoped her spirit was here, too. I bowed my head, closed my eyes, and spoke aloud, "Oh, Anna, I'm gettin' hitched! You know Jonas is THE one, the love of my life … I so wish you were here with me." I cleared my throat and changed my tone. "Dear Lord, take care of her. And if it's not too much trouble, take care of my brother, Timmy Lee, too, and keep him locked up in the mental institution for as long as you can. And help me to be a good wife and friend to Jonas. Thank you, Lord, for this day, a weddin' day I never thought I'd have. Amen."

There was a soft tapping at the hollow door and one of Tisha's big eyes filled the crack of space as the door inched open. "Stella!" she hissed. "It is almost time. Jonas is getting antsy standing up front and the girls are ready to go."

I didn't say a word. My creamy velveteen dress fell into place as I stood. It was too fancy for an old country woman like me, but was plain compared to the frilly things that Tisha and Eliza pushed on me at the dress shop. It was fitted and

1

Chapter 1

beaded up top and hung straight down from my armpits and covered my knobby knees. Having friends with sense enough to dress me and put together a wedding on short notice during the holidays sure was a great thing. Plus, the church was already decorated with battery-powered candles and fresh cut evergreens and pinecones in every window and wreaths on all the doors with fresh new bows courtesy of Tisha. A Christmas tree twinkled on one side of the sanctuary and a nativity rested on the altar between two poinsettias.

It was quiet in the sanctuary now. I knew it was time. Time to get this show on the road. At the last minute, I unpinned the short veil. It felt silly to wear a veil. I wanted Jonas to see me, to know me, well, except for that one secret, until I got up my nerve. I stuck my head out the door trying not to tear up my new upswept hairdo and gave Tisha a thumbs up. She quit wringing her hands and scurried to the sanctuary entrance to signal to the piano player who started playing a wordless version of Jonas' favorite Beatles' song, "Hey, Jude," as the processional. I studied my little bouquet of baby's breath, mistletoe, and red roses as Tisha got everyone lined up and heading in the right direction. The bridesmaids and the ring bearer disappeared through the door of the sanctuary. Then it was just the flower girl who entered the aisle. She was tossing poinsettia petals and trying to catch them in her mouth. Weren't they poisonous? If her mother had not been busy being a bridesmaid up front, she would have swatted that child. Eliza was in the sanctuary and she knelt down to talk to her, and the little girl nodded, refocused, and marched towards the center aisle, tossing petals by the handfuls as soon as she entered. A few seconds of oohs and aahs and it was my turn. Tish was motioning wildly and mouthing, "Where's the veil?" silently. I stuck my tongue out at her.

No one was "giving me away." I thought of my father, dead since I was in third grade, and my crazy brother, Timmy Lee. Even if Daddy had been there or Timmy Lee had been sane, I would have balked on being escorted. I was giving myself to Jonas, as much as I could anyway. The piano player came down hard on the opening chords of "Here Comes the Bride" and I gulped my courage back down before it got away. Tish looked at me with questioning eyes and I grinned and nodded. She rolled her eyes and I thought I saw a tear. I filed that image away to enjoy later; my tough friend getting emotional, probably over that dang veil.

I stopped at the back of the church and the guests stood in a rustle of fabrics and a fragrant breeze of flowers and pinecones. For a second I had the urge to cover my heart as if the national anthem was coming next, but every eye was on me. Can this be happening? This must be the way that a queen feels. Then again, I might not be queen material. My next urge was to wave. Fought that off, too, but I could feel my grin widening as I made eye contact with church friends and business friends and a whole crew of men that worked with Jonas at the Celanese plant. I took my time going down the aisle; little steps like Tisha and Eliza had coached me. When I finally sought out Jonas with my eyes, they locked with his. He was sweating. I could tell his collar and tie were tight and wished I could loosen them for him. His shiny dark hair was trimmed so it fell just over his collar in the back and across one eyebrow. He was clean-shaven for the wedding. I knew he was trying to hide the grey in his beard by shaving, but there was a little white in his sideburns. He stretched and twisted a little like he was uncomfortable in that black tuxedo but he filled it out just fine. That little smile pulling up the corners of his lips as he looked at me was real. This was going to be okay.

All the hurried preparations had sucked the energy right out of me. I had rushed around like a deflating balloon whooshing this way and that to the floor. And it was for all the wrong reasons, like the length of my dress or the color of the flowers. But when I saw him, my mountain of a man, silhouetted against the pale blue of the church walls, the balloon spirit inside me just grew and grew until it was nigh on ready to bust. With his tux, he wore a grey sealskin vest and matching knee high mukluks decorated with fringe and beadwork. His sister, Barbara, had sent them from Alaska by priority mail to get these symbols of his Inupiaq heritage here in time for the wedding. I had never seen them before but I could tell that he wore them proudly. He also wore that tight black bowtie. I figured he was wearing it so our wedding would fit in with what was expected by friends here and maybe me. It was clear that he was gracefully walking in two worlds.

Reverend Beau Booth was at ease, in his element in front of our little country church. He motioned Jonas and me to front and center. "Friends, we are gathered together to witness the marriage of this man and this woman." He stopped and looked at the audience. "I love weddings." He laughed a little. "I love baptisms. These are ceremonies of celebration with God."

Chapter 1

Then he grabbed Jonas by the arm and asked him out loud, "Would you like me to just get on with it?" Jonas nodded and there were chuckles from the guests. Loretta Cecil sang "I'm a Believer," my song to Jonas. Then Clarence Price from church sang "Something" to me from Jonas.If I hadn't been old and strong, I would've blubbered right there. Reverend Booth asked us to kneel before him and there were some more chuckles and I figured they were laughing at Jonas being so stiff at getting his knees on the altar cushions. The preacher prayed and I felt Jonas' shoulders shake and I peeked at his face. His eyes were squeezed shut and tears were dripping. Weird.

We struggled to our feet, helping each other. The ring bearer was a perfect doll handing us each a ring, and we repeated  our vows. The preacher was so comfortable that we were starting to feel at ease, too. He pronounced us husband and wife and Jonas kissed me so hard that he dipped me, his hand supporting my neck as he leaned me backwards. His buddies all cheered and we hurried back out the aisle to the Fellowship Hall. The photographer took some pictures as the ushers and bridesmaids joined us, then we lined up and greeted all our guests. Eliza and Tisha were always in the background, checking on cookie platters and refilling the punch bowl and checking on me.

Everyone was so kind, the men telling Jonas that it was about time he married me and the ladies telling him that they hoped they would see him more often. Even Doc hugged me and shook Jonas' arm half off.

The party was lively. A band had been thrown together just the week before and was playing in the far corner, finger sandwiches and cookies were disappearing and punch was flowing. By the time we hugged and shook hands with every guest, people had started dancing. Jonas loves the Beatles, so we slow-danced to "Let it Be." I was awkward; I guess I had never danced in front of people before, but after a few sips of punch and some divinity candy to sustain me, I warmed up and it became fun and I hardly noticed anyone else there while we danced.

The ladies of the church had brought the food and made the punch and it was awfully good. I heard my friend Sally corner Macie Amos, "I want that punch recipe, Macie, you've outdone yourself. It is really good." Macie stared in her cup and told her, "Same things as always: orange sherbet, orange juice, and ginger ale. But, this is good, we must've gotten a good 'do' on it today."

The preacher came through the refreshment line several times smacking his lips and pretending to dance by shuffling his feet and wiggling. I was resting in a folding chair under the braided rebar cross, hoping it wouldn't fall on my head, when I looked up to see Jonas, Ben McDaniel, his best man, and both ushers playing air guitars to the band's version of "Johnny Be Good." They were jumping around, shirttails out and bowties dangling. It was good to see them having a good time, but the average age on the dance floor was about fifty. Their muscles were going to be sore in the morning.

I watched the festivities from a folding chair near the refreshment table. Jonas had slipped out the back door to get a breath of fresh air I figured and I was startled when he reappeared waving an envelope. He flopped down in the chair beside me and threw an arm around me pressing his mouth to my ear. "Sorry about the punch," he choked and laughed. "The boys hit it pretty hard with booze." My eyes must have widened because he hugged me tight as if to pin my arms to my side and continued whispering, "... but it tasted good and the church ladies are drinking it and no one knows ..."

"What else have they done?" I sputtered, remembering the laughter when we knelt.

He pushed back from me and hung his head, shoulders shaking silently, laughing so hard he couldn't speak. I didn't know whether to laugh along or get aggravated. After I pondered my choices for a few seconds, he looked up, wiping tears from the corners of both eyes with the closed fist holding an envelope.

He stood, grinning from ear to ear, and faced the guests. "Listen up, I have an announcement to make." Then he turned to me and cleared his throat. "Stella, my family wants to meet you – they made us tickets." He waved the envelope overhead and did what may have been an Eskimo dance around me. "We're going to Alaska in the morning!"

I may have swooned.

5

Chapter 2

She Warmed my Soul

Jonas

Those boys I worked with at the Celanese were in prank heaven. Me marrying Stella gave them the perfect setup for practical jokes. I had taken day after day of teasing at work after I thumbtacked up an invite in the break room. Might as well've painted a big target on my back. But it was all in good fun, and maybe a little bit deserved. Maybe I had taken part in a few funny tricks myself. Like the time somebody hid the music chip from a musical card, you know, the part that plays a tune when the card is opened, above the dropped ceiling in our supervisor's office. The ceiling tiles muffled the music so he could only hear it sometimes. Thought he was losing his mind when none of us admitted to hearing anything. That thing played for almost six weeks until he found it. Good fun! He got us back though; told us that our paychecks were gonna be held until the company got through some auditing, maybe for three weeks. Some of the boys were scurrying around trying to borrow money and collect old debts so they didn't have to face their wives. All a lie. Payday came right on time and the boss grinned that whole day.

Ben McDaniel, my best man, had brought me with him to his home in West Virginia years ago when we both left the oilfields, found me work and let me rent-to-buy a house he owned.

Now we waited together in a Sunday school classroom before the wedding. He checked my tie and patted my chest. "My truck is gassed up and parked by the kitchen door if you've changed your mind." He grinned and pointed to my mukluks, "Are those boots guaranteed against getting cold feet?" He laughed at his own joke and thumped me on the back as I turned to check out my unfamiliar tuxedo in the mirror. "If you duck out the back, Stella will probably hunt you down, though, so be sure you want to be on the run for the rest of your life." He kept grinning, trying to make me uncomfortable.

"Oh, quit. I've done this before, remember?" Ben had been there for my first wedding thirty years ago at the Barrow courthouse. I shook my head remembering that tiny beauty that had stolen my twenty-year-old heart. The joy and wonder that she could love me quickly became heartbreak. Turned out that I was her ticket off the North Slope. She disappeared with my truck a few months after we moved to Louisiana never to be seen or heard from again. I spent two decades unsuccessfully searching for her to divorce her. Ben kept telling me that I could run an ad in the paper and finalize a divorce, but that didn't feel right to me. I knew I didn't owe her a thing, but I wanted to tell her in person. We had only learned three weeks ago that she had been killed in a car crash in the Philippines long ago.

This wedding is different. Middle age wisdom, at least the grounding and confidence life had given me, was calming. Stella didn't need me, but she wanted me. When I was near her, even in my thoughts, she warmed my soul. We were equals and I wanted her beside me the rest of my life. There was no worry about this ceremony. My only regret was that we hadn't married twenty years ago.

Finally, the preacher pecked on the door and we went into the hallway where Eliza, Stella's friend, straightened ties and checked for the ring. Then Stella's hyperactive friend, Tisha, inspected us and sent us on in the sanctuary. While I was gussied up at the front of the church waiting for Stella, I was wondering what those boys from work had planned. All of them knew or were kin to half the congregation, had been to church or Sunday school off and on all their lives here at the Lindside United Methodist Church, or to benefit dinners or after the game parties in high school, so they knew the layout and the people. A great prank needs attention away from it and here we had a long-anticipated wedding. Perfect storm. The main reason I was sweating as I stood between Preacher Booth and Ben McDaniel was my concern for whatever joke those boys would try to pull off in the church.

Some of the sweat was caused by my clothes. This collar was killing me, but the mukluks felt so comfortable and right, they balanced out the pain. The faint Arctic smell from the sealskin reminded me of home and I shifted weight from one foot to the other thinking of the surprise I had for Stella after the wedding.

Then, the recorded songs ended and the sanctuary fell silent. The church ladies had used evergreens to decorate and during that moment of quiet I breathed hard and the spicy pine smell filled my lungs. I could hear the wind whistling through the old stained glass windows and spent a moment watching the candles on the altar dance in the wisps of wind that leaked inside. Then, the opening chords of "Hey Jude" started and the bridesmaids and ushers strolled down the aisle. Every groomsman made faces and winked at me when they got close enough to the altar that the guests couldn't see them. I was having a hard time keeping a straight face. Then the flower girls appeared tossing red petals and then there was Stella. She looked real nice, her face was relaxed and she was smiling. Finally, as she got closer to the altar, she looked me dead in the eyes.

Beau, the preacher, was a good guy. He joked around a little and some songs were sung and we knelt to pray. I heard a man choke and cough and I knew they had been up to something. Sure enough, when I helped Stella up, I saw white shoe polish on the bottom of her shoes. They had written something there. Which means they had probably written something on my shoes. Lord knows my shoes were big enough for a message. So, I tried to hide the bottom of my feet when I knelt by keeping my toes flat and bending my feet in the middle. Azaa, I even got tickled. Don't know how I'll explain that to Stella. Clumsy, but I managed and the preacher wasn't too long winded, so I got through it.

The kiss was great, but it was more than just a kiss. It felt like we were free at last to show off how we felt in front of God and everybody. The boys enjoyed it more than they should've, but I didn't care. After that, we suffered through handshaking and pictures with Stella pinching my butt when she thought no one was looking, really being a scamp. Those boys were contagious, I guess.

Then the band started up and the punch started flowing, and I loosened my bowtie and just went with the flow. In half an hour, shirttails were out, the Fellowship Hall was half full of guests dancing and even the most serious church ladies were smiling and tapping their feet. Those rascals had spiked the punch. I don't know how they got in the kitchen with booze, must've used a girlfriend or wife to help out; probably the spiker didn't even know, that's how good those fellows were. Maybe Tisha, Stella's friend, helped out. That girl could've pulled it off. I laughed to myself just thinking about the plotting and scheming that got the job done.

Tisha had sure helped me. She made Stella pack a honeymoon suitcase with plenty of warm clothes "just in case" we took off for the weekend. She also made arrangements for Stella's animals to be fed and promised to check on the heat during the holidays.

Thinking about Tisha and my coworkers reminded me, I checked the bottom of my boots. "SAVE" was written on one and "ME!" on the other. The soft caribou hide had absorbed some of the shoe polish but it was pretty clear. I thought I would just clean Stella's shoes and never tell her.

Stella danced awhile then rested, sipping the delicious orange punch, chatting with friends. I weighed my timing, tell her now or let her drink some more? She didn't know that my family had sent us tickets and the flight left DC at 6 AM. Our first night of married life would be spent with Ben McDaniel in my truck driving to Reagan National Airport. Then, we'd fly on 15 hours to Barrow and finally home to Atqasuk, Alaska, for a Christmas homecoming and wedding reception. I hadn't been home in a decade and I was plenty excited.

So I got everybody's attention and showed her the boarding passes and told her about the trip. I sure didn't see it coming. My tough, brave, independent Stella fainted dead away. Guess it was good I didn't tell her it was a one-way ticket.

Chapter 3

I Sighed and Got Down to Business

Stella

I recovered pretty quickly from my little spell and someone brought me a cup of that delicious punch and life rolled on. I didn't dance any more, though. My mind was racing about meeting Jonas' family and childhood friends. That had to be reined in. I would have time to think about that later.

The wedding reception was winding down when we left about ten o'clock. Jonas drove us home through the cold and carried me over the back door threshold, the wind howling through the open door. He closed the door with his foot and sat me down gently at the kitchen table, rubbing his hands together and breathing hard.

"I hate to be in a rush," he said, "but we kinda need to hurry."

I'm sure I looked at him in amazement, not knowing where this was going. I was ready to crawl between the lavender scented covers and snuggle.

"The flight leaves at 6:23 AM." He paused and rubbed his forehead. "Tomorrow."

"What?" was all I could manage.

"Looks like our honeymoon will be a trip to DC." He paused and grinned. "Wifey." He tried that on for size and I had to smile back.

The smile faded as I grasped the reality of the moment. "But it's a six-hour drive to DC."

"Yep, that's why we have to hurry. Grab your suitcase and maybe change clothes. Think warm."

Chapter 3

"What?" Again, it was the best I could muster.

"I'll put up the chickens and throw the goats and sheep some hay and feed the dogs and cats." Jonas grabbed an old jacket from the coat rack near the door.

Watching my new husband in a rumpled tuxedo getting ready to go out the door into the night with a flashlight and a feed bucket pushed me over the drunken edge where I'd been unknowingly teetering. I cracked up, then cried and stumbled to the kitchen sink for a glass of water. Jonas waited and stood beside me smoothing back my hair, but I don't think he said a word. Wise man. He escorted me back to the chair and silently eased out the door. When he returned I could smell the chicken manure. "Why in the world did you wear a tux to the chicken house?" I mumbled.

"Figured it was better than getting the clothes I'll be traveling in dirty."

I couldn't argue with that logic.

I trudged upstairs to take off the wedding dress. Smoothing it on the hanger, I laughed again realizing that my life of glamour had been shorter than expected. I sighed and got down to business, putting on jeans and a long-sleeved shirt with a fleece vest. "Can we not change the ticket date?" I was slowly coming to my senses.

Jonas answered as he tossed his jacket and vest into a chair. "Nope, my family all donated mileage and the fee to change it is too steep. Shake a leg, woman, we have only eight hours to make a six-hour trip and the clock is ticking." He dressed quickly.

I pulled on warm socks and a pair of sturdy shoes and went slowly back down to the kitchen, touching familiar things along the way; the rail on the stairs, the back of the couch, the door facing at the kitchen as if to reassure myself that this was really happening.

He grabbed our packed suitcases and thumped back down the steps behind me, "Oh, one more thing: we are picking up Ben. He is going to drive the truck back from the airport."

"Who is taking care of my animals? And getting the mail? And keeping the plumbing from freezing?"

Jonas held me while I whined. "Shhhhh, Baby. Tisha has it all taken care of. What she can't do herself, Eliza will do; and if they can't, they will call others. You know they will look after things. Take a minute while I load the truck and check the weather."

Tisha knew. Eliza knew. Ben knew. Thoughts to revisit later. All I could think about now was that my first night of my first honeymoon was going to be with Jonas' best friend Ben, in a pickup truck; something I had never, ever imagined.

Jonas

We finally got home and changed and loaded up the truck. Stella sure didn't seem too excited about driving to DC or going to Alaska. Maybe she could take a nap on the way to the plane and feel better. I guess the wedding and the party and the trip was too much.

We are Alaska bound – I'm going home!

Stella

Jonas drove up Interstate 81 with me cat-napping under his right arm. Ben had the window and took care of the music selections on the all-night radio stations. I could listen to anything as long as it wasn't too loud, but probably heard enough from Willie's Roadhouse to last me a good while. The men talked about things that needed to be done in the coming week. Ben was taking back the tux and checking with Tisha to be sure the house was okay. They had packed up boxes of Jonas' belongings the week before, and Ben promised to get them moved into my house while we were gone.

Our path led through the Valley of Virginia and around the DC beltway, stopping only once for gas at White's truck stop in Northern Virginia about two in the morning. It felt good to get out of the pick-up; my legs were stiff from sitting still so long. The air was cold and crisp with a hint of diesel fumes, the smell that reminded me of the long ago night I rode the bus away from home.

I went inside and played the Elvis quarter machine there while Jonas got gas and Ben bought Subway sandwiches. As a bride on my honeymoon, I figured I was entitled to a little fun. I won pretty big, a plastic cup full of quarters. Also, a lighter and some folding money fell over the moving waterfall of money. Maybe it was a sign of good luck to follow.

Two hours later, Jonas pulled over at the airport curb under the blue Alaska Airlines sign. He reached over the tailgate and unhooked the mesh net securing our suitcases inside the truck bed. Ben got out and they thumped each other on the back in a kind of man hug and Ben waved at me as he pulled out, heading back home.

Chapter 3

We checked in at the counter, gave up our bags, and found a seat in the shiny chrome and black airport. If I hadn't been so tired, I might have enjoyed the early morning busyness more. As it was I was fascinated, pretty much paralyzed, but fascinated. Men in suits were scurrying around, sleepy families with children still in their pajamas and oh, my, the strangeness ... women swathed in fabric, only their faces showing with turbaned men, cowboys wearing ten gallon hats and pointed boots and carrying briefcases, a young woman with cats in two soft bags. I swear I could've just sat there all day long and just watched.

Chapter 4

We're in Alaska and We're Married

Stella

After a few hours on the flight between DC and Seattle, I started to visualize a winged metal tube of people hurtling through the sky. Jonas was sleeping, making funny little snoring sounds and leaning against me. What a honeymoon! I nodded and napped from time to time, but I fought it. Someone needed to stay alert in case there were problems with the people or the plane. I had no plan of action to handle suspicious persons. This was my first flight and it was all too exciting to sleep anyway, but I thought it was important to keep watch. Finally, I was pretty convinced that everyone around us was asleep or reading or on a computer, so I relaxed about an hour before we got to the Seattle airport.

That airport was wonderful. Partly because we got to stretch our legs, partly because of the huge glass wall that let us watch the airplanes coming and going, and partly because of the food court. Oh, my goodness, we could get any kind of food we could imagine.

"Whatcha wanna eat?" Jonas scratched his head looking at all the choices. We had walked the kinks out of our legs and cleaned up a little bit in the shiny chrome bathrooms.

I feasted on the colors and textures in the huge Sea-Tac food and shopping arena. I couldn't speak for looking around.

"How about clam chowder?" His eyes rested on a blue neon sign and he seemed excited.

"Sure, I like chowder."

15

Chapter 4

"Let's get bread bowls." Jonas headed toward the blue sign. Ivar's, it said, but I thought it said "Ivan's."

"Sure." I had never heard of Ivar's or bread bowls, but I knew I liked clam chowder. He ordered and picked up the tray of food and I was amazed. The bowl was actually a short fat loaf of bread with the middle carved out like a pumpkin. It was filled with steaming hot chowder. We had to wait for it to cool. No problem, we were facing that big glass wall and I thoroughly enjoyed the airplanes moving around out there.

Then, out of nowhere, music. A baby grand piano that was sitting empty when we entered the area was now being played. Not just played, but stroked with passion; kisses and hugs of musical love filled the room. Christmas music was the choice, making the emotional pull (on top of my exhaustion and newly-wed status) even stronger.

"Might want to shut your mouth, unless you are catching flies," Jonas pointed his spoon at me, obviously enjoying the rapture I felt. It was a wonderful moment. As soon as I could tear myself away from the joy, I ate. And ate. And watched my husband eat. When he tore bits of chowder soaked bread from his bowl to eat, I did the same. We just sat and grinned at each other between bites.

The mood was broken when Jonas looked at his watch and at our boarding passes. "Babe, we better scoot. Our flight boards in ten minutes." We cleared the table and studied monitors and backlit maps and found our way to the gate. Then got on the next leg of our long journey, another Alaska Airlines flight, this time only three hours, to Anchorage.

We settled in for the shorter flight and Jonas was talkative. "You'll like the Anchorage Airport, named for Ted Stevens."

Another new name for me. "Who's that?"

"He was a Republican who served in the senate a really long time, like forty years. Got in a little trouble with the FBI over accepting gifts. That mess went on for a long time. I can't even remember how it ended up. Anyway, they named the airport after him."

Jonas patted my hand on the armrest. "Let's get rid of this," he said, and in a flash, he folded it up and we had a few more inches of space. Then our bodies could touch full length at least on one side.

"Whatever happened to him?"

"Killed in a plane crash." Jonas chuckled.

A tiny gasp came out, "And still they named the airport after him?"

Jonas shrugged. "He traveled a lot on planes. Everybody in Alaska does. Not unusual to die in a plane crash. The airport was named for him while he was alive and well, not a memorial or anything."

The sound system crackled and we were told that the plane was about to land. I couldn't see anything below but mountains and frozen mud. My heart pounded and I sent up a prayer for us all when I couldn't see a thing, much less a place to land. Then, out of nowhere, a runway, and quickly, a roar and we were on the ground. Whew, Jesus was hearing from me more than usual on this trip.

We gathered our carry-on bags and waited for our turn to trudge down the center aisle to the back door of the plane. The stairs led to the windy outdoors, not to a warm tunnel to the terminal. We followed a painted path, directed by ladies in Alaska Airlines parkas waving what seemed to be light sabers to show us the way. It was chilly, to say the least, and our pathway was icy.

Our final flight to Barrow was two hours away so we "bath-roomed up" and looked around. Jonas wanted to show me the huge stuffed animals. Not toys, the real thing. There was a musk-ox, big sad-eyed creature with horns that met in the middle of her forehead, a polar bear, and a larger-than-nightmare Kodiak Bear, standing upright on his back feet. I hope the display case could hold him if he somehow came to life. Then, I realized how silly that sounded and figured even my mind was getting tired.

"Look over here." Jonas motioned me over to a side hallway with more, smaller displays and showed me artworks, things I had never imagined.

"Here's a baleen basket. My cousin makes them, too, but he puts an ivory knob on the lid. This one is good, too." Jonas tapped on the glass of the case he wanted me to see. Then, he moved ahead and found soapstone carvings of hunters and motioned for me to come and see them.

"Wow. That took some time to make," was all I could come up with. The miles were catching up with me and I didn't much care about all the new things at the moment, but I tried to be interested. I really did. The way Jonas was coming alive as he got closer to his childhood home made me happy, but the joy was balanced out by my need to rest. In a bed. In a quiet place.

We headed back to a monitor screen to figure out our gate and hiked to the end of a wide, windowed hallway to wait for boarding. This gate was the most alive of any we'd visited. Small dark-haired children were playing tag around the benches; adults were greeting one another and visiting. But the teenagers, like their peers we had seen around the country, were sitting still, furiously typing on cell phones.

"Everyone seems to know each other," I whispered to Jonas.

"Yep, this flight is to Barrow, non-stop. You can see the long-time residents, mostly Inupiaq, are glad to see one another here in the city. They may even live beside each other in Barrow, but it is good to see familiar faces out in the world."

"Do you know anybody here?"

"I know who some of them are. Darryl's grandma is over there," and he pointed his chin in her direction, "and those must be Okpeaha children."

"How do you know?"

He shrugged. "Just by looking."

I remembered my trouble understanding the Anchorage airport's name and asked, "What's the name of the Barrow airport?"

"Wiley Post – Will Rogers," He answered quickly.

"But, that doesn't make sense, they were both from Oklahoma."

Jonas shrugged and tried to hide a smile.

Then it hit me, "They died in a plane crash, didn't they?"

"'Bout ten miles from the airport, there's a marker there." I hit him on the arm, mostly from the giddiness of traveling for 20 hours, but some because it scared me that so many people in Alaska died in plane crashes.

The uniformed employees started to assemble and I knew from the previous stops this was a good sign that things were about to happen. Sure enough, the flight was announced and we lined up to get on board. This time, we walked down inside stairs and out across the cleared pavement to climb the wheeled stairs to the plane. The wind was howling and the sun had dropped below the horizon, so the warmth and wind free cabin was very welcoming.

The interior was busy much like the gate; children jabbering and crying, people stowing their belongings overhead, lots of greetings all around. It could have been a bus going to a family reunion. I sighed with relief; there was not one person that looked like a terrorist to me.

Two and a half more hours and we'd be in Barrow. I tried to summon up nervousness at meeting the Akpik family, but I couldn't. Too tired, I guess. Jonas was sitting upright, eyes sparkling, the power of simply going home radiating from his body. I wondered if I went back to the dairy farm near Atlanta where I spent my short childhood, even if the place still existed, would I feel such delight. No, my father and mother were both dead, Daddy died when I was a child. The only member of my immediate family to share those memories was my mean brother, Timmy Lee, now residing in an institution awaiting a diagnosis of sanity to stand trial for murder. No, I would not be feeling any great pleasure to go home. But, I was glad that Jonas' home was a place that brought him joy.

Then I must've dropped off to sleep because the next thing I knew the plane had jolted and bounced and jolted again and I thought we had crashed. The plane crash ended with a mighty roar from the wings and we bounced and skidded until I resigned myself to certain death. I even had time to be angry about it. Then, the passengers cheered and I thought, "What a crazy bunch of people on this plane."

Barrow (Utqiaġvik), Alaska Airlines Terminal. Photo by Aimee Romeijn-Boen.

Chapter 4

"Rough landing, Darlin', but we are here!" I watched open-mouthed as Jonas and other people jumped up out of their seats to unload the luggage overhead, staggering around as the plane continued to roll. The flight attendants had given up after warning them twice to "Take your seats until the plane comes to a complete stop." It seemed that the importance of being almost home trumped safety and indeed, everything else.

"Jonas, the lady said to sit down," I pulled on his shirttail as he was standing up.

"What's she gonna do, throw us off the plane?" He laughed and so did the young men in the seats behind us. When the plane finally stopped, I could see the lit windows of the turquoise and blue Alaska Air terminal, people waiting and watching. We waited a lot longer before the back door was opened. "Better put on your jacket and gloves and hood." Jonas whispered. "How come?" I pointed to the terminal, "We are just going over there." He chuckled. "Whatever you think is best, Dear." Good Lord, that sounded like I better do it. So, I did. One of my better decisions.

We walked through the strips of heavy plastic in the plane's doorway that protected the crew from the fierce arctic wind. It hit me at the top of the stairs. The cold took my breath away. Next, my nose hairs froze and then I felt my earlobes ache where earrings filled the piercings. I couldn't decide whether to rub my nose or take out my earrings, but I had to keep moving down the steps so did neither. I stopped halfway down and watched a snow dust-bunny swirl over the icy runway just for a second then kept moving down the stairs. When I reached the paved runway, a smiling Alaska Airlines employee, dressed in a warm-looking parka with a fur trimmed hood was waving me on towards the terminal door. An ice-cream headache was beginning. I shuffled my feet on the ice to keep from falling and held my hood together at my mouth to keep the wind off my face as much as I could.

I trudged through the ice and light snow across the runway to the terminal door. When I looked up long enough to inspect the distance beyond my immediate surroundings, the pitch dark seemed to go forever. No mountains, no skyline, just blackness. The smell of diesel permeated the cold wind and something else, something new to me, something of the earth and of wildness. I accepted that heated jet ways were a thing of the past. Little did I know how many other new sights and smells were in store.

Baggage claim Barrow (Utqiaġvik), Alaska Airlines Terminal. Photo by Aimee Romeijn-Boen.

The sound of howling wind was replaced by happy voices as the terminal door swung open to let me enter the crowded terminal. I focused on the sounds and warmth of the room as I slogged through the crowd. For a second, I thought people were rushing at me and I held my backpack tightly against my chest, but they passed by. They were rushing toward Jonas. I turned around to check on him and women were hugging him and men slapping him on the back. I was so glad for him, but I was dog tired and just wanted to get wherever we were going.

The stream of people flowed to an opening near the exit and stopped. Luggage was starting to appear through the strips of plastic. Not on a conveyor belt, but just pushed or tossed through the air to the metal ramp where we stood. People would grab a bag or box, read the names and pass it to the owner. Looked like a bucket brigade for putting out fires. We were pressed together so tightly that we jostled each other by just turning or waving. I moved to the wall of the terminal for some sense of security and to conserve energy. No way I could move that luggage and still have the strength to move myself. It was fascinating, though and I watched, hypnotized by the coordination of it all. Then someone called "Jonas Akpik" and there were whoops and shouts of welcome.

Chapter 4

He was handed his suitcase. "Thank you boys," he hollered and then, "Find Stella's," to a man on the edge of the ramp. "Purple," he added, and they did. We were somehow transported back outside into that dreadful cold and loaded into an old Explorer with more people than it should hold. Jonas reached for my hand through the luggage and children on our laps in the back seat and I was glad he hadn't forgotten me completely.

We were taken through the dark to a blue, two-story frame house with the hind quarters of a deer or something like it tied to the railings out front. There was a pile of boots and a wall of coats just inside the front door and we added ours. Then we pushed open the inside door and entered a warm room full of people: old people, tiny children, middle-aged folks, and teens. The faint smell of cigarettes and the stronger odor of a wet diaper made it hard to breathe. They all wanted to hug Jonas but I felt invisible. Jonas introduced me and hugged me, but that just interrupted the back-slapping story telling he was part of.

I found a place on the arm of a chair and leaned against the wall, watching the room, but eventually I nodded off. Jonas woke me, whispering, "Hey Babe, how about we hit the sack?" He led me as I trudged behind him through the living room and into a back room. Through my sleepy haze, a few children appeared. Some of them seemed to be sitting on an air mattress watching a big screen TV. Others were sleeping; little bodies stretched out or curled up all over the place. I didn't see my suitcase and I was too tired to care. I slid off my jeans and hoodie and unhooked my bra underneath the t-shirt and crawled under the comforter on the mattress. Jonas was moving little bodies off the bed and shooed the conscious kids back to the living room. "Go on, find your mama, now. It's late." Then he joined me, crinkling the plastic mattress as he rolled over behind me.

"We're in Alaska and we're married." I murmured and smiled in spite of myself. He snuggled up behind me and I felt the heat from the full length of his body. Then, the thirty-hour trip caught up with me and I gulped sleep like a thirsty woman.

Chapter 5

Haven't Been This Excited in a While

Jonas

Man, I hated giving my truck keys to Ben and watching my truck head back to West Virginia without me, but I loved heading home to Alaska with Stella more than I hated that.

Could feel my age – must be getting old. The flights were longer than I remembered and the airplane seats must have shrunk. My knees and hips were stiff and I had to walk the aisle during every flight. That achy feeling that I get in the dentist chair when my body needs to stretch started setting in near the end of each leg of the trip.

The stewardesses all looked like teenagers, smiling and seeming to care whether we wanted water or coffee, but there was a tired, grown-up look behind their eyes. I felt sorry for them.

I couldn't keep from grinning when I thought about seeing Mom and brothers and sister and nieces and nephews. Hadn't been this excited for a while. Glad to have Stella beside me to share it. Made it all new again. Wished I had a picture of her eyes in the SeaTac Airport. They were really big.

It's been a rush since we learned about Anna's death. Anna's daughters had needed Stella. Timmy Lee framed her for a robbery at church, then broke into the house and tried to kill her. We found out that my ex was dead so then we could get married.

All this must be why Stella gets quiet every now and then. She doesn't exactly withdraw but she is quiet and doesn't show her true self, at least the Stella that has always reacted quickly and sincerely. Maybe I'd just imagined it because we've been together so much lately. I guessed time would tell.

Aerial view of Barrow (Utqiaġvik), Alaska. Photo by Vanni Prichard.

Chapter 6

Time is Ticking

Jonas

We slept all night and through the daytime hours of the day after we arrived, got up and ate, then went back to bed. Mom was living in the big village of Barrow with my sister Barbara and her family. We stayed those first days with them on Karluk Street. Early the second day, my youngest brother, Leo, tiptoed in to wake me up.

"Hey man, get up," he whispered. "We gotta plan the reception. Time is ticking!" This was especially hilarious since I used that phrase on him a few hundred times waiting for him to get ready for school or to go hunting or to play ball. Now he was using it on me.

"Azaa, man, give me just a few minutes." I sat up and rubbed my eyes and yawned. He left to go get Richard and James, my other brothers, while I tried to wake up my mind by getting oriented. Slowly it seeped into my head where I was, why I was here and who was in the bed with me. Barbara's house. Wedding reception. Stella.

We didn't need a big shindig at all, just being home and seeing my family was enough for me. But, the purpose of the trip was to let Stella meet them all and them to get to know her; and they had collected the money and sent the tickets, so we were having a wedding reception. A big one. This week, the Friday night before Christmas. Where it was happening was not as definite.

I tried to be quiet when I rolled out of our makeshift bed in the back room. There were two kids sleeping next to our

25

air mattress in the floor and an adult on the couch all bathed in a blue glow from a silent TV. It was on but muted and on a channel that didn't come in. Guess it had been on all night. As I pulled on a shirt, I reached down to the air mattress on the floor, shook Stella's shoulder and whispered to wake her up, "Get up, Babe. Remember, we're looking at places for our reception this morning."

"Hunh-uh, not me." She pulled the sleeping bag tight around her and burrowed back under the pillow. The kids stirred in their sleep.

"C'mon Stel' you gotta help me with this." I didn't like begging but it was going to be a long day without her. I had forgotten how much could be said without words and my family members were experts. There needed to be two of us to just see it all. I expected to see both raised eyebrows of approval and wrinkled noses of distaste.

A muffled "Nope" from the mattress followed by, "Sorry, Jonas, you're on your own, big boy. I am cold and tired and staying in this bed for awhile. Besides, I don't care where the reception is ..."

I was about half pissed at her so I stomped around making more noise than I needed to. For added effect, I sat down and got up a time or two and jiggled the air mattress until she started laughing. "Aw, Jonas," she sat up wrapped in blankets and quit giggling, "I'm not really that cold." She chewed a nail, "I don't wanna go 'cause I have not yet said a thing that anyone in your family likes or agrees with." She looked at the blue screen on the TV for a second. "It's kinda discouraging." She pulled me back down onto the mattress and hugged me for awhile and I thought she had changed her mind. Then she blew in my ear, "Thanks for going without me. It won't be that bad."

I knew I was beat and changed tactics; I used my finger to trace the marks on her cheek caused by the pressure of the pillow while she slept. She giggled again and rolled over.

"Oh, no, not happening." I caught her words from deep in the cover.

A man deserves a better honeymoon than this. We sure didn't join the "Mile High" Club on the long flight to Barrow, and so far, we'd spent two nights on the floor in a crowded TV room. The air mattress crunched as I rolled over to get up, this time for the day. I pulled on yesterday's limp socks under the elastic leg bands of my sweat pants and tippy toed between children to the kitchen to start the coffee maker.

Mom's was the first sleepy body to walk zombie-like into the kitchen. "Pour." She motioned with her hand to the cupboard and the coffee maker. I poured her a cup, black and strong, set it on the table, and watched her. It amazed me how her face had changed. Still beautiful, but more skin on it. Skin that hung looser, like little drapes. Her eyes were the same, sparkly almond slits, and I swear she was wearing the same glasses she did in the 1980s: great big pinkish frames. The main difference was her mouth; it was so much smaller than before. That big smile had shrunk up to a puckered little opening. Hadn't seen her smile much since she welcomed and hugged me at the airport. Need to get her to smile more. She was walking slowly and carefully picking the places for her feet, even inside the house. She was nearly 80 years old; maybe she was doing okay. Maybe this was just how it was.

"You're up early." I threw out a greeting as I sat down at the table with her.

"Huh." She grunted and held her mug with both hands and stared at it. So much for getting a smile. I shut up and drank my own coffee. A toilet flushed upstairs and signaled another family member's entry into the day. Sure enough, Barbara soon appeared into our little world of silence and coffee aroma. I guess if any of us were close, Barbara and I were the closest of all my siblings. She was five years younger, widowed ten years ago and raised three kids alone. I had sent her money from time to time, but we were down to a Christmas card and a couple of phone calls a year now. She and some of the grandkids lived with Mom. Most of our conversations were about growth of the children and their activities and her sporadic relationships. She still worked at the borough offices; had been since the family moved from Atqasuk to Barrow, and I knew she had moved in to help Mom, not the other way around.

"Good morning, brother." She held out her arms to me and we hugged. She used the moment to ask in a low voice, "How is she today?" I held her at arm's length.

"Who?" I wasn't sure if she meant Stella or Mom.

She cut her eyes at Mom and nodded her head sideways at her.

"Oh-h-h. Don't you know you gotta be pretty plain with me, sis?"

27

Chapter 6

She laughed. "Oh yes, remember when we were kids and I asked you if you thought my boat would make it across Meade River? I was about seven and you thought you were a big man. You walked around it and told me, 'should make it fine.' I got in it and drifted almost half a mile before people came and got me. You didn't tell me I needed oars, Knucklehead." She punched me on the shoulder and laughed.

Then, lots quieter, she whispered, "How does she seem to you?"

I wasn't sure whether to talk out loud or whisper, too, so I shrugged and said, "Haven't been around her all that much."

Barbara nodded and cradled her hands around a coffee mug, her face long. She nodded towards Mom. "We have good days and bad. It was good that she knew you when you got off the plane. My granddaughters practiced with her for a couple of days, showing her your picture and making her repeat your name until she screamed at them that she wasn't stupid."

My heart fell. I hadn't realized that she was in this kind of shape. Thinking back, though, our phone conversations in the last few years had been pretty much one-sided. She'd usually give up the phone to someone else in the room. Surely they had been to the doctor to see what was wrong. "What does the doctor say?"

It was Barbara's turn to shrug. "Old age, dementia, Alzheimer's, sundowner disease, senility, mild cognitive disorder. We've heard it all. Nothing that we can do anything about." Barbara breathed a deep, shuddering sigh. "It's been coming on for several years. My older grandkids and I have taken over paying her bills, and buying all the food and her clothing and shoes, and giving her a cash allowance to play bingo or buy treats and cigarettes."

I didn't know what to say, so I turned the conversation to Mom, laughingly. "Are you hearing this, Ma? How come you don't pay your bills?" She looked at me hard, then laughed and shook her finger at me.

"What?" I turned to Barbara.

"She reacts to your tone of voice more than your words. She knows you are playing with her, but she might not know exactly what you are saying. Sometimes, she does and she is fine, playful and smart. If she gets frustrated, look out because she responds with anger and confusion."

"Is she always like this?"

28

"No, no. She will come around later in the day and get more like her old self, then by bedtime she will be restless and, God forgive me, I'll give her a sleeping pill, mainly so I can sleep. Physically, she is fine; we've checked for anything that could've been causing this, but there's not." She got up and refilled her coffee cup and turned away from me, then turned back quickly and faced me head on. "You might as well know. I worry about her leaving the house at night and freezing to death."

So shocked that my once brilliant mother was living even part of the time like a zombie of her former self, unfairness screamed in my head. I was sure glad when I heard the floor creak signaling footsteps. Josie, the oldest of Barbara's grandchildren, shuffled into the kitchen, long hair tousled and eyes half closed with sleep. "Uvlaalluataq, Uncle." She reached to hug me, and I loved the feel of her warm flannel pajamas against me and the smell of strawberry shampoo in her hair and Tide detergent in her clothes. She leaned against me, yawning, for a few seconds longer. In the face of Mom's deterioration, it felt good to have a child, young and strong in my arms. Josie was a tiny little girl the last time I was home, laughing and sailing a piece of Styrofoam in a big mud puddle.

Barbara and the teenaged grandkids, my nephews and nieces, wanted the reception to be at the middle school gym, but my brothers all wanted us to reserve the Inupiat Heritage Center. Somebody was going to be unhappy. I hadn't been inside either of the buildings; they had both been built while I was in the lower 48. Today was the day I was going to visit

Inupiat Heritage Center, Barrow (Utqiaġvik), Alaska. Photo by Aimee Romeijn-Boen.

both places and decide. I sat watching my mother sip her coffee across the table and she caught me staring. Snake-like, she stuck her tongue out at me then laughed so hard that she had to sit down her coffee.

"Ah, Ma, I love you." I got up and walked around the table to give her a hug. She patted me on the arm and then we looked up at the sound of the outside door squeaking open. My brothers came stomping through the inner door, pulling off knit caps and gloves and throwing snow everywhere. A big German shepherd dashed in behind them and the kitchen was in chaos. Leo and James and Richard loudly welcomed me; Josie started rattling coffee mugs, getting one for each uncle. Mom had eyes for only the dog, sitting at her feet waiting patiently.

Mom dug in her robe pocket and dug out something and gave it to the dog, who carried it under the table and began to crunch it. Then she clapped her hands with delight and said "Riley, Riley, Riley."

Richard laughed, "Mom, you and that dog have a love/hate relationship. One day you give it treats and the next day you chain it back out in the cold." She seemed to be warming up and smiled at Richard.

"Sometimes Riley is the only one who understands me," she said.

Riley. Photo by B. Crabtree.

Chapter 7

Yes to Going Somewhere Alone with You

Stella

No one else was awake except Jonas and I, and the silence of the house was sacred, like being in a cathedral. After making oatmeal for Jonas, I played with my half cup of cocoa, moving my wrist so the brown chocolate circled and sloshed around as I thought about things.

Jonas had not heard his mother screech during our short time here, but I had. I suspected she ranted about me; she spit in my direction at least. He hadn't seen his brothers' gesture about me among themselves in my presence, or watched the grandkids' friends kick Riley for sport as they went by. I didn't know quite how to tell him. He loved his family dearly. I wasn't sure he would believe that his Mother, Mary Jo, was a lunatic, and dear sister Barbara and the brothers enabled her by just doing everything Mary Jo wanted. The other sister that was in jail may be the lucky one. The Bible says that the first stone should be thrown by the person without sin or something like that. I am not that person, so I'd decided to hold it all in. My biggest sin was a secret, but I felt it growing into a wall between Jonas and me because I couldn't talk about it. I was not totally open with him on other things because of it. Was the treatment by Jonas' family payback because I had done wrong?

No, I will never believe that I was wrong. Anna had bone cancer. The pain was racking her, every breath. Her suffering was unholy. She doubted God. I did not, but I doubted his mercy. The insurance had paid all it would pay. She had sold everything except the house because she wanted to have something to leave for her daughters. My evil brother had tried to get her to sign it over to the church so he could live there, even forged her name, but that didn't work out.

Anna begged me to give her my pistol because she was scared of prowlers on the mountain. I figured out that was a lie; she wanted to shoot herself to end the pain. She begged me to help her die. We came up with a plan and I did it. She dressed up for church and lay back in her bed and smiled and thanked me before I held a couch cushion to her face and smothered her. But it was not easy. She fought and kicked. I really had to be strong to hold her down. She had told me that she would never change her mind but I started to doubt it as she thrashed around. It was horrible.

When it was finally over, I rushed around to tidy up. I could feel her spirit above me as if she were watching and willing everything to be neat, like she kept her house. That I could feel her then gave me comfort when I looked back, but at the moment I was pretty shook up. I straightened her clothes, the covers, smoothed her hair, and got out of there.

Evidently in the rush, I didn't pick up the couch cushion. I sure didn't notice that her partial plate was hooked onto the loose fibers of the orange plaid cushion cover. Timmy Lee didn't either when he broke in later to get her to sign over her house. All I can figure is that the teeth wires were stuck on the edge and hung down out of sight. He replaced the cushion on the couch and lost the pocket hanky from his suit coat, evidence which proved he was at the scene and was the main reason he was charged with murder. A murder that I knew he didn't do. I figured he deserved jail time for all the things that he'd done but didn't get caught at.

"Any more oatmeal?" Jonas' voice startled me, and I wondered if he somehow heard my thoughts so close across the table. I got up stupidly to scoop more out of the pan and he hugged up behind me. "Where are you, girl? Not in this kitchen, that's for sure."

If I told him, what would he think? Would he hate me for killing my best friend? For not trusting him enough to tell? Would he leave me immediately? No, I couldn't bear not having him in my life. I couldn't tell yet. But I needed to. Soon. I had to quit thinking about it for now. Change the channels in my head and savor happiness with him while I could. I moved the dial on my personality to sassy.

"I tell you one thing, I am not sitting in this house another day watching the snow blow sideways under the street lights."

His grip on me relaxed a little. "We can go to the holiday basketball tournament at the high school if you want," he offered.

"How about something alone with you?" I turned and lay my head on his chest.

"I can think of something to do. This is our honeymoon, after all."

"No, sir. Not with kids at the foot of the air mattress."

"They sleep pretty hard." He rubbed my sides tenderly, up and down, and kissed me. I was considering it but came to my senses just in time.

"My body says yes, but my mind says no." I broke away. "Your oatmeal is getting cold." My mind, ever practical, was moving on.

"Wait a second, how about if I borrow a car and we'll go out to the point and look for nanuuqs?"

"Yes to going somewhere alone with you. If that means polar bears, no to looking for them." I draped my arms around his neck and we kissed some more, not down-to-business kisses, just for fun kisses.

"We gotta look for them in case they are looking for us! They can break five inches of ice to grab a fish or a seal, so the windshield isn't much of a challenge."

I lowered my eyebrows because it sounded like a tall tale.

"Seriously, Stella, they are at the top of the food chain around here. We'll just keep a lookout, it'll be fine." He made a phone call to one of his brothers. "Woke him up, but he says we can take his pick-up. Get dressed. Warm, just in case the heater isn't good. Leo is known for his broken-down truck. That boy is not mechanical minded at all."

We tromped through the snow to Leo's, got the keys and climbed out of the wind into the cab of his truck. The engine started after several discouraging clicks and within a few minutes, the heater blew warm air.

It was early morning, with just a tiny glow of light on the horizon; the sun didn't really return for another month and then just for a few minutes a day. Jonas had explained the strange long winter days of darkness and the continuous hours of summer light caused by the tilt of the earth toward the sun, but I wasn't sure I really understood it or even believed it before I got up here. He wasn't kidding.

We bumped along a gravel road running parallel to the frozen ocean. Nothing was moving except streams of smoke or steam from chimneys. It was as if we were the only people left

Chapter 7

on a frozen planet. When we were well away from town, we saw a little settlement and a building supply store and the only billboard in town advertising Ilisagvik College. There were old Quonset huts left over from the military and a metal runway on the inland side of the road. A big white round structure loomed off in the distance beyond the runway.

"What is that golf ball like thing?"

"That's the radar for the DEW line site, Distant Early Warning Line. The employees, some military and some civilian, have a mission to protect us from the threat of attack. Used to be Russia that we were afraid of." He laughed. "I sure had some good times at that DEW line station. They are outside the town limits so can have liquor, but they were real careful who they invited to keep down trouble. Those guys were a lot of fun, smart and with a lot of time on their hands. They had a totem pole with a pink toilet on the top and a history to go with it. They built a cool bar out of the inlaid wood from a bowling alley, had great food, music." He sighed. "Great guys to share their site with locals every now and then. Wish I'd stayed in touch with those men. They'd traveled everywhere and told great stories."

We drove another mile or two until there was a stenciled sign, "Northernmost Point in the United States," just below the "Danger Polar Bears" sign. It was full of bullet holes. Target practice, I guessed and Jonas confirmed. I figured this was the end of the trail because it also said "No Vehicles Beyond This Point," but Jonas wheeled on around and we went further out.

"Out here is really the point. There is water on both sides in the summer, the Beaufort Sea on one side and the Chukchi Sea on the other." It all looked the same to me, frozen water and land just the same. "Erosion is changing the spit of land. I wouldn't come out this far in the summer, but we're safe now with the ice beneath us."

"Jonas, I don't like the idea of being on ice. What if it breaks?"

"It won't. Do you think I would put us in danger when we just got married and have the rest of our lives together?"

I don't know if it was his soulful eyes or his loving voice or the tender way he pulled me over to him, but I was charmed. Again. And so, amid much twisting and giggling and groaning about the small space, our marriage was consummated in a vehicle parked at Point Barrow, northernmost point in the United States. No one was watching for bears, either.

Chapter 8

Stella was Rescuing our Honeymoon

Jonas

The reception was to be at the Inupiat Heritage Center. Stella had joined Barbara and Mom and me for the final inspection of the sprawling three-story building on Tuesday. Barbara carried a clipboard, making a list of all that needed to be done. We'd decided the big assembly room lined with chairs was perfect, light colored and bright, and a nice opposite of the cold and dark outside. Posters of Inupiat elders gave the feeling that they were watching and blessing us, too. Stella's eyes got pretty big at the life-size, 55-foot model of a bowhead whale suspended from the ceiling of the entranceway. The building was dedicated in 1999 and was a National Park. It documented the history of whaling which determined much of the history of Inupiat people.

"Wow! People really chase them in little skin boats?"

"Yep." I was proud that she got how difficult and dangerous whaling is. I teased, "It's an Inupiat tradition to say your vows under the bowhead whale." Stella had enough sense to laugh, she was used to my kidding around.

"We've already said our vows." She crossed her arms and stuck out her tongue at me.

I egged her on. "Then, we can renew our vows." Barbara overheard me and thought my fake enthusiasm was real. God knows (and so does Stella) that I hated the formality of saying vows last time; well, and the time before that, when I was just a dumb kid.

Barbara added "vows under whale" to her list.

35

Stella growled under her breath so low only I could hear, "Only been married a few days. Reckon we need to renew our vows every week?" I wanted to hold her and maybe tickle her, but Barbara hustled me into the big kitchen and I couldn't tell if Stella was getting mad or just kidding around.

Reception planning took over our lives. We spent the next three days decorating and making petty decisions about colors and clothes and music and hauling food and drink to the Heritage Center. We ate aluuttaġaaq from a crock-pot while Barbara baked cakes and cooked I don't know what all else. I had never really looked forward to this reception, but now I wanted to get it over with so much that I wished it would hurry up.

The results of all the trouble and work really paid off.

On Friday night the Heritage Center rocked. The place looked great and a crowd showed up to wish us well. Stella grinned as we repeated our vows under the whale and everybody clapped. Then Stella and I shook hands or hugged every single person that came. It was slow work. If I knew the person, we had a 'remember when' story to tell. If I didn't, it took awhile to determine our connection. Like the woman

Point Barrow DEWline site. Photo by Aimee Romeijn-Boen.

who said, "My sister's baby's daddy worked at the water plant in Atqasuk with your brother, and his auntie married your uncle, so I feel like we are cousins. Congratulations, Cousin Jonas!" Then we hugged. Just greeting everyone took two hours and my feet hurt, but when I took the time to look around everyone else seemed happy. Josie brought us both cups of punch every now and then. No one was going hungry; there were plenty of refreshments.

Every now and then there was a toast with punch. Barbara had laid down the law about alcohol. It had caused a lot of problems in Barrow, enough so there were no legal sales of alcohol in Barrow. I had heard enough of her side of a screaming phone conversation with someone, probably one of our brothers, and was sure she wasn't including any liquor in the festivities. I had laughed at the boys in our WV wedding spiking the punch. It was fun, even funny, but here, drinking was more serious. Barbara was doing the right thing keeping this party alcohol-free, but knowing Leo, Richard, and James, there had been a pre-party somewhere.

After we cut the cake and nibbled on the frosting on our pieces, everyone else was being served and I drifted over to a group of old friends. We revisited the past, mostly stupid

Polar bear walking on pack ice. Photo by Andreanita.

things we'd done when we were young. I walked away when the stories started repeating. One version of the time the Barrow Whalers basketball team all dyed their hair blue before a game was enough. Another friend met me and whispered that a stag party was planned for me at his house as soon as I could get loose. "Man, I am too old for that stuff," I whispered back, "but y'all have a great time without me." The glint in his eye gave him away. That party was happening with or without me. Likely, more happily without me. It was nice to be remembered, though.

"If you change your mind, stop by later." I gave him a thumbs up and headed to the far corner where my brothers stood in a circle of men, laughing and talking. Photographs of whalers from years gone by were displayed on the wall behind them and I wondered for a second how the men of today would have measured up a hundred years ago. Probably not made of the same stuff, I reflected before joining the group. Easing my way into the conversation, I thanked them for the party and told them how honored I was that so many people came out in spite of the bitter cold. It was 30 degrees below zero.

Leo teased me, "Your blood is thin because you've been off the slope so long. This is not that cold!" He looked to the others for laughter and found it.

I thought, Brother, if you knew how pretty the mountains and rivers of West Virginia are and how full of deer and trout

West Virgina meadow and forest. Photo by B. Crabtree.

and how great life is in a four-season climate, you'd trade your thick blood and bragging rights for my life. But, I said, "My blood is still Eskimo blood, but cold is cold." I pretended to shiver and they all laughed some more.

Then we started talking about school memories. All of us remembered Ira, back at Meade River School. I was older and my brothers were younger than Ira, but we remembered that he tried to impress the daughter of a white teacher by telling her that Eskimos didn't get frostbite. He tried to prove it by playing out without covering his ears. Both ears turned black and swelled double. He told her that it was caused by strep throat and she believed him. We laughed at how dumb those two kids were.

"Ira drives a bus in Fairbanks now," Richard shared. I was glad to hear that Ira had gotten to town and made it.

We talked about boating on Meade River and hunting and the day a rabid fox chased us home from school and Mom shot it with an old shotgun then poured bleach all over it and wouldn't let us get close to it. Then, the ever-popular tricks on new teachers came up. James giggled and remembered saying "Atchu" to teachers until they said "God bless you." It took a few weeks for teachers to figure out that "Atchu" meant "I don't know" in Inupiat. My brothers still thought this was hilarious. I told myself that it was great to have someone to share grade school memories with, but the truth was I was restless and getting tired of all this reminiscing.

James dredged up the stories of a ghost in teacher housing. "Was there anything to the reports of a little girl's ghost appearing in the back hallway?"

"I heard she was buried in a red dress and that's what the ghost wears." Leo lowered his eyebrows, a sign of deep thought, and took a sip of punch. Leo had always had the timing of a story down to perfection. "My friend William manages the new security camera in that building. He says the video goes to static every now and then." He paused for effect. "And a glimpse of a little girl can be seen just before and after the static. William's seen it, he has it on tape."

"Will still smoking weed?" I had to ask. Leo grinned and shook his head, not denying it. He just knew when he was beat. His eyes focused on something behind me and he pointed his chin over my shoulder. I looked back to see a short, heavy woman huffing and puffing in my direction. She set her cup and plate down and faced me, arms outstretched.

Chapter 8

"Jonas, Akpik, give me a hug." She lowered her voice and gave me a hint. "You left me for your first wife, Leeza."

"Lucy?" I didn't recognize her but she looked exactly like her mom had years ago when I hung out with Lucy. It was her and she was right. Leeza had swept me off my feet, swept me off the slope and away from my family. Then, after a quickie wedding and a three thousand mile move to the Louisiana oil fields, she left me. Leeza was tiny and gorgeous, and, I learned too late, a scam artist. I spent years looking for her and only recently found a record of her death, a long time ago. She'd messed with my mind so much, I even wondered for awhile if the death certificate was real. But it allowed me to marry again and I regretted waiting so long to make Stella my wife.

Lucy was sturdy and practical and loyal, the opposite of Leeza. I had kept up with Luce through Barbara; she'd married Tony Kaleak and they'd had four boys in four years. Tony was killed on the ice, hunting seals, when the baby was three. She'd been left alone to raise a houseful of little boys.

"How've you been?" I asked as soon as she quit hugging and pounding on my back. "And how're the boys?"

"Men, now." She nodded across the room and pointed to each of her sons with an outstretched arm, Vanna White-style, pausing at each name, "TJ, Brian, Eli, and Joe." They were gathered together talking, each juggling interruptions from

Whale bones and skin boat frames, Barrow (Utqiaġvik), Alaska. Photo by C. Taylor.

kids and girlfriend or wives. "All of them look like their daddy, don't you think, Jonas?"

"Yep, sure do." I wasn't sure what else to say. "You've done a good job." Her smile faded when she looked up at me.

"Jonas, sometimes I think about the what-ifs." She looked away and took a deep breath so full of emotion that I closed my eyes. "But, Jonas," she patted my arm and I opened my eyes, "finally I am happy with my life. They say everything happens for a reason. Just so damn hard to understand the reasons." She kept patting my arm. "Your Stella is a lucky girl."

My mind rolled with all the ways Stella was not lucky, but I knew a compliment when I heard one. "Thanks, Luce," I sighed.

She chuckled, "Is your mom ever going to speak to her?"

I froze. "What?" A quick search of the room found Stella sitting alone, picking lint off her wool skirt. Was Mom not speaking to her? She hadn't said anything.

I turned back to Lucy. She'd already picked up her cup and plate and was shaking her head.

"Men ..." She laughed and elbowed me. "Go to her Jonas and help her through this day, not much fun for her, sure. Your mom, Jonas, can be any much difficult." She shuffled toward her sons and I mumbled more thanks, but I needed to go to Stella.

I waved to get Stella's attention, but she was concentrating on the specks of lint. By the time I reached her, she was looking at me but there was no light in her eyes.

"Hey, Mister." She plastered on a phony smile.

"Hey, Babe. How goes it?"

She answered me with a shrug. I knew not to push her, but I knew something needed to be done. I sat down beside her. "Want something to drink?" She shook her head no.

"Piece of cake?" Again, not a word, just a headshake.

"Time to go?" Her eyes met mine and I saw the yes in them, but she didn't say anything. My God, what has happened? I took her hand and helped her up. She gripped my hand like it was a lifeline.

I whistled to get everyone's attention then announced, "Quyanapak, everyone! You made us so happy by coming. We'll be Barrowmiuts for a few more days, then y'all come and see us in the West Virginia hills!" I heard my cousins making fun of me saying "y'all" and somebody made a crack about us being pretty old for newlyweds and I waved goodbye and we went to get our coats.

Barbara ran up before we could put them on. "The drummers are just getting here for an Eskimo dance. You can't leave now."

Barbara, my dear sister, overworked and trying so hard to make our visit memorable, was distraught. I heard Stella beside me, head bowed and spirit wilted, say, "It's okay Jonas, we can stay." A moment of relief then a pinprick of pain at the memory of the wrong choice I had made between love and family years ago. This was different. Stella was real. Our love was real. I took Barbara's face in my hands and kissed her forehead, "Thanks, Sis, I'll never forget this shindig, but we've gotta go. Newlyweds, don't you know." And I winked and she relaxed and grinned and we were okay.

"Mom's gonna blow a gasket," she warned, "and promise me we'll talk later?"

"Sure thing, Sis. Tell Mom bye, we'll see her later." I helped Stella into her parka and grabbed mine. A cab waited at the front door and we hurried to it.

The Korean cabbie asked and I opened my mouth to tell him the house number, but Stella was quicker. She leaned over the front seat and spoke loudly and slowly, "Top of the World Hotel, please, on Brower Street."

The driver nodded, "The new hotel?"

Top of the World Hotel, Barrow (Utqiaġvik), Alaska. Photo by Aimee Romeijn-Boen.

"Yes, sir." Stella leaned back and smiled at me, "I get one night with you on my honeymoon, with a real bed and some privacy. One night in a hotel."

My first thought was that I needed to let Barbara and Mom know where I was and I shared that, but Stella reminded me that I was nearly 60 years old and had just gotten married and that they might not be too worried. And then she swore like a sailor for an entire minute about every child in our bed and every dirty diaper and even how badly the dog was treated. Then, she cried. I held her and my happiness started deep in my belly.

Stella was rescuing our honeymoon, something I was too slow-witted to do. I hugged her as the cab crept along following the above-ground pipes to stay on the snow-covered road. Stella was ready when it stopped and bolted up the metal stairs as I fumbled through my pockets for cab fare. Holding my coat together, I braved the blowing snow to the lobby where she met me, flashing a swipe card key to a room. We giggled like giddy teenagers and stumbled up another flight of stairs to find our room.

Chapter 9

Santa Isn't Coming Here Tonight

Jonas

The prefab unit of the new hotel was cozy even though we heard the wind whistling in the dark most of the night. We didn't sleep much. Just touching each other's bare skin led to other things pretty quickly. Then we talked about how good it was to be alone and all the things we hadn't had a chance to discuss during the week. It was 4 o'clock in the morning and the Today show was on before I napped. I did call Barbara around midnight and told her I wasn't coming home. She thanked me and hung up. It was so loud at her house that I was extra grateful not to be there.

Stella woke me by accident a few hours later calling Osaka Restaurant for breakfast delivery. We had a double order of tempura vegetables brought to our door. Stella's southern accent and the Japanese ear that took the order just didn't jive. Stella looked at those vegetables and looked at me, "I said breakfast, not veggies." Then she fell over on the bed in a fit of laughter.

It wasn't the first time Stella's twang got others confused. The day before, at the grocery store, Stella had tried to help an Asian man find ChapStick when he was looking for chopsticks. Everyone was speaking English but it was still hard to make little sound distinctions.

I was deliriously happy eating the veggie mistake alone with my wife. My world was righting itself. Any guilt at not going home was washed away by remembering how much I loved Stella and how much I loved being with her. I didn't

45

have as much in common with my family as I thought, and what little we had was pretty much exhausted during this trip. I did feel badly about leaving Barbara with the cleanup and a dance without the guests of honor. As I replayed the reception, it hit me why we left.

"Hey, Lucy said Mom wasn't speaking to you. Any truth there?"

Stella flopped back on the bed and put the pillow over her face and screamed.

I pulled the pillow off her, "Dish, Stella, what is going on?"

"Dish? Really, Jonas, where did you hear that?"

"Josie says it all the time. Now talk to me." I fell backwards beside her.

She rubbed her eyes and pushed herself up on one elbow, staring at me. "Jonas, we have been here six days. Your mother grunts at me and I have to figure out what she wants. She slaps at my hands or pushes me away when I don't guess right. She speaks to me only in Inupiat, so unless she says 'quyanaq' or 'uvlaalluataq,' I don't understand because all I know is 'thank you' and 'good morning.' She yells or laughs then depending on her mood." She pressed her lips together hard. "Let's face it, your mom doesn't like me."

I tried to deny it but Stella was having none of it. "You are too busy to see it, but know it is true. Josie notices. For a fifteen-year-old she notices a lot and tries to smooth it over. She told me that your mother will never think anyone is good enough for you or for Barbara or Leo and James, for that matter."

I moved the pillows to prop up my head and stared at the ceiling. "Why would Mom treat you badly? We are already married. It's too late to change your mind or mine." She put her pale arm up against mine.

"Hmmm," she said. "Have you noticed that we are different colors? I'm white, Jonas. Your mom doesn't like white people, not just me, not any white people."

Anger started to burn. Mom was not a bigot. My mind raced. A dozen incidents flashed through my head, every one proving Stella's words to be true. Mom hated the BIA schools. She'd been sent home for refusing to speak English and never graduated. She'd disagreed with the white teachers and white police officers for enforcing western rules and laws. She allowed us to miss school to go fishing or hunting caribou because that is the way we lived. She despised the booze that came in with white people and said that all bootleggers could be traced back to greedy Tuniks. Mom wanted us to learn the old ways. Until this moment, I had seen all her battles as cultural. She fought for her way of life. Could she have evolved into hating Stella just because she was white?

I tried to explain all this. Again, Stella wasn't buying.

"All I know for sure is that she doesn't like me. She doesn't even know me. I'm not taking you away; you already left." Her voice was firm. "I smile at her and I bring her food and something to drink. She won't even look at me, much less thank me. Riley, the dog, likes me better than she does. At least she comes to greet me when I come to the house." Stella paused for breath. "That's another thing. Why is that beautiful dog chained outside 24/7 in this cold with only a barrel for shelter? The dog needs a better home." She leaned over and kissed a line up my naked chest then got up to shower.

"Will you hunt up our return tickets today? I need to plan a few things, and oh, Jonas, today is Christmas Eve. Merry Christmas Eve, Hubby!"

I had a lot to think about, but Stella called from the bathroom, "The water is hot, wanna join me?" Then she shut the door. I chuckled, pushed the covers out of my way and promptly forgot about Mom and the fact that our tickets were one way. We took so long that it was almost the noon deadline when we finally checked out and headed back to Barbara's.

The relatives sitting around in the living room cheered when they caught a glimpse of us kicking off our boots in the outer hallway, the qanitchat, I translated for Stella. Her face was flushed from the cold and she was smiling shyly. My aunt was making cracks about her new happiness; lewd enough that I decided this was not the time to ask them all to speak in English so Stella would understand. Mom was participating fully, saying off-color things and nodding her head at Stella to lead her into nodding as well. Then Mom led the laughing at Stella when it looked like she was agreeing with the risqué things being said.

In a flash, I realized what they were doing and the anger went straight to my head. I pulled Stella to my chest and hid her face and waggled my finger to the group in the room and boomed in Inupiat, "THIS IS MY WIFE! WHEN YOU MOCK HER, YOU DISRESPECT ME!" After my roar, all I could hear was the TV. No one said a word. I stared Mom down until she glared at me and muttered something about a Tunik.

Chapter 9

Barbara appeared from the kitchen, clucking, "Tsk, tsk, I told you guys to back off." Then to me, "It needed to be said, Brother, now they know." She switched to English. "Josie and Stella, could you come help in the kitchen?" I joined them, still too hot for socializing in the living room. Barbara handed me a cold Coke, "You okay?"

"Yeah, but we need to stay somewhere else. We appreciate you having us, but things are a little close here. I'm going to end up ruining Christmas if we stay."

"Azaa, it will be fine." She waved off my concern. "Mom was just showing off for Auntie Phoebe." She kept cleaning. "Mom." She stopped wiping the counter long enough to straight arm it and sigh. "Josie, you and Stella knead this bowl of dough and make the donuts and let them rise. Then get the deep fryer ready. Stella, you okay with that? Josie will help you."

"Sure, let me wash up first." Stella and Josie began to chatter at the sink and Barbara threw the sponge aside and dried her hands on a towel. "Brother, I need to talk business – let's go upstairs."

My eyes met Stella's. She nodded for me to go. Stella liked Josie. They'd be fine.

Barbara led the way up the narrow steps and cleared wrapping paper and gifts off the hope chest at the foot of her bed and had a seat. She patted the space beside her. I wasn't sure that it would hold my weight so I eased down on it gently. She faced me and took my hands. "Brother, we need you." She gave that a few seconds to sink in. "Mom's arthritis isn't getting any better. Her fingers are almost too messed up to hold a Sigaaq. The dementia isn't getting better either, it is getting worse. No need to bother you with all the details, but there may be a personality disorder diagnosis if we had any competent medical professionals. You know how doctors come and go up here. Even with the new hospital, if the doctors are not thorough, well, you know, doesn't matter how shiny the building is. I've taken her to Native hospitals in Fairbanks and Anchorage. She gets test after test run and then pain pills are prescribed and for a few weeks she is mellow. Then, she gets like ..." She pulled a hand free and pointed downstairs, "... like she is treating Stella today."

"Barbara, what do you want me to do?" I was stumped. "I've been married six, no seven days. I haven't bought return tickets yet and Stella is more than ready to go home."

"Jonas, we don't need money. Mom has yearly Alaska Permanent Fund dividends and quarterly dividends from her Native corporation. Plus, she gets a little pension check from the state, she got some years of employment in between firings," she snorted.

"I don't get where I come in."

"Jonas, I have lost several good men and a son-in-law at least partly because of Mom's behavior. My daughters have left the slope except for Josie's mom who is in the blue hotel, you know the North Slope Borough jail, awaiting trial. All of it is related to our mother and her mood swings and wicked temper. Josie and her little brother and sister deserve some peacefulness in this household, to be children at play instead of hiding in the closet when their Great Aaka screams and threatens us all."

It came to me in a white flash. They wanted me to take Mom. "Oh, no. Huh-uh, nope. Not taking her with me. No way." I pulled my hands away realizing why my relatives were so generous in sending us tickets. It was a set-up.

"Jonas, I have dealt with her for a lifetime. No one else can take her. She will go with you, her golden son." Barbara hid her face with her hands and cried.

I had yelled enough for one day, but my voice grew louder inside my head. I had to speak and I stood.

"You set me up to visit, making it seem like you all cared about me and Stella. You have a big party for us and I start believing that it is good to be home. Then I finally realize that nobody is treating Stella right, and you want us to spend all our waking hours watching Mom? Sorry, Sister." I stomped down the stairs, grabbed my coat and stepped into my boots. I had to get outside to think. The cold air made me gasp but I got my coat zipped and flipped my hood up quickly and ducked into the AC, short for Alaska Commercial Store. Everything, even the prices were blurry to me, I was so mad. Colors and textures blended into one another as I marched up and down the aisles, fist clenched and jaw set. I had to sweep the anger away and think clearly. I focused on just breathing as I walked.

At work, I used the mental exercise of overlaying a schematic of the known, especially for electrical problems. Solutions appeared when I thought of the facts first and then considered options. One truth materialized as I walked through the store: no matter how hurt I was, I would not hurt Barbara any more. We'd be there for Christmas Eve tonight and again tomorrow on Christmas Day. Before we left, I wanted to show Stella Atqasuk, the village where I grew up. There were friends and relatives there that I'd like to see. Maybe for a night or two. Mentally, I drew lines from today to December 28, after the holiday and after a quick trip to Atqasuk. I was not sure I wanted to stay at Barbara's any more, so I sketched two junction boxes on the line, one for each night remaining in Barrow. Then, I added a box for Mom's care, needing to explore options there. But, before that, another big junction box that I would've labeled 'STELLA' if it were on paper. I needed to talk to her to complete the circuit.

I quit pacing around the store and stopped at the customer service desk to borrow the phone. I called the hotel we had just left and let it ring six times before a clerk picked it up. They had plenty of rooms available this weekend and I reserved us one. Alaska Airlines was the opposite; there were zero empty seats leaving Barrow until after New Year's. There were no seats on smaller airlines, Raven and Frontier, but I did make arrangements to fly out to Atqasuk and back. That was a fast $1,000 spent. Meanwhile, the manager had been staring,

Alaska Commercial Store in Barrow (Utqiaġvik), Alaska. Photo by Almee Romeijn-Boen.

but when I hung up and thanked him, he lightened up. My muscles relaxed and I headed back to Barbara's.

The house smelled like yeast bread. Dozens of fried golden Eskimo donuts were stacked on cooling racks in the kitchen. Stella and Josie were dotted with dough and sprinkled with flour and spots of grease. Happy chatter filled the kitchen. Mom and Aunt Phoebe slept on two recliners in the living room. The little kids were sitting close to the television watching an old Burl Ives Christmas special about Rudolph. The volume was turned way low. I mouthed, "Barbara?" and Josie pointed up the stairs. Tiptoeing up the steps, I could see Barbara wrapping gifts before she saw me. I cleared my throat and she turned.

The look on her face nearly killed me. Fear. Pure gratitude. Regret. Exhaustion. Humbleness. Love. She fell into my arms and sobbed.

"Shhh, Little Sister." I stroked her hair. "We'll figure something out."

Later, we got ready to go to the Utqiagvik Presbyterian Church, a tradition for my nieces and nephews. If Stella knew what was going on, she didn't show it. Whenever my mother needed anything, she was right there, helping her put on her coat, finding mittens for her, waiting patiently in the wind waiting for her to get in the cab, and helping her shed her outside clothes and slide into the pew at church. Stella was a saint.

Most of the service was in Inupiat and the vocal music was terrible. I could only hope that members of the choir that could carry a tune were gone on vacation. Josie giggled at the Virgin Mary so hard that Barbara put a hand on her leg, but when the three wise men entered, Josie got so tickled that she had to cram her fist into her mouth to keep from laughing out loud. I even gave her the evil eye and she whispered, "Jonas, they are the dumbest three boys in school." She had to take a breath to compose herself enough to go on. "Look at their robes! They are all on wrong-side-out."

She was right. I had to look down at the floor to swallow my chuckles. It was good to hear the angels singing because I knew the end was near. We stayed after for cookies and punch then piled back into a cab. We could hardly see the Christmas lights for the swirling snow, but Stella wanted to drive around and look. She clasped her hands together at her chest and ooo-ed and ahh-ed. When she had seen enough, she said, "It's

51

like a little of the life and sweetness inside these dreary houses are leaking out." She turned to me and I kissed her. I knew that she was the sweetness in my life.

After an hour or two at Barbara's house, I asked Stella to pack her stuff.

"All of it?" she asked as I threw dirty clothes in my duffle bag.

"Yep, Santa isn't coming here for us tonight." I kept looking for socks and shoes in the floor.

"Oh?" Stella was tapping her foot, and I looked there first then lifted my eyes up to the hands on her hips and then to her face which was one big smile. "I guess it's not far to the North Pole from here. Are we going on up to meet him and the sleigh?"

That made me grin myself. "Just pack, Woman." I gathered up the rest of my scattered clothes and stuffed them in the bag and zipped it.

"Just a second, I'll get our toothbrushes and toiletries from the bathroom and stick them in my bag. Everything, right?" I nodded and slipped out to tell Barbara that we were leaving and we'd see her tomorrow and hugged Mom and told her I loved her. I wasn't sure she knew me, the meds may have dulled her mind, but at least she was pleasant. Josie had called a cab and we crawled in. Stella clapped her hands as we pulled up to Top of the World Hotel.

In answer to Stella's raised eyebrows and upturned hands, I whispered, "Two nights, baby." She had absorbed non-verbal Inupiat communication skills quickly.

Our suite had a large bedroom with a kitchen and a living room. It seemed so quiet and huge with only two people in such large a space after life at Barbara's. Once we had settled in, I took a couple of deep breaths, determined to explain my family's situation. Stella was checking out the refrigerator, standing with the door open, and I turned a kitchen chair around and sat in it backwards and jumped right in. "Stella, what would you think of someone from my family coming back to West Virginia with us?"

"Sure," she said, "we've been talking around it. I told her it would be a big change. Maybe she could have the guest room and I could take her wherever she wants to go." The refrigerator made a sucking sound as it closed and she turned around.

I might've been too shocked to formulate sensible words. "What?" came out of my mouth but I hardly knew I had spoken.

"I think she'd like it in Lindside; she could help with the goats and it would be kinda nice to have another female around."

She poured two glasses half full of eggnog, and I didn't even question where it had come from. She lifted one for a toast, "To family."

I ignored the toast. Something was off track. "What about the extra work for you?"

"Not that much extra. I have to cook and wash clothes anyway." She cocked her head at me looking for all the world like her little red dog, Sugar. She smelled a rat. "Who are you talking about?" she finally asked.

"I was wondering who you were talking about."

"Josie, of course, who else?"

"Oh, Baby, I was talking about my mom." The temperature in the room dropped to nearly the temperature outside. I was leery, but I set my jaw and kept eye contact. Hands shaking, she tried to set her glass down gently but it rocked a little before it landed. She grasped the edge of the table and I knew I was in for it.

"YOUR MOM? Have you lost your mind? Your mom in Lindside?" Her voice became mocking. I didn't much care for her sarcastic side. "Wouldn't that just be the cat's meow? Can you see her Jonas? Screaming in Inupiat at all the white people, and 95% of Lindside is white."

"Yes, I've noticed." I thought that might be funny, but it didn't seem to be.

"Dear God in heaven. And you want me to take care of her. In our home? Light her cigarettes and eventually change her diapers?" The slamming bedroom door added emphasis, if any had been needed.

I spent Christmas Eve night on the couch. Can't say I slept. I tossed and turned all night listening for a sound from the bedroom.

One thing I got right was that Santa would not find us Christmas Eve.

Stella came out early in the morning, red-eyed and sad. She led me to the bed. I told her everything I knew about Mom from my childhood to Barbara's plea for help. She didn't say much but she paid close attention.

Chapter 9

When we were done, she rummaged through her clothes, dressed, and struggled into boots and parka. "Wait here," she said, grabbed the hotel key and left.

What now? Voices in my head were troubled, but the call of the bed was louder and I answered it, curling up in the place our bodies had warmed.

The smell of turkey woke me. I stretched and rubbed my face and then remembered where I was and the shadow hanging over me.

Was that delicious smell really turkey?

I stumbled out of the bedroom to find a smiling Stella who had cooked four 'Hungry Man' TV dinners and was dumping the food onto two plates.

"Merry Christmas, Husband." She gave me a big ole bear hug. "Pull up a chair, Christmas dinner is served."

I was not sure what was happening. Something had changed while I had slept. Stella was happy. So, I was happy and I did what I was told. But, a part of me was worried.

We spent the afternoon at Barbara's. Stella had bought some gifts and gift bags at the AC store when she went out earlier. She kept telling me I'd get my gift later. Surprisingly, everyone at Barbara's was also happy. And they were nice to Stella and they spoke mostly in English, even Aunt Phoebe and Mom. What in the hell was going on?

Chapter 10

Christmas Day Ended Better than it Began

Stella

Taking care of his crazy mean-ass mother for the rest of my natural life. Ha, that was not going to happen! I felt like a poor old hound dog under the table being kicked every time someone moved, but I stayed put with the hope of the next crumb that might fall.

Ridiculed, ignored, looked down on to the point she might as well have spit on me. Not once, but once an hour, every day here.

The Inupiat value of respect evidently did not include a white woman your son married and brought home. And now she needed a place to live.

Precious Jesus," I prayed, "please get me through this. It's for Jonas." I kept telling myself, we're only here a few more days. Over and over I repeated, like a mantra, "I can do anything for a few days."

Good grief, that bitter old woman in our home. I couldn't even imagine her poison attitude on the farm. My sweet dog would probably snarl and bite her, she was so hateful.

I took myself to Barbara's on Christmas morning, early. The storm was over and the streetlights were bright enough for me to find my way. Thank goodness, she was up. The kids were all still sleeping. We had a good talk and I got her side of the story. Her mom had health issues, but she was mostly old and mean. Dementia had begun but she was hard to live with even before that. Years ago, she'd taken all her children's PFD checks and gone to Anchorage and stayed playing bingo and riding limousines until the money, about ten thousand dollars, ran out. Another time she locked the grandkids outside because they were too noisy. She especially targeted boyfriends with her cruelty. She had reloaded a cigarette with a firecracker that had bloodied the face of a man that Barbara was dating. Barbara had dumped another boyfriend after Mary Jo started the lie that he had a boyfriend and AIDS. She told Sissy, the sister now in jail, that her husband could have been her brother because her dad had an affair with the man's mother. All lies, made up to torment others. Barbara was trying to save her grandkids from the abuse her kids, grandchildren, and boyfriends had suffered at Mary Jo's hand.

She let me borrow her cell phone to call Eliza, back in West Virginia. Only a true friend will talk to you on the phone early Christmas morning. She went online and worked her agency magic, found assisted living available right in Barrow at the Senior Center. Mary Jo was old enough to be eligible and finances were not a problem. I could see the Senior Center from Barbara's front door and I trudged on over there. Preparations for a big Christmas dinner were starting, workers were moving slowly. No administrators were there, but I found the woman in charge at the moment. She told me there was a waiting list for single rooms but a double room was opening on March 15 with no applications on file. Mr. and Mrs. Nungasuk were transferring to an Anchorage facility to be closer to their daughter. So, Mary Jo needed a roommate.

I walked back through the snow to Barbara's, starting to be a bit more aware of my surroundings. The snow squeaked in places and crunched in others. This time, I felt the cold rushing in through the shoelace holes in my boots, felt my metal earrings get cold and my earlobes start to ache. Should remember to take out earrings.

The kids were still sleeping and I started whispering before I took off my coat, "Barbara, there's a double room coming available. So we need two residents to get the room. Can we marry her off?" Barbara laughed so hard that she pretended to pound the table for relief. I tried to laugh quietly, but holding it back with a hand over my mouth resulted in tears. When I wiped my eyes and we sobered up and could breathe again, Barbara snapped her fingers.

"I've got it. Aunt Phoebe. They get along. She's younger, but not by much. They've lived together off and on over the years. Phoebe can take care of little things, like sneak her cigarettes and talk to her in Inupiat and gossip about everything. Yes, and she can afford it, too." Then, a light came on in Barbara's eyes. "And her kids will thank me forever. She travels from household to household until there is a fuss and they kick her out, then she moves on to the next child's home. Been doing that for four years."

"Will you do the paperwork, fill out the applications?"

"Yes, ma'am," Barbara replied with gusto, "but will you take them both until March 15?"

Less than three months, I reasoned. Phoebe can take care of Mary Jo. Shoot, they can live in Jonas' little house. It ran through my mind like a runaway train and I closed my eyes and said, "Yes."

Barbara did a dance right there in the kitchen and told me she would get the airplane tickets made.

"But I don't know the date on our tickets."

She smiled a knowing smile, "Jonas only has one way tickets. We'll take care of four seats. I know someone at the desk at Alaska Airlines; we'll get the first four seats that they have." She giggled, "Our families will be more than happy to contribute to that fund."

"Wait, wait, we are going to a village tomorrow. Jonas wants to visit there a day or two." I was thinking fast. "Oh, and make those tickets for Mary Jo and Phoebe round trip returning March 14." What else, what else? "And one more thing, I want your dog."

"Done. The kids loved her as a playful pup but now I do everything. She is miserable, too, tied up all the time."

Her mental wheels were turning so fast, I could hear the gears meshing. "I need time to get those two ready. Let's try for New Year's Eve." She rolled her eyes, "They'll be thrilled to go on a trip."

We heard footsteps upstairs and Barbara jumped to her feet. "I've got to turn on the Christmas tree lights. Will you stay?" I was already up and getting dressed for outdoors. "No, I have Christmas shopping to do." We hugged and the die was cast. Even Riley was happy; she wiggled at me as I left and I blew her a kiss.

If I could've skipped through snowdrifts to the store I would've, but the deep snow and frozen chunks of ice made that hazardous. I felt like dancing but I didn't need a twisted ankle.

Chapter 10

AC was open a few hours this morning so I stopped by for food and gifts and something to wrap them in. A necklace for Josie, toys for the kids, driving gloves for Barbara, warm socks for Phoebe and a fruit basket for Mary Jo. I knew she hated fruit but they were on sale and I figured she deserved it. Then I felt bad and hid a carton of Marlboros in the back. Knit caps for Leo and James and Richard, but that wasn't very much so I added bags of Christmas candy. They each had a sweet tooth. I got a mushy card for Jonas. His gift would be me with a bow on my head, warm and willing. More than he deserved; he brought me here with a one-way ticket and didn't tell me.

I stood in the frozen food aisle thinking. When should I tell him my plan? I'd better wait until it all gets set and find the right moment. Maybe while he's eating? Then, I remembered to get food. By the time I paid the cashier, there were eight plastic bags on eight different fingers. I headed down the street to the hotel.

Christmas Day ended better than it began. We spent a few hours at Barbara's exchanging gifts. Everyone was positively radiant. Then, a wonderful night, a real honeymoon night. I was practically purring before I finally went to sleep.

The next morning, we rolled out early, took one duffle with a couple of changes of clothes for us both and put the rest of our things in hotel storage.

As I climbed up two teeny steps into a tiny airplane, I wondered if this was a joke. There were only three seats, one already occupied by a large woman. Jonas followed me and the pilot, who looked like a high school kid, helped each of us with an ancient harness-like seat belt. Jonas tossed our duffle behind the netting in the back where the freight was stored. Looked like the freight on this trip was all cases of pop. The windows were edged with duct tape and when the engine started, it sounded like a lawn mower. Surely this was not big enough or safe enough to fly. But it did.

The frozen ocean was on the right, a whiter, smoother texture than the land. An orange pipeline cut this way and that across the tundra. We never lost sight of the ground and I was fascinated by the white expanse of Arctic scenery, or lack of. No trees. No houses. No lights. No colors except black and white with some pastel pinks from the Arctic sun, which was below the horizon, and some blues on the ocean ice.

The engine was too loud for us to talk so Jonas rapped his knuckles against the window in front of me and pointed below. A herd of reindeer or caribou or something with big-daddy antlers was pawing at the snow and eating whatever was underneath. Before I knew it there were blue lights lining a short runway and a cluster of colorful houses frosted with snow like a Christmas card scene. It was only a sixteen-minute flight to go sixty miles from Barrow, but no roads existed to connect Atqasuk to any other settlement. It felt like we were landing in another world.

When the plane rolled to a stop, pick-up trucks came out onto the tarmac all the way to the plane. We unhooked our seat belts. "There's Mick to get us." Jonas pointed with his head at a big white truck as he grabbed the duffle. "We're staying at his mother-in-law, Gwennie's, house. She's away in Anchorage and they use it when repairmen and guests get weathered in out here." He was so excited; he forgot he told me this already when we were at Barbara's. "She was always good to me, gave me extra cookies at school. She taught Inupiat."

Then he turned to me and slaughtered an old saying in his crazy way, "Let's miss and cake up." We kissed before we climbed down the tiny steps, our bodies twisted awkwardly in the cramped space. The ridiculousness of it all lightened my mood.

When we made it to the white pick-up, the driver jumped down and the two men thumped each other on the back and looked at each other for so long that I started thinking about the truck heater. Finally, Jonas thought to introduce me, "Mick, this is Stella. We got married ten days ago." Mick was very nice and took his glove off to shake my hand, so I did, too. I put it back on pretty fast afterwards. The men high-fived and I shook my head and climbed into Mick's running truck and sat right in front of the warm air vents. Jonas and Mick unloaded all that freight into the truck bed and hurried into the cab from different sides at the same time. They both breathed clouds of ice fog that disappeared in the warm air. They pushed me to the center and for an instant, I felt very much like a little girl on an adventure, safely surrounded by two burly men who knew where they were and what they were doing, unlike myself.

Chapter 11

Part of my Heart Stayed in Atqasuk

Jonas

Riding the mile or so with Mick and Stella to Atqasuk, I was thinking about that thing Stella says to Granddaddy Longlegs spiders, "Granddaddy, Granddaddy, where is your home?" or something like that and it eventually points with one of his long legs. If I were a spider I would point here, to the bluffs above the meandering Meade River where my mom taught me to fish, and the tundra beyond, where I heard the clicking tendons of massive numbers of caribou. I'd point to Second Creek where I picked a million orange aqpik berries and ate another million, and to the dirt streets of town and the little siksriks that pop up like prairie dogs in the summertime, and the snow machines and four wheelers and boats that made a young boy's paradise, especially during twenty-four hour days of daylight. They say home is where your heart is. If memories make up your heart and life has room for more than one home, it's fair to say that part of my heart stayed in Atqasuk because it sure felt like home.

Mick let us in Gwennie's house and the smell of caribou stew filled the room. He lifted the lid of a big crock-pot to show us the simmering broth, chunks of meat, and potatoes. His wife Gaye had made it for us along with a big zip-lock bag of Eskimo donuts. "Help yourself to anything in the cupboards or refrigerator," he said, "and don't forget to come over to the school this afternoon for the Christmas games. I'll put the word out on the VHF that you are in town and people can stop by there to see you." He waved his hat at us as he turned

Chapter 11

Meade River in Atqasuk, Alaska. Photo by Molly Ahkivgak.

to leave then added, "My number is still 2525, half a buck; call if you need anything else. Oh, and Kristopher has an extra skidoo if you want to go out. Customized. Pretty powerful, though. Might be too much machine for you." He slapped his leg and chuckled as he left.

"What is he talking about?" Stella wanted in on the joke.

"Oh, a schoolteacher wanted to sell me a snow machine when he left one spring and he said those words to me. He didn't know that I had rebuilt the engine when I was in 7th grade. My buddies got a kick out of it and looks like they haven't forgotten even fifty years later."

Stella went to the bathroom. I had forgotten how many times a day women went to the bathroom. Gwennie's framed photographs covered her walls; and I moved around the rooms remembering her grandchildren, Charles, Kristopher, Samantha, and Sondra. Now they all had children of their own. Mixed in with group pictures and newspaper clippings were school pictures of dark students, tanned at the end of a summer spent outdoors, and photos of little boys posing with their hunting rifles. Bet they don't allow guns in school any more. The pictures really took me back in time.

Stella's voice startled me, "Hey you, how about some stew?" As skinny as that woman was, she sure ate a lot. I joined her and enjoyed sopping up the rich tuttu broth with my Eskimo donut. Stella finished hers first and looked over Gwennie's extensive video library. There were dozens of old fashioned VHS tapes. "Would it be all right if I watched a movie?"

She was always easy to get along with, but not this sugary sweet. My suspicions were on high alert. I decided not to call her on it just yet. "Absolutely, movie watching is big in the Arctic. Gwennie sure won't mind."

She picked some old movie that didn't interest me in the least, popped it in the player, figured out both remotes and snuggled on the couch to watch. Focused totally on the TV.

Last night was great and the flight out here was fun, but not a word about Mom or about leaving. Strange behavior. It was time for me to take a walk.

Atqasuk, Alaska moon in winter. Photo by Doug Armstrong.

Chapter 12

I Needed to Share it all with Jonas

Stella

The phone rang so soon after Jonas left that I was afraid he'd hear it and come back in. I scrambled across the room to answer it before the second ring. In my new world of cell phones, it was a blast from the past to have to move to find an old landline phone. It was Barbara. I had told her where we'd be staying as we left her house last night. She had explained that we'd be out of the cell phone service area. She had gotten applications from the Senior Center for both Mary Jo and Phoebe. This afternoon, she would sit them both down and explain what we wanted to do, then, hopefully, help them fill out the papers. Also, she was waiting for Alaska Airlines to open so she could see about tickets for us. I reminded her about the dog and she said that there was an old kennel in an outbuilding for Riley to use to travel. After we hung up, doubt flashed through my mind, just for a second, but long enough that I realized I needed to share it all with Jonas. I had kept one big secret from him for months and I didn't want any more terrible feelings that came with secrecy.

Within the hour, Jonas burst back in stomping off the snow. "Not much has changed around here. A couple of new houses and the school has had an upgrade since I was here last." He unlaced his boots and stepped out of coveralls and helped me up from the couch. "Ah, reunited and it feels so good." He tried to sing and then grabbed me to twirl me around in a sort of dance move. We fell back to the couch holding hands.

"What's on your mind these days?" He was blunt and caught me off guard.

The plans Barbara and I had put in place came pouring out. I discussed them all. And then listed them in a summary, "One, we reserve a place at the Senior Center for both Phoebe and your mom. Next, we take them home with us until the middle of March. They can live in your house. Then, we carry them back up to Barrow and settle them in their new place. Oh, and Riley is ours." I studied his face. The dark eyes sparkled and he chewed on the inside of his cheek before he nodded.

"What was the holdup on telling me? I knew that something was off; you came back on Christmas Day all happy. Is that when you and Barbara talked?"

"Yes." I felt muscles relaxing.

"Mary Jo Akpik in Lindside. That paints a picture to ponder."

I very seriously asked, "What can go wrong?" After a moment of silence, both of us exploded into hoots of laughter. Then, we wiped each other's happy tears.

He hugged me and whispered, "I love you. I don't understand you, but I love you. Thank you for dealing with all my mom has put you through and what she surely will do in the future." We headed for the bedroom and it occurred to me that I would need to wash the sheets before we left.

The gym at Meade River School was packed. An announcer called events and age groups and I watched the strangest sports I have ever seen.

"Most of these games came to be because of the long, cold winters and limited indoor space," Jonas explained, "and some of them are events in Native Youth Olympics. There are world competitions, usually in Canada, that are a big deal for kids in Alaska."

"Are you kidding with me? Butt walking is an Olympic event?"

"Well, some of them are just for fun and some were added more recently like hula hooping; but the one-foot-high kick, two-foot-high kick and head and finger pulls have been standards." Sounded weird to me. "They're calling women, your age group; wanna give it a try?" I declined. "Twenty dollars for first place." He nudged me.

"Are you going to compete when it's the men's turn?" I was sure I knew the answer was 'no' but I got a surprise.

He shrugged, "Maybe."

"What time do they end?" I could see me sitting on the bleachers for hours today.

"They end when they are all done, usually on New Year's Day. If they finish earlier, we compete as a village, teams of married people against those not married."

"That's a week, Jonas. People really come here every day for a week?"

"What can I say, there's not much else to do in the dead of winter when family members come home for the holidays. Remember, we don't have shopping malls or theaters or restaurants, so this is a very popular event, the place to be."

"Aarigaa, Jonas Akpik, welcome home!" An old friend spotted Jonas and approached us. Jonas stood to shake hands with him, introduced me to the man, Thomas, who introduced all his family and joined us. That was the pattern for the afternoon; people of all ages came up in the bleachers to visit then drifted away in little groups. Babies were carried on their mother's backs under fur-lined parkas tied with a sash to hold the baby in place. Some of those parkas were spread out in between the bleacher benches for a bed and little ones slept through the talking and cheering. There was always entertainment on the court, races and cash prizes given by age group, but the bleachers buzzed with activity, too. It was a very cozy feeling, like being in a huge living room.

When 50- to 59-year-old men were called for leg rassling, (he said wrestling) Jonas joined the group of six men who shuffled down to mid-court, poking fun at each other's age and strength. Jonas was the biggest man down there. They all tried to lose the draw to go first and I understood why shortly. The winner of the first match kept playing and as soon as a contestant lost, they were out. Jonas was fifth to compete, making it easy to beat his exhausted opponent and then the next to win first place. The crowd cheered and he held clasped fists overhead after he was helped to his feet. He proudly carried the $20 prize money up to me. I was concerned. "Think this will buy enough painkiller to cover everything that will hurt tomorrow?"

He said, "At least I didn't lose and get flipped backwards. That would've hurt. I have done this before." I hugged him and rubbed his back, knowing that it was going to ache.

"I just didn't know what an athlete I married."

"Now, it's your turn."

"Oh, no, I've never leg-rassled in my life."

Chapter 12

I had the feeling he was going to take me down the bleachers and become my coach, but Mick came in and scanned the bleachers, saw Jonas waving, and joined us. Thank goodness.

"Hey Jonas, wanna go out on ski-doos? There's caribou about five miles out."

Jonas looked at me, then back at Mick. "Can I take Stella out, too?" He looked back at me, "That is, if she wants to go." I raised my eyebrows like the people all around me would have done to say yes.

Mick clapped his gloves against his leg and sat down and turned to face the games. "Sure. Like I said, Kristopher has a sweet machine. Gaye may have a warmer parka and fur-lined mittens and hat if either of you need them."

"When do you want to leave?" Mick was talking to Jonas but watching the women leg-rassle. Jonas' eyes wrinkled up in the corners like he was about to laugh.

"How about after this event?" Then he added, "Gaye will skin your ears if she sees you enjoying the women's events."

Mick just grinned. "Good point, meet you in 30 minutes at my house." He stayed behind as Jonas and I walked out of the gym holding hands. The feelings of pride and possession that I had day-dreamed about forty years ago when I yearned for a boyfriend were as glorious as I had imagined.

At the bottom of the front ramp, Jonas stopped, "Are you sure?"

"Yes, Jonas, I need something to do. Thanks for including me."

He arched his eyebrows at me. "Stella, it's 30 below."

I raised my eyebrows.

Jonas shrugged. The lack of words needed to hold a conversation here was a major change from home.

We walked back to Gwennie's and scrambled to get ready. Jonas pulled on his heavy outdoor gear while I got bathroomed up. I had borrowed Barbara's full-length parka, lined with sheepskin and trimmed with wolverine fur. She had heavy boots with wool liners, too. They were a little big for me, but would be warm enough.

It took twenty minutes to get dressed; he was determined that I find good gloves in the box in the qanitchat overflowing with gloves, mittens, knit caps, neck gaitors, and stretchy face masks. "They don't have to match but they can't have holes and they have to be warm." He finally fished out two mammoth sized, fur covered, and fur-lined mittens and reached them to me. They had a distinctive odor and I thought that Sugar would've probably attacked them, which made me a little homesick and strengthened my resolve to get home soon.

The wind had picked up since we left the school. As soon as we stepped off the front stoop, it caught my face and took my breath away, its icy fingers reaching back into my hood and touching my ears and neck. Jonas turned and fastened my hood tightly, compressing the opening into a tiny fur-lined tunnel about three inches across, just enough to see out. I could feel a reminder of the cold through every seam of my boots, wind pants, and even through the stitches in my gloves, but I was plenty warm. As we walked over to Mick's, I was never so glad of anything as those smelly, warm mittens.

Jonas started Kristopher's snow machine to let the engine warm up. Mick had his machine already running. Jonas had explained to me earlier that oil thickened in the cold and had to be given some time to warm and thin and circulate around the engines. Cars and snow machines had to idle awhile before their engines were ready to go. I sat sideways on the frozen seat while he stomped the snow off his boots and went back inside with Mick. They came back with two rifles, one strapped across Mick's back and the other he handed to me. I lowered my head into the loop made by the strap and he helped me

Arctic snowmachining. Photo by Vanni Prichard.

69

put it on. He nodded approval and turned me around and checked it all then patted me on the back. I felt like a good ole packhorse, but it was better than being cooped up inside with a movie.

He threw a leg over the snowmobile's seat, a Mad Max sort of cowboy, and motioned me to get on behind him. I thought my borrowed parka would be too long to allow me to straddle the seat, but it wasn't and I realized why the zipper didn't go all the way to the bottom hem, to give the coat a sort of split for me to move my legs. My thought had been that it was poorly made. Funny how we judged based on our own background and don't wait to see the reasons behind other people's actions. I congratulated myself on keeping my mouth shut this time and vowed to be more open to new ways.

Then my neck whipped back as Jonas revved the motor and we flew out of our parking place. I could see a rooster tail of snow pluming behind Mick as he pulled out and reckoned we had one behind us, too. I tried to hold on but couldn't grip Jonas' parka with my hands; it was too thick and so were my mittens. I wrapped my arms around him and held on for dear life with hands flat against him. We went through town on streets, hitting enough gravel beneath the ice to cause sparks to fly out from the snow machine's skids. After a few minutes we were out on the tundra, away from town, and to my surprise, from the lights of town. Our headlights led the way and we roared through a flock of ptarmigan, white feathers flying as the nearly invisible birds scattered out of our path. They'd fly only a few feet and then land again. What kind of sport was ptarmigan hunting? It would be like shooting chickens.

We only slowed down enough for me to see them: Jonas stretched out an arm to point and I had to look twice because even though they didn't go far, their white bodies blended into the snow-covered tundra nearly perfectly. Mick was riding parallel to our path about fifty yards away.

Then Jonas sped across open spaces and I could see the orange pipeline. We kept in sight of it for an hour before Jonas pulled up beside Mick who had stopped, checked on me, and took a drink from an old green thermos. "Should be close."

"What should be close?" I had gotten stiff and cold on the way and my backside was tender from hard landings going over the bumps. I didn't much care what was close, but I felt it was something I should know.

"Tuttu." Both men replied at the same time.

I knew that meant caribou and I figured we weren't going there to pet them. The meat was delicious and I knew Jonas was a good shot, so clearly we were hunting, not that anyone said so. Men all over the world tend to lose their minds when hunting is involved, I guess. The cold and dark were enough to discourage me and I did wonder how we'd get dead caribou back to town. My forehead hurt from the cold, a brain freeze of sorts, and I pulled the knit cap down over it as we took off again.

Within a few miles, we met the massive herd and went to the side of it to a knoll to admire hundreds of animals. It was getting late in the day and the dim, hazy light was fading, but we climbed off the snow machine to watch. Mick, ahead of us, picked out a target and shot it. The nearby tuttu scattered away from the fallen beast. Then Jonas reached for the rifle on my back and shot another one. We rode down to the dead caribou and the men quickly field dressed them for travel and lashed them on the back of Mick's back seat and rack.

Mick asked me, "Alappaa?" and I was stumped.

"Are you cold?" Jonas translated.

I fought the urge to say, "Duh!" and just nodded my head. They talked and Jonas explained that they would shorten the trip back, but we'd go up and down some bluffs and ravines. I didn't understand how the caribou could stay put on the bumpy tundra, much less ravines, but the men didn't seem worried. They high-fived each other and celebrated their success with some cocoa laced with butterscotch schnapps. I thought there was coffee in the thermos. The cocoa was rich and sweet and warmed me for a moment. Mick smoked a cigarette and we headed back to the village. I didn't think I could bear the cold another minute when we pulled up to Mick's house.

They were going to hang the meat in Mick's garage and skin and butcher it, but I headed to Gwennie's for a warm bath. So weary that I could barely guide my spoon of stew from the slow cooker to my mouth, I gave up and went to bed. After midnight Jonas slid into the bed beside me. He smelled soapy clean with butterscotch on his breath, and I went back to sleep pressed against his chest, cuddled in his arms.

Landed at the Barrow (Utqiaġvik) Airport. Photo by B. Crabtree.

Chapter 13

A Force to be Reckoned With?

Jonas

Azaa! I was so tired and so happy. Just wandering around Atqasuk was terrific, but then to get to see some of the Christmas games, and on top of that, to get to go out on the tundra made for a near-perfect day. The smell of the snow machine's exhaust in the midst of fresh cold air was such a powerful reminder of my past that I got lost in it all, even with Stella sitting close behind me. When I wasn't bursting with joy, I tried to imagine how it looked to her. "Otherworldly" was the best word I could think of. I know her eyes wouldn't have distinguished slight rises of land or groups of plants to identify a location. Mine were just getting back to those fine Arctic differences. It was cold. "Airish," I bet she'll say like those mountain people do when it's cool and crisp out. She was a good sport though, and both Mick and I were impressed. Not the first complaint had come out of her mouth.

I had forgotten how the cold temperature zaps energy. Mick did most of the work cutting up those caribou. We packaged them and hung them out to freeze. I looked forward to taking some cuts of meat to Barbara.

Afterwards, it was all I could do to hike back to Stella, take a shower, and go to bed. Gwennie's house was warm as toast and when I raised the covers, the scent of baby powder and vanilla filled the air. I guess from Stella's old flannel nightgown or shampoo or something. She must have awakened some because she "ummed" and "oooed" and snuggled up to my bare chest. God, I loved being home and I loved being married.

Chapter 13

Before sleep overtook me, I tried to absorb the plan that Barbara and Stella had cooked up for Mom and Aunt Phoebe and wondered if it was going to work out. Those two interacted powerfully. Alone, it sounded like they could be pretty awful, but manageable. Together, they might be a force to be reckoned with. They had grown up in hard times as little girls carrying sacks of coal from the mine in Atqasuk home for heat. As adults, they had scraped by.

Their parties of yesteryear were legendary. Uncle Walter died at one of their bashes and they posed him so his face was hidden and pretended he had passed out so they could keep on partying. Later, they said that's what he would've wanted. Lindside may not be ready for them. The last thing I remember was a shadow of doubt about the whole thing and then I slept.

The next day I woke and started to stretch in bed. My usual, "I could stretch a mile if I didn't have to walk back," didn't cross my lips because nothing happened. My back was locked up. Either the leg wrestling or the skidoo ride did me in. Stella got me extra strength Excedrin and I took a couple of them. So much for visiting around at the Christmas games. By afternoon, I could roll out of bed to the floor and Stella helped me stand but I couldn't get to a sitting position. My choices for the day were lying or standing. Stella started calling around for something stronger, and the health aide in the village found some muscle relaxants, little home-plate shaped pills, that sent me into a wonderful dream world and enabled me to move a little late in the day. We were supposed to fly out the next morning, but Stella moved those reservations ahead a few more days.

"Champ-ee-un leg rasslers bound to have some aches and pains," Stella teased. "Am I gonna have to give you a sponge bath or are you gonna be able to take a shower in a few days?" Her humor was evil, but she waited on me, helped me up and down for 48 hours until I felt like I could move. Mick and Gaye came to visit and he commiserated and said he was sore after that ride, too, but he was probably just being kind. After three days, I felt that I could sit in a truck a mile to the airport and then fly for less than twenty minutes back to Barrow. By then, those planes were all full so we waited another day until we could get out. Thank goodness, the clear weather held. Stella carried the big cardboard box of frozen tuttu meat and I carried the tiny duffle on board the Cessna 172.

Aerial view of Barrow (Utqiaġvik), Alaska. Photo by Vanni Prichard.

We made it back with a minimum of conversation. Stella had volunteered to sit in the co-pilot seat and kept looking back to see if I was okay. Leo picked us up at the Barrow terminal. "Might as well just leave you here," he sniggered. "Barbara has helped pack and Mom's raring to go. All the applications have been submitted and approved and they are having their checks mailed to your old address in West Virginia. Now, just waiting for four seats to open up."

I moaned, I think from back pain, but it cracked Leo up. "You and Stella," he looked at her for a second, "have our deepest admiration for taking these two away from here, even for three months." He paused. "Stella, you must really love this guy." Then he whistled.

"For the first time, we are getting a break from spreading untrue rumors, picking at the kids, screaming at us. Mood swings and confusion that knock you down then hit from the other side." He sighed. "I swear I love her, but sometimes she is just hard."

His mood lightened, "Barbara told her that if she talks to Stella in Inupiat, she'll be sent back to Barrow. She cussed a blue streak in Inupiat, said it was just like the BIA days. She threw things and pouted and went to her room until Barbara got worried and checked on her and found her packing, all happy. Mom told Barbara in English, 'Do not worry, I'll be good.' Makes you think that she knows when she is being so awful. I thought it might be out of her control like Alzheimer's or something. We even tried to get mood enhancers prescribed for her. She said that we needed to take them, she was fine." He pounded the steering wheel, laughing. "And Phoebe's kids may have a party when the plane leaves with her on it." We were coming to a four-way intersection and Leo needed to know which way to go.

"So, where we going, Bro? Hotel or Barbara's?" Stella cleared her throat in the back seat and I got it.

"Hotel. It sounds like we may be heading home soon."

"10-4, at your service."

He left us at the front door and I went slowly up the steps without much pain. They had vacancies, thank goodness, and we got our luggage out of the back storage closet and headed to the room. Our cell phones lit up with texts and missed calls as soon as we got service again. Not anything important, but lots of holiday greetings from West Virginia and a report on Stella's animals from Tisha. All was well.

The big news of the day came late, when Barbara texted, "Get ready, you are on the red-eye flight tomorrow night." I hung my head. It was hard to look forward to New Year's Eve on a plane for seventeen hours with Mom and Aunt Phoebe and a bad back.

Chapter 14

Things Started Falling Apart

Stella

The night before we were scheduled to fly home, I think Jonas took two muscle relaxers instead of just one. He took one at bedtime and woke up in a few hours and took another one, in spite of me telling him it was the second one. Anyway, he was still sleeping hard when we should've been up and at it. I sure hoped he would wake up before check out; if'n he didn't, we'd have to pay for another night. All I needed to do was tie up some loose ends and pack our clothes which could be done with him sleeping. I'd had time to wash all of the ones we took to Atqasuk at Gwennie's, thank goodness, but he needed to be mobile by noon.

Our flight was to leave just before 7 PM. Hallelujah! Check-in was an hour before. So, I had about twelve hours to get everything settled with Jonas' kin people and get us ready to leave. The dog was supposed to have a health certificate to travel, so I needed to get her to the vet sometime today and check out her kennel to be sure it was clean and the door latch worked. Poor thing was gonna love Peters Mountain and running free. Me too, for that matter. I was spending too much time here getting dressed to go outside and then undressing to come inside. Spent too much time inside, too. Missed my dog and the chickens and sheep and goats, too. Tisha and Eliza and my church family were on my mind as well. My crazy mean brother, Timmy Lee, even crossed my mind for the first time in weeks. He was being held and treated in a hospital in Huntington, West Virginia, until he was determined fit to stand trial on a murder charge. My friend Tisha called it the 'loony bin' and I always shushed her, but she wasn't far off. Even though I probably should feel sorry for him, I didn't. I felt like I had been away for months, not just ten days. It was time to go home.

Things started to fall into place. Riley passed the health certificate exam with flying colors. All she needed was a kennel cough shot and we were good to go. All the clothes got washed and packed and Jonas woke up enough to go to Barbara's before noon and saved us another night's expense.

Then, things started falling apart. For no good reason, his mother was throwing a fit about being called Aaka, the Inupiat word for grandmother. If she had to speak English, then she was demanding to be called "Grandma" by everyone. It was an odd request from her.

"But, Mom," Jonas tried to be logical even if he was still groggy, "you are not my Grandma, you are my Mother."

"Not to matter. If we are speaking English, then we are speaking English. All around." She pointed around the room at everyone. "Say with me, 'Grand-ma'." We all did. This was not a battle worth fighting. As far as I was concerned, she could be Grandma.

Barbara was cooking an early bon voyage supper. She had baked and sliced one of the big caribou roasts and had rice and a tableful of side dishes. The savory smells of cooked meat and more delicate garlic and celery alerted my stomach; it growled to be fed. We all sat around one table and the mood grew somber as we finished the delicious meal. Silverware clanked against dishes less often, and it was quiet for long moments. Finally, Barbara spoke.

"I'm going to miss you, Mom." Barbara paused with her fork in the air, waiting for a response. Nothing. "Mom, I am going to miss you around here," she repeated.

Her mom looked around as if she were looking for someone, "No Mom here. I am Grandma." She cackled at her own joke then grew a bit more serious. "I will miss you all, too, but what's ten weeks?" She threw her arms up like a cheerleader. "I'll be home before you know it." Then, she slurped the caribou broth at the bottom of her bowl and Barbara muttered, "Not gonna miss those table manners."

The children watched, big-eyed, as their Grandma calmly sat at the table smiling, speaking only in English, and not screaming at anyone. Jonas was still too out of it to do much more than shake his head at me.

Dessert was served: a pineapple-upside-down-cake with candied cherries in the center of each pineapple ring. It was buttery and sticky with brown sugar and I could've eaten another piece, but Mary Jo pushed back and announced, "It's time."

The little kids hugged and kissed her and she squeezed them hard and told them to mind their mom. They hugged me and shook Jonas' hand. We told them we'd bring their Grandma home in March. They nodded and ran off to the TV. Josie came and hugged us all. She was staying home with the children, not riding with us to the terminal. I promised to bring her jewelry when we returned in March. She shyly thanked me for marrying Jonas and added, "He might come back more often if you ask him."

"Maybe you'll come and visit us sometime, too." It was hard to leave her.

She nodded and hugged me again.

Barbara was coming with us to the airport. It was a good thing because we needed her to help with all the luggage. Mary Jo had three huge suitcases and Jonas and I had two. The cabbie had to use a bungee cord to fasten the trunk because it wouldn't close. Riley in the kennel took up more room in the back seat than we had expected, so the four of us didn't have space to sit. Jonas called Leo to come with the truck and get the dog. Phoebe was going to meet us there. Barbara ran a last minute check to see if Mary Jo had her ticket, her credit card, cash, and an ID. She showed them, meek as a child, then zipped them in her shoulder bag and jumped into the back seat, ready to go. Maybe she behaved in public?

Phoebe was sitting in the plastic terminal chairs waiting when we got there. She greeted Mary Jo warmly and they snuck into a corner to chat. We checked in our bags then joined Barbara to visit Phoebe's family. Her oldest son spoke softly, "We were going to leave her here by herself, but we were afraid she would change her mind and come home, so we are staying here to be sure she gets on the plane." There was an undercurrent of laughter but no one contradicted him. He wasn't kidding. Aunt Phoebe must be a character. Ten weeks isn't that long; it'll be a good break for her and them, I thought.

All went well at boarding. We went through security and walked thirty yards across the windblown runway to climb the stairs of the plane. I stayed behind Mary Jo and Jonas trailed Phoebe, just to be sure the old girls didn't fall. We found our seats, we were nearly in the front of the plane, and Phoebe and Mary Jo were ten rows behind us. Jonas wanted to trade seats with them so we would be able to watch them, but I pooh-poohed the idea. It was less than a two-hour flight to Anchorage; surely there was nothing that could happen. Turns out that was a mistake.

After the safety announcements including, "Take your seats and find the nearest exit. Please note that the seat belt light is on," I turned to see them settled in, could just barely see the two gray heads over the seat backs. I started to prepare myself mentally for the takeoff. The announcements were repeated in a firmer tone. Good grief, people, sit down. Then, the captain sternly reminded everyone to sit down. I looked around and realized who was up. Mary Jo and Phoebe were both cruising the aisle visiting with people they knew and were pretending to not understand English when the flight attendants spoke to them. I elbowed Jonas. "You've got to go get them." He struggled to his feet in the small space.

"Grandma," I was proud that he remembered what she wanted to be called, "You and Aunt Phoebe need to sit down."

"Sir?" The perfectly-groomed flight attendant, her hair slicked back and the creases in her uniform pants crisp and unbroken, was raising her voice just a tad. "Sir, are you traveling with these women?"

Jonas shook his head up and down, "Yes, ma'am."

"They are refusing to take their seats. We cannot taxi until they are safely seated."

"I'll take care of this. Sorry ma'am." I stood and watched

Jonas get close and speak with both of them. The women seemed to be grumbling but shuffled back to their seats, stopping long enough to hug Jonas. The flight attendant seemed to be thanking him and he sidestepped back down the aisle to me and squeezed back in his seat.

Nicole, the flight attendant, before she met Mary Jo and Phoebe.

The plane started to move and under the cover

of the engine sounds I asked him what happened. He tried not to laugh as he explained that Phoebe and Mary Jo were excited when they saw an old neighbor on the plane and then someone else they knew and rushed to talk to them. "They are pretty excited anyway, and they were all speaking in Inupiat and ignoring the attendant as if they didn't understand or were invisible or something." He twisted in his seat and confirmed that they were in place as the plane reached its cruising altitude. We both closed our eyes and began to relax.

A few minutes later, Nicole, the attendant, was standing beside us, "Excuse me, sir, your relatives have cigarettes out and are asking for a light. They rang their service call bell and asked me for a light." A tendril of hair had escaped her ponytail and her voice was less firm. "Could you please come and speak to them? I'm not sure if they understand the consequences of smoking on board."

Jonas pushed on the armrests to get up and followed her to the back. He returned with two packs of cigarettes and angrily stuffed them in the chair back pouch in front of him. "They understand just fine. They are just like children wanting attention. I think they just wanted to push the service call button."

"What did you tell them?"

"That an open flame in the cabin will ignite the oxygen that is pumped in and we'll be blown to kingdom come. The stewardess wanted to confiscate their smokes, so I took them. Mom actually showed me her lighter when I took her cigarettes; she didn't need a light."

"Oh, goodness, what else can they get into?"

"Oh, they'll think of something. They're on a roll."

We heard the ping of a service call button and then another. Nicole was responding and then brought them both glasses of water.

I checked my watch. An hour until we landed in Anchorage. The seat belt light was turned off allowing passengers to move about and here they both came, visiting with people until they got up to us, smiling and thanking us for taking them on this grand trip.

Phoebe was looking around and called out, "Mary Jo, there's a bathroom and a kitchen back there! Did you know that?" They both looked toward the rear of the plane.

"You didn't know that? C'mon, I'll show you." They pattered away.

Chapter 14

"I don't think two people can get in that little bathroom, but if they can, those two will figure out a way. Mom will probably want to demonstrate all the features to Phoebe." Jonas turned often to monitor the bathroom visit and I tried to disappear. What if someone else needed the bathroom while these two knuckleheads played back there?

Sure enough, here came Nicole, shirttail peeking out and jacket rumpled. "Sir, your relatives are causing a disruption, can you come?" He grunted and stood up again and followed her. He returned to get me. "Stella, come and talk to them, they are stuck in the bathroom and tell me that it is a ladies' room and I can't open the door." I groaned out loud and followed him to the back of the plane where several had gathered.

Faced with a closed door and several pair of expectant eyes, I went into Sunday school teacher mode and steeled my will and voice, "Grandma! Open the door right this minute."

Fumbling noises came from inside and the little red sign on the door slid from 'Occupied' to green 'Vacancy.' I pulled the door open and Mary Jo started to fall out, shoulder first, her tummy wedged in against the sink. A distinctive odor accompanied her. Phoebe was seated and had her pants around her ankles. "Can either of you reach the flush button?" It was like talking to six-year-olds. I turned away to get a breath of fresh air and got a mouthful of air freshener that Nicole was spraying. I turned back into the fray.

Softly, Phoebe spoke. "I'm not done."

"You can flush it and finish and flush it again." My voice was as soft as hers.

"I think I can reach it," Mary Jo lurched backward in her zeal to be helpful and pressed a button which caused water to pour from the spigot and drench her other arm and front of her shirt. Phoebe must have gotten splashed, too, and I heard her pee a little in the toilet. They both got tickled which didn't help my mood.

"Mary Jo, I am going to help you out the door. Twist around and get free of the sink."

"But I'm all wet." Her whining was almost as irritating as her behavior.

"You turn and pick your foot up and take a step out of there! Right now!"

She did, and as she staggered out, remarked, "Might have to sue Alaska Airlines."

"Whatever for?" I was amazed.

"Bathrooms are too uutukuu. Dangerous."

I was so done with her, and Jonas appeared to lead her to her seat. The door had self-closed on Phoebe who was still finishing up. "Aunt Phoebe, you okay?"

In answer, there was a flush. She came to the door, red-faced with little curls from her recent perm pressed against her forehead with sweat. "Do you have any lipstick? I look too pale."

"You look fine, Phoebe, let's move out of the way. People are waiting for the bathroom."

Jonas was waiting, too. He explained that during this fiasco, Nicole had talked the couple in back of the girls into moving up front to our seats and we were reseated behind them. We all sat down. They were quiet, except for some giggling as they discovered the crossword puzzle in the travel magazine, summoned Nicole for pens and amused themselves by filling in the boxes in Inupiat.

"We should be grateful that they didn't land the plane and put them off," I whispered to Jonas.

"Yeah, well, we have a long way still to go. Are all the flights on Alaska Airlines?"

"Yes, I think so, both families combined their miles for discounted tickets."

Jonas sighed. "You guess they'll call ahead to warn the staff?"

Relaxing was over, and our journey had only just begun. Jonas and I were on high alert the rest of the short flight.

Nicole brought me a slip of paper. I thought I saw pity in her eyes when she asked if I was also traveling with a dog. The form letter said Riley was doing fine in the cargo hold and would be watered and transferred to the next flight during the short layover. We only had an hour between flights.

The exit door was in the rear so we were among the first to get out. By now, Nicole looked like she had been ridden hard and put away wet. No one could fault her for effort, though. She was exceptionally attentive, helping the girls with their carry-on bags, smiling and wishing them well. Jonas and I both thanked her as we exited. She should get the Medal of Honor for flight attendants.

The gate for our next flight was nearby and we found it easily. We decided to get a snack at Chili's but Phoebe and Mary Jo wanted to go get a Cinnabon, just around the corner. We kept their bags and they toddled away happily.

"Jonas, should we let them out of our sight?"

He took a long breath. "They are grown women. Mom has been in and out of this airport dozens of times. They should be fine. Actually I need some space."

His voice sounded worried, too, but he was trying to calm me. The next flight left at 9:55. It was 9:10. They had plenty of time to get a Cinnabon and get back to the gate, so we ordered and tried to forget the previous two hours.

Within half an hour, Mary Jo or Grandma or whoever she was at the moment showed up at Chili's with a big to-go box of cinnamon buns, arms flailing, babbling in Inupiat.

"What is going on?" Jonas listened, wiped his mouth and pushed back his chair. He glared at his mother. "Which bag is Phoebe's?" I handed it to him.

"These two women of the world left the terminal to go smoke and Phoebe can't get back in because she didn't take her ticket or ID." He dug through her things and found them. "Meet us at the gate, Babe." The two of them walked away and I watched them disappear, one short and one tall shape silhouetted in the huge hallway. Mary Jo took two steps for every one of Jonas' strides and I felt sorry for her for a moment until I remembered this was all likely her fault.

Chapter 15

These Two Ladies Have Special Needs

Jonas

As I hobbled behind the two elderly delinquents I was herding back to the boarding gate, I felt guilty for yelling at them to be responsible and to find something to do that didn't require Stella or me getting them out of trouble. On one hand, I was plenty pissed at them, but on the other hand, I admired them for their spunk. Still sneaking around to smoke a cigarette at 75 years old.

I looked at them, marching ahead of me as fast as they could, meek for the moment, at least. I could barely keep up, muscles in my back let me know they were still angry, but we needed to keep moving to board on time. I didn't want Stella to have to decide whether to get on the plane or wait for us. I was afraid of which choice she would make. Maybe these two would be tired and sleep on this leg of the flight. I could feel my back muscles knotting up again as the muscle relaxants in my system wore off. When the drugs wore off completely, I was afraid my back would hurt too much to bear, but I didn't dare take another pill and leave Stella alone to deal with whatever Mom and Auntie cooked up.

When we boarded, I leaned in to the lady at the podium and told her, "These two ladies have special needs and we need to be seated near them." It wasn't a lie. "It's a full flight, sir, but I'll try." She checked her computer and pressed the screen a few times and new boarding passes printed out. I took them all and assigned seats myself. Stella and I were together and they were in the row ahead, with another person between them. Poor guy. I chuckled.

Turns out it wasn't a guy; it was a young mother with a baby boy. I didn't know what to expect, but those two grandmas enjoyed the infant the entire flight. They fed him, rocked him to sleep, and cooed to him. They may have actually been useful except when they fussed at each other about whose turn it was to hold the baby. He didn't cry and I caught a nap. Stella said that she was afraid to sleep, but that our girls stayed seated except for letting the mom out to go change the child and one bathroom trip each, alone. Just after 2 o'clock in the morning, we landed in Seattle and had a three-hour layover. Surely Mom and Phoebe would slow down; they hadn't slept a wink all night. I was so wrong.

There were some shops open in the gigantic terminal and a lot of places to eat. Stella left the girls at the famous Ivar's restaurant and went to get Riley to walk her and take her back to the check-in for the next gate. I wanted to go with but couldn't make it the entire way; just gave out. I waited on a bench just inside security. Riley had cozied up to Stella from the beginning and I bet she danced when Stella peeked into the kennel. Stella joined me in twenty minutes or so; she had taken the dog outside for a walk. "Sorry I took so long. Do you know how hard it is to find grass near the terminal? Riley smelled every blade of the tiny patch of grass before deciding where to do business. She was good on the leash, though, and no trouble getting back to the kennel. I gave her a treat and a drink. She'll be fine. How's the back?"

I told her that I'd live, but I wasn't convinced.

We should have known that by the time we got back to Ivar's, there would be no familiar faces. We found Special Needs 1 and 2 in a newsstand/souvenir shop. They were examining magnets and Seattle postcards. "Stella, do you have one of these in West Virginia?" Mary Jo pointed to a Space Needle photo.

"Nope," Stella said.

"Then maybe we just stay here," the girls giggled.

I needed to nip this in the bud. "Mom, we don't have time to see the Space Needle this trip, maybe on the way home." I knew as I spoke that it wasn't going to happen, these two could not be trusted in downtown Seattle. My back was starting to really hurt and I knew I had to stretch out in the floor soon to relieve it.

I asked Stella if she could babysit and get them back up to the gate in an hour or two. She agreed, but she wasn't exactly filled with joy. When I left, the shoppers were examining souvenir shot glasses. I headed up to the gate, found a quiet corner, and stretched out.

When I woke up, three women were sitting over me on the black plastic bench singing, "This Little Light of Mine." When they finished, they wished me a loud, "HAPPY NEW YEAR!" Aarigaa, I had forgotten it was New Year's Eve. Or was. It was now New Year's Day.

"Stella?"

She shrugged her shoulders and said, "Atchu?" and they all three looked at each other and burst into laughter. I rolled over and tried to get up, but I had to go slowly to keep the pain at bay. When I finally stood, they were still giggling.

"Listen, Jonas," Stella stumbled to me. "I'm not so very drunk. They found a bar that was nice enough to STAY OPEN just for us so we could get a couple of drinks. I tried, Jonas, I did, but they wouldn't listen to me and I am just as tired as all get out." She did a drunken spin on one foot and fell to the bench. "You know what you always say, 'if you can't join them, beat them.'"

I faced her and held her shoulders, to sit down would have hurt too much. "You've all got to sober up or they won't let you on the next plane."

"Well, that would be ... not fair ... what do you call that?" Stella leaned forward. She was in rare form.

"Discrimination?" Phoebe volunteered.

"Yep. Discrimination." Then Stella flopped back on the bench.

"Azaa. You three stay right here." I limped to an automated snack bar and bought big bottles of water.

"Drink every drop," I warned them all and forbade them to get up.

"Yuk." Mom spit out the first mouthful on the carpet.

"Oh, no," I shook my finger at her. I am so close to changing this ticket and sending both of you back to Barrow. You drink that whole bottle."

Then the only sound was water gurgling as they drank. They conferred among themselves.

Stella raised her hand. How much has she had to drink? I played along, "Yes, Stella?"

"We need to go to the restroom. Please."

Chapter 15

I was almost afraid for all of them to go together. There was power in numbers. "Sure, one at a time. Mom, you go first." Phoebe stuck her tongue out at me and she and Stella fell over laughing.

Mom did her looking around joke and said, "No Mom here, only Grandma."

I didn't fight my fate. "Grandma can go first."

She headed to the ladies' room and came back quickly; then Phoebe, then Stella. The water was all gone and boarding had started. I prayed we would be allowed on the plane.

This was a big jet and we were seated in the center section, all in a row, all behaving nicely. I had the aisle seat on one side and Phoebe on the other. It was 5 o'clock in the morning and we'd be in Atlanta by noon. I couldn't make it without another pill, took it and must've passed out within minutes.

Stella was shaking me as I woke up. Bright light was shooting through the windows. "Jonas, I need to get by you. I waited as long as I could."

"Go the other way." Sleep and pain were speaking as I stirred back to life.

"Jonas, your mother has been throwing up off and on for awhile. I have the bag of vomit to take to the trash. Could you move?"

"Sure." I pushed up and stepped aside to let her out. Mom was hunched over her table tray, littered with little liquor bottles. Phoebe was leaned back, mouth open wide, snoring. The row smelled like a bar. My God, they'd kept drinking all night.

The pilot came on the PA and announced that the plane would be landing in 20 minutes and to expect turbulence.

Perfect.

Stella returned before I sat back down. She was holding one hand above her eyes to block the light and covering her mouth and nose with the other as the plane started bouncing.

"Hangovers are hell, Stella." I know my eyes were glistening with laughter, I could feel the tears about to overflow, but I was able to keep my mouth from joining them. "Hung over with Grandma. Who would've thought you'd become drinking buddies in just one night." I saw her chin quiver and a tear starting down her cheek and I had mercy and pulled back.

"If I laugh, I will throw up. My head is pounding and every joint aches. If I laugh, I will throw up. Or worse. So, shut up. Just shut up."

I didn't make any sounds, but I couldn't help it that my body shook with silent hilarity. Stella kicked me once, hard, so I guess she noticed. I focused on a spot at the front of the plane as it rose and dipped and ignored the retching two seats over. Stella was keeping it together enough to help Mom.

We were a sad-looking little group as we plodded off this plane to find our last flight on a small plane into Roanoke. I decided not to call my buddy, Ben McDaniel, to come get us. Instead, I'd just rent a van for the 90-minute drive home. We should be home by bedtime. I planned ahead to leave Mom and Phoebe at my house and Stella and I would head on up to the mountain. The only question mark was the weather; the temperature in Roanoke was 35 above, about 70 degrees warmer than Barrow, and it was raining. Home would be a few degrees colder, prime time for snow.

Snow-covered forest road in winter landscape. Photo by Nina Malyna.

Chapter 16

We Survived the Nightmare of a Trip

Stella

I promised God I would never touch hard liquor again if He would allow me to live through this hangover. I never should have started drinking shots with those two. I have never had more than one shot at a time in my whole life and that was awhile back, like thirty years ago. The drive home was going to hurt. Good thing Jonas felt like driving. I would've found a hotel room in Roanoke.

The snowplows and cinder trucks had been out on the main roads in Virginia so the roads were passable. We had to stop six or seven times on Route 81 at truck stops because Phoebe or Mary Jo were either hungry, thirsty, had irritable leg syndrome, whatever that was, or had to go to the bathroom. Finally, I had to go because they always bought me something to eat and drink when we stopped. By that last one, Jonas was mumbling things that were really not very nice. Travel can be a little bit hard on a marriage.

Then we hit little winding Route 100 and it was slick as owl poop. The van was light in the rear and Jonas made us all go sit in the back seat to get us out of a ditch. Oh, yes, we slid into several ditches and one fence. Mary Jo started putting her hands up and squealing like she was riding a roller coaster. She had seen it on a commercial according to Phoebe; neither of them had ever really ridden a roller coaster. They were blissfully unafraid and chatted and giggled. Jonas threatened them every now and then, but they didn't pay him much mind.

Chapter 16

The worst roads were closest to home, on the West Virginia side. The earlier rain must've changed to snow so there was a layer of ice underneath. Not many cars were on the road and I kept thinking that was a plus, but Jonas was concerned that if we got stuck there would be no way to get his elderly passengers home. It was not a concern that they shared. They were weirdly encouraging, cackling, "Keep driving, Jonas, spin some wheels some more," and chanting, "We think you can, we think you can, we think you can," as we crept up hills. How they could be so lively while I was holding my head, I did not understand.

When the windshield wipers on the driver's side quit working, Jonas stopped to look for a string to attach it to the other wiper, because he couldn't see. "Oh, I got it," Mary Jo shouted and fumbled around in the back seat. Then, she squashed her pudgy little body between the second row of seats to hand Jonas something. He said, "Really, Mom? Pantyhose?"

She harrumphed him and demonstrated how to double it and twist it together and make a rope. He opened the door into the storm and stood in it to reach the wiper and tie a knot in the toe, then got out and tied the other end to the working wiper. And that is how we watched Grandma's perforated cotton crotch stretch across our viewing field for the rest of the trip. I was horrified at first, but hey, the wipers both worked. It is amazing what the human mind can ignore, and hopefully, forget.

We survived the nightmare of a trip against great odds and delivered the Golden Girls and their luggage to Jonas' house. There was not a crumb of fresh food or bread except for the pop and circus peanuts and potato chips and pork skins left over from their gas station greed.

Jonas and I braved the slippery mountain road to our house. Jonas stumbled to the house holding his back. I unloaded Riley into the run with Sugar. The dogs were both girls, they probably wouldn't fight. Mary Jo and Phoebe would find frozen dinners in the freezer if they got hungry enough. I called Barbara and left a message that we were home safely and then fell into the bed. My body said it could sleep a week and my mind agreed. I guess Jonas was in the bed beside me. I hoped so. Somebody was but I was too exhausted to care who.

Jonas

We got home. It wasn't easy and I am not sure it was even in our power to resist. This great land has deep roots that entangle our souls and pull us home. I felt it more powerfully than any other reason to keep going, more than love or responsibility, more than a normal homing instinct. Something divine had to have touched me because no mortal man could have stood up to the struggle. This must be how conquering warriors feel when victory is won against all odds. I slept like the dead.

Phoebe

That was some kinda trip. Mary Jo is still one crazy old Eskimo woman. Love her plenty. Always good laughs. We had big fun, but both of us are getting too old to bounce back fast from that much booze. Might have to rest all ten weeks before the trip back. Nice house Jonas is letting us borrow. I like my bed.

Mary Jo

Oh, my head. My eyes hurt, too. I gotta rest. My stomach is not so good, either. But my mind has been true all the way from the North Slope.

Sometimes the waves come and wipe my mind clean. I don't know where I am. Nothing looks right. It's scary. Doctors don't know, pills don't help, but I know. I am getting ready for the next world. Don't want to go yet, want to wait so have to deal with waves.

Phoebe and me have to live fast. We have lived slow and hard and now we have to live full and not miss any little thing we can see or do. Unless we get irritable leg syndrome or anxiety in crowds or all the things TV warns us about. More trouble than my head waves out there in the world.

Maybe Stella is okay. Hee-hee. When she said "atchu," Jonas looked plenty surprised. Ee, maybe Stella is okay. We'll see.

I will sit up and watch out the window as long as I can stay awake. Snow and air is soft here when it touches my face. Maybe I will go outside.

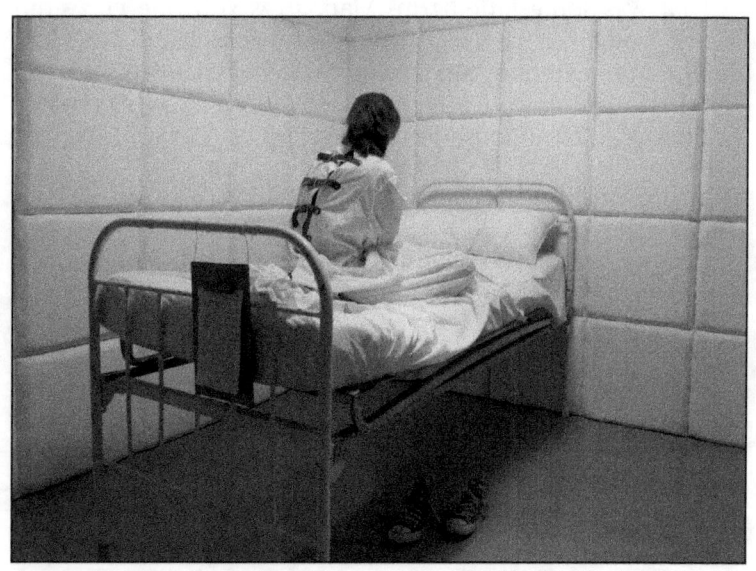

Straitjacketed in a psychiatric ward. Photo by Alvaro German Vilela.

Chapter 17

I am Winning this Hide-and-Seek Game

Timmy Lee

Another day, another nosy orderly. "How are we today, Mr. Davis?" The door clangs then the guard's key rattles in the lock as the certified nurse assistant comes near. He is carrying a basin of water, a bar of Zest soap and a towel over his shoulder. He is so close I can smell the soap. Two guards wait by the door, just like always. I despise them, I hate this hellhole and I hate Stella the most for putting me here.

"Time for a sponge bath, Mr. Davis." Damn. It takes all my self-discipline to watch another man wash my body. Sicko.

It's been forty days. I haven't said a thing. I can't write anything down or show any emotions. I slobber. I wear a diaper. When I figured out they were going to stick a feeding tube in me, I started swallowing when they filled my mouth with food or drink like a damn baby bird.

But I am winning this hide-and-seek game. Nobody knows I am here and I am going to stay hidden until I can get home free. It's getting harder, though. I pace most of the day to keep my muscles ready. I walk into the block walls sometimes to fool these idiots. There are cameras in my room, so I flex and move in the night under the covers. That way, it will look like I am dreaming and moving in my sleep. They are easy to fool. When my eyes are open, I keep them fixed. No one suspects a thing. My eyes are always red when I look in the stainless steel panel behind the toilet, because I stay awake as long as I can every night and put soap in them when I can get by with it.

Today's guy, now wiping me off, moves slowly like a retard. I know I could make him feel sorry for me. He is big and dumb. His nostril flares while he works like he is careful or maybe angry. I could make him feel sorry for me, have him eating out of my hand if I wanted to. He's humming now. I miss music. Hell, I miss everything.

I tell myself that I will eat a good meal again. I will dress in nice clothes, smile at broads, and drive a flashy car. But, not yet. First is freedom and then revenge. Revenge on my slut of a sister and her stinkin' Indian boyfriend for putting me here. The look on Stella's face when she gets what she deserves and a truckload of money is all I want. I remember my wife's eyes and mouth when she misbehaved and I had to hold a lit cigarette to her skin. Beautiful. How did she dare to eat supper before me? The strong eat first. Just making Stella pay makes my body spasm. I can hear the orderly call for help.

"Looks like another seizure," he calls to the guard who flips a headset in place and turns it on.

"Trauma in 514," the guard says. I hear the door open and when I can peek I see a doctor, a young intern, and another nurse standing beside my cot. They check my heartbeat and blood pressure and say the numbers out loud. The readings sound sky high. They look in my eyes and mouth and ears and get a needle ready, but they decide not to use it. In a few minutes, my body relaxes. This must be a teaching hospital because the doctors explain themselves a lot. He says, "This doesn't require outside medical attention."

The intern asks, "What determines if the patient needs to go to the hospital downtown?"

Oh, yeah. Good question. I want to hear that answer.

"Not much. Broken bones, which rarely happen here, drug interactions, especially EPS with psychiatric drugs. More likely in this hospital are excessive bleeding or evidence of internal bleeding and some suicide attempts, those that we can't suture up ourselves. Each case is evaluated individually." The intern takes notes. My mind is racing. Do these idiots not know they are giving me the way to get out?

The nurse is female. Must've been hiding behind the door when they handed out looks. She is ugly as sin and her body smells stale. She is writing on a clipboard, too, and asks, "Are this patient's seizures on a regular schedule, possibly related to food intake, meds, or other environmental events?"

Sister, my body reacts like this whenever I think of my dumbass sister that left me at home with a dumbass mother. I showed her, though. When a drowned woman wasn't identified, I said it was my sister. She got buried in a grave and has a headstone and everything. Dead and forgotten. Then she might as well have come back to life because she made my life miserable, ruined a good job and a perfect scam. She pinned a murder on me that I didn't do, and she knows I didn't. The bitch will pay for that.

The doctor speaks and I pay attention. "That would be a good angle to check, why don't you chart the times that they occur?"

Good, he put it back on her. That bitch must not be a nurse, must be an intern, too. Bitches don't know their place any more. I focus on what they were saying. The staff talks too much about shit I need to know. I file it away. It surprises me but I guess it is a compliment to my act. People don't mind talking in front of me. I know which nurses and doctors are sloppy and who plays by the book, who needs money and who is cheating on their wife.

They check my pulse and pressure again and it is near normal. The doctor pats me on the back, "You're okay Mr. Davis. You're going to be fine."

I hear the key rattle and the door creak open and the trauma team leaves. Then the creak and rattle repeat and I know the armed guards are in place on either side of the locked metal door.

When I was admitted, even in my supposedly messed-up state, it was explained to me in a monotone that every thirty days I would be checked to determine if I was sane enough to stand trial. Flunked my first test by doing absolutely nothing and felt proud. I've been thinking about it, though. I've never stepped foot out of this grey room and only got rid of the "chemical restraints" shots during meals two weeks ago. Ha, won't be smacking at the hand that feeds me anymore. I can't see much future for me here. I get angry remembering why I am here. My body starts to knot up again. It has become a traitor just like her. I have to focus on something else to get control of my body. I think about standing in front of a church, singing my heart out while studying all the suckers in the pews, figuring out who is the easiest mark. I can see the guilty, the phony, the superior, but I go after the godly. They turn the other cheek and forgive me after I use them. I am

97

Chapter 17

damn good at reading suckers. Damn good. My muscles begin
to relax.

When I weigh my options, which I do every hour, I have
started to think it might be better to slowly become sane. I could
move and talk and would probably be taken to the Southern
Regional Jail to be near the courtroom during the hearings
and trial. I will defeat the system at the Mildred Bateman State
Psychiatric Hospital one way or another. Besides, I haven't
forgotten the doctor explaining that some injuries get you to
the hospital downtown. Could be a better place to run from.

The nurse pulls me to a sitting position in the bed. "Now
Mr. Davis, you stay calm. I just need a few minutes to shave
you." He moistens my face with a wet washcloth and pats me
with shaving lotion. I desperately wish he would hum some
more and decide to take a chance, bob my head and hum two
disjointed notes, then keep bobbing.

"Why Mr. Davis, I believe you are at home somewhere deep
inside. You like my humming." He stops and stares at me.

I close my eyes, so tired, and take another chance. I pant
like a dog. "Haa, haa, haa, haa, haa." Maybe he will think that
means I am happy. It is the first time in 40 days I have tried to
communicate.

"You hold that wobbly head of yours still so I can give
you a nice shave, and I will hum all you want. Your last little
episode put me behind schedule, so I would surely appreciate
this to go quick and easy."

He starts humming 'When the Saints Go Marching In' and
shaving me. I can't move. That little bit of music lifts me up
and carries me away. It is better than dessert, strong enough to
remind me of the urge of the revenge I crave.

I remember trying to find a beat in the pipes popping and
in the heater fan coming on and off, but I don't know how
much I am hungry for the patterns, the feel of music. The
desire makes me weak; I need to block that cursed tune in my
head, but I can't. He finishes shaving me and cleans me up. He
helps me lay down and tucks the sheet over me. The seizure
made me tired. I'll think about it again tomorrow. Tomorrow,
I will figure out how to get out of here. Now, I sleep.

Chapter 18

My Kind of Homecoming

Stella

I woke before daylight and made a little something to eat for breakfast, cinnamon bread from a loaf in the freezer and hot cocoa. I texted Eliza and Tisha to tell them I was back. Not sure if they were in school on January 2, but they needed to know there was no need to come up here in the snow to feed and water animals.

The ground sparkled with the remnants of last night's blizzard, a soft, warm layer of snow compared to the Arctic shards of ice and squeaky snow. The ankle boots I was wearing were four inches tall and the new snow fell over the tops, so five or six inches had fallen. My path to the dog kennel was quickly erased when I let the dogs out and they hopped and twirled and played in the snow. I fed them and the cats and traipsed on out to the barn and threw some hay down for the sheep. Their water just had a skim of ice on it, so I broke it with a shovel handle kept nearby just for that reason. By then, the sun was peeping up over the mountain and I stopped to watch it rise. After my time in Barrow, I had a new appreciation for the sun and I didn't ever want to take it for granted again.

Jonas was still in bed. I tried not to disturb him when I got up. It felt so different to have another person in my bed, my house, and my life. I had to start adjusting; one thing was to catch myself and say "our" instead of "my" for all the things we shared. After all my years alone, it was just delicious to be "us."

Chapter 18

Probably ought to apologize for the mess in the airport. Shucks. That conversation may take awhile. Putting up with his relatives was not easy, but I did try to kill them with kindness. That should score me enough points to balance out one drunken New Year's Eve. Who cares, anyway? That terrible hangover was the worst punishment I could've had for my lapse in judgment. I had a fun time with those old girls and we had needed to unwind together, so Jonas could just put that in his pipe and smoke it. I laughed out loud and slapped my leg as I walked back to the house.

Relatives are complicated. I only had one, my brother, Timothy Lee. Dad died in an accident in the dairy barn when I was little, then Timmy pretty much ruined my life until I left home on graduation night. That was all a long time ago and until he showed up in Lindside as a gospel singer last summer, I had not laid eyes on him or his wife or son, Adam. He invaded my church, accused me of stealing the Harvest Festival money, took money from the church and got me arrested. Oh, Lord he was born pure trouble and he hadn't changed.

I reached the house and banged my toes against the back door to knock the snow off. Jonas was in the kitchen helping himself to toast and warm chocolate. He looked at me the way he does with crinkles at the corners of his eyes and the tip of his tongue touching his top lip and my heart flip-flopped. He wasn't mad at me; he was still here, we were still married. Our life together was real.

Winter farm house. Photo by B. Crabtree

His kiss tasted like dark cocoa and was so yummy I shivered.

He pushed me back to arm's length. "You're not cold, are you, Stella of the Arctic?"

I stepped back into his arms. "Oh, you silly man, how could I be cold around someone so hot?" We held each other, no one else in the room or even in the house, no TV blaring, or housekeeping staff knocking on the door.

"Quarter for your thoughts."

"I think it's a penny. You always get those sayings wrong, Jonas."

"That's because your thoughts are so valuable. Besides, I know what you are thinking." His eyebrows rose.

"Atchu?" I tried to look innocent but I was ready to run. He tried to chase me but he grabbed his back with one hand and the handrail with the other. I led him up the stairs where I knew we both wanted to be, so it wasn't much of a chase. I stumbled and grabbed the handrail while he missed a step and bumped his knee behind me. We were both too old to run up the steps. He had to move slowly on the bed because of his lingering back trouble and I kicked and squealed gently until the kisses deepened and distracted me. My kind of homecoming, for sure.

The shrill train whistle of Jonas' cell phone busted our bubble. It was Mary Jo, oops, Grandma. She'd like some fresh strawberries, please. I got so tickled that Jonas threw a pillow at me while he was on the phone. "Yes, I'll get some for you, and some macaroni and cheese. And a rack of Dr. Pepper." I hunted for something to write with; he and I together couldn't remember all the things Mary Jo absolutely had to have. A pencil and legal pad was on the nightstand and I grabbed it. He called the items out and I wrote them down until she finally finished.

"So, we're going to Bob's Grocery?" I asked.

"Bob's changed to Jewell's IGA ten years ago," he yelled from the bathroom.

"I miss Bob, I think I subconsciously still call the store Bob's so I don't have to accept the fact that he sold the business."

"You are in denial about Bob's," he paused and added, "and a few other things."

"Like what?"

"Like Timmy Lee. You haven't even patched up the holes in the paneling from the night he snuck in the house to do you harm, Stella, remember? You shot at him, you could have

101

killed him. I'm just saying that you may need more time to deal with all the damage he caused."

"I've been busy, getting married and what-not." I looked at my nails, pretending to be concerned about my non-existent manicure. "Besides, I missed and it all ended pretty well. He is crazy. No denial here."

"But you haven't worked through all the crazy and checked it off your list like you do everything else."

He was right. I needed to talk to somebody about the awful time before we got married. Jonas was my best friend in addition to being my husband, but I had a big ole secret that I wasn't ready to tell just yet. "Okay, I'll make a list. Number 1: Patch bullet holes in hallway and try to forget that night. Number 2: Call the courthouse and see if Timmy Lee passed the sanity test. Number 3: Check on Anna's grave. Number 4: Check on Anna's girls. What else?"

"Have you checked on the young woman's family? The one that drowned in Georgia that your brother identified as you? That needs to be taken care of. And he practically admitted to killing your mother in his last lucid hours. That is pretty big emotional baggage."

"Number 5: Go to Atlanta and find that girl's family and tell them she died long ago. Number 6: Check on Mom's death certificate, talk to any officials who might have been present at her death or funeral." I choked back tears. She'd been dead nearly thirty years before I knew it. There was no psychic awareness, no sense of her passing. Jonas was right. I did need to think about that. I shook it off and tried to be cheery. "What else?"

"I know that you are taking all this lightly, but maybe talk to somebody, Preacher Booth maybe? He knows you and he knows the situation. Heck, he was involved about the church money and hiring Timmy Lee at the church. He knows your brother is a snake."

I tossed the list to the foot of the bed. "How about if I go to Preacher Booth and get him to help me come up with a list that I can manage? Jonas, I can get through this but we are going to have our hands full with your mom and Aunt Phoebe, so we're going to be busy."

"And a new dog and a new marriage and whatever happens to us in the future. I will help every step. Speaking of which, we better go get groceries for Grandma." He nuzzled my warm neck with his two-day-old whiskers.

"Owee, you better shave or grow your soft beard back."

"Whatever you say, Wifey."

"Oh, Jonas, grow the beard back." I was shy about telling him anything about his appearance, maybe because I would be so hurt if he commented on mine. But fair is fair, so I asked, "What would you change about me?" The pause was so long, I held my breath.

"Really? Anything?" His eyes gleamed with mischief.

"If I can." Boy, was I nervous.

"Okay. Here goes. Throw out all your cotton panties and wear the silky kind. They feel so nice." He rubbed my bare butt. "More like you."

"Jonas!" I squealed, but I knew I would do it. It seemed so risqué that I giggled as I jumped out of bed to get dressed. Wished he'd asked a decade ago.

Chapter 19

If We Only Had a Car

Mary Jo & Phoebe

"Hey." Mary Jo pressed the TV remote button and laid it down, then flipped the recliner upright. She raised her voice, "Phoebe, where are ya?"

Phoebe toddled into the living room, yawning. "Whatcha doing? Whatcha hollering at me for?"

"Phoebe, something is wrong." She shook her head and gave Phoebe time to guess what was wrong, but Phoebe sat down on the couch and crossed her arms and waited. She was good at waiting.

"In Barrow, we could walk to the store. We could call a cab to get us some pop or a pizza. The bus runs everywhere. We could take a cab. We can't do that here. No good."

Phoebe stretched her arms. "We have the whole house to ourselves. We can smoke, we can stay up all night without hearing 'Be quiet, it is school night.' We are not cold, even outside. We don't have to go anywhere, we can watch TV and movies and no one interrupts and changes channel to Paw Patrol." She yawned again. "I hate Paw Patrol. Stupid shows for kids these days. I liked Lassie and Flipper and Fury. I like it here, too. I might get Jonas to get me some yarn and a crochet hook and start crocheting again."

"You are ready for the senior center, Pheebs. I want to get outa here and do something. We are prisoners in this house and have been for a week. We need a car! I gotta driver's license. Let's call Jonas and tell him we need a car."

"Azaa, where would we go? We would get lost on this zig-zagging mountain road." She moved her arms up and down to illustrate. What makes you think we could find home again? We are two miles from a paved road. I didn't know people really lived like this. Where do you want to go?"

"I read the newspaper – there's bingo and pull-tabs in a town called Rich Creek. Sounds like a good place to win money. And they have a Dairy Queen with $5 lunches. If we only had a car." Mary Jo drummed her fingers on the wooden trim on the armrest of the recliner? "How much money can you lay hands on?"

"Atchu. What for?" Phoebe was notoriously frugal.

"We can buy our own car." She shook the newspaper at Phoebe. "Good deals."

Phoebe had lost money with Mary Jo's big ideas before. "Let's try Jonas first. Maybe he has an extra." Their eyes met and MJ got her phone out and pressed his name.

"Jonas, honey, we need a car. Phoebe has a doctor appointment next week and," she shushed Phoebe who was protesting.

"Don't lie, Mary Jo, you know that's not true."

Mary Jo covered the phone with her hand and whispered, "Shhh, maybe he and Stella don't want to take us to our appointments. Then we get a car."

"But, we don't have any appointments."

"We will make some, not hard. Shush up."

"Yes, Jonas, Phoebe really feels bad. Stomach and, and, well, maybe gout in her feet. She might have to go to the hospital. In the night. Would hate to bother you and Stella." Silence. "Okay, but we need soon." Silence. "Thank you, Son; oh, and we need yarn and two crochet hooks." She pressed the hang up button.

"You don't know how to crochet. You never listen or pay attention long enough to learn."

"Oh, pshaw, I can learn." She lit up. "You can teach me in the waiting room at the doctor. I always hate sitting in the waiting room."

"What doctor? We don't have a doctor. And I never had gout in my life. Where did that come from?"

"Sometimes I can't lie quick and words just spew out of my mouth." She shook her head. "I think Jesus must put the words there. I don't even know what gout is."

Phoebe muttered, "More likely the devil, telling such tales."

"If we get a car by the weekend, we can go play bingo Saturday night at the Lions Club. They have that club in Barrow, too. Nice people. Big money."

Phoebe rolled her eyes. "I'm going to make burgers for supper. You hungry?"

"Yeah, I want one. Don't use that little countertop grill though, it takes the fat out of the meat. I don't want a dried-up burger, no taste."

"You want to do this yourself? I like this grill. Easy clean-up. Healthy, too. You need to think about healthy, MJ. You're not getting younger. Or skinnier." She laughed. "What you in now, size 22?"

Mary Jo was miffed. "Size 20, Petite." She pouted and then added, "At least my feet don't slop over the sides of my shoes."

"Petite?" Phoebe whooped while she patted out burgers. "I thought petite means uutukuu. You never have been uutukuu. You need to work on making nice. Maybe it's the gout that makes my feet swell." Then she whooped again and punctuated it with a sizzle as she closed the grill on the raw meat.

There was silence. Mary Jo opened the paper. Phoebe puttered around in the kitchen getting all the burger fixings ready. "Come and eat, grouchy old woman. It's ready. Or have you gone on a diet since you said you wanted a burger?"

"Hey, hey, forget all that. Look here. There is a real live liquor store in Pearisburg, Virginia, just 20 miles away." Phoebe stopped what she was doing to go and look. "They are having a sale."

"What? A sale? Like cut prices or buy one, get one? On liquor? I love a sale."

"All we need is a car, Pheebs."

"Well, my gout is acting up, we better find a doctor tomorrow and make an appointment. You look up those used cars over there in case Jonas doesn't see things our way. If we have to buy a car, we cancel the appointment."

"Deal."

"And, Mary Jo, old buddy, old friend, I think my cataracts are acting up. If we can find a liquor store, we might find something for my cataracts, too." She winked three times.

"I didn't know you have a cataract. What do you need for a cataract?"

"We need something to help us sleep, too."

Mary Jo still looked confused.

Chapter 19

"Really, Mary Jo, Queen of the Joint. Weed, you ninny-head, weed." Phoebe's skirt twirled as she spun around then did a halting version of an Eskimo dance, stomping and acting out with the motions of smoking with dramatic hand and arm movements.

"Oh, yes. If we only had a car." They both sighed.

The phone rang. It was Barbara checking on them. It was 3 o'clock in the afternoon in Alaska and 7 o'clock in the evening in West Virginia. Josie and the kids weren't out of school and Barbara was on break at work.

"She worries too much," Mary Jo remarked when she hung up.

"Huh. At least she cares enough to call. Not one of my kids called this week. Can't say that I mind too much. Will have more money with no one bumming money. Money for our car, come to think of it. What kind we gonna get?"

"I want a red one."

"Red is okay with me. I want four doors if we ever have to get in the back seat."

"It's our car, we are never getting in the back seat. We always ride up front."

"The car ads don't say what color they are. That's messed up. How do they think we can choose what color car we want?"

"Mary Jo, look at that ad on the back of the paper. 'Rent-a-car, any model. Low weekly rates.' We want that kinda deal, probably a lot cheaper to rent. We can give it back when we leave, no problem getting rid of it."

"I bet they have a red one, too. Let's call them first thing tomorrow morning. Forget about Jonas, he's gonna wait and see. Let's get a doctor appointment, though, so we have a reason to get one ourselves. We need to figure out a ride to Pearisburg, too, one way, so we can get our car."

They ate supper and Mary Jo cleaned up the dishes. That was the way they rolled, one cooked and the other washed the dishes. Then, they relaxed in front of the TV, watched the news and then a movie. As the credits rolled, Phoebe spoke. "MJ?"

"Yep, what?"

"I want to live with you forever."

"Looks like we are going to be together for awhile, Pheebs."

"Let's don't go so far that we get in trouble here, okay? When we drink or smoke dope, let's do it only in the house where no one will know."

"But what about parties? We might make some new friends."

"No parties at other houses. We don't know our way around well enough yet. Only parties at our house and we keep everyone inside. Jonas will never know."

"Wanna sleep in the recliners tonight?"

"No, but I'll bring you a blanket."

"That would be nice."

Phoebe found a soft fleece blanket and tucked it around MJ right in the recliner, then lumbered off to her room. She called back into the living room when she was stretched out in the bed, "This is the best time of our life. Remember when we were little and the nights our bellies were full and we were warm, we thought those were the best times in our life? We were wrong." Phoebe cuddled with her pillow, pounded it, and snuggled in again.

"The best time is now."

She waited a few seconds and finished. "Good night Mary Jo, I hope you dream of red cars."

"Huh," she grunted, "this ain't John Boy, but good night."

Chapter 20

Talking with My Best Friend

Jonas

I was at my desk at work, just thinking about things, when Ben McDaniel swung through the door. "That desk was empty too long, man, glad your ugly face is back where it belongs." We shook hands. "How's it going? You look even more stressed than you did at the airport a month ago. I didn't think that was even possible."

We both laughed at the memory of that early morning curb drop-off. "Thanks for asking. Mom and Aunt Phoebe have been here a month and it hasn't been as bad as it could have been. Other than Stella and I running our legs off getting them whatever they need, they have been more self-sufficient than they have been in quite a few years. They cook for themselves, clean up after themselves, put the garbage out for me to get on Tuesdays, and watch TV or stay on the phone most of the day and night."

He sat down on the only other chair in my tiny office. "I haven't met your mother. What's she like?"

"Depends on where she is and who's with her, I guess. My sister, Barbara, warned us about Alzheimer's and mood swings and bad behavior, but since the flight to get here, they've been pretty good. Now that I've gone back to work, I don't even see them much. They pay for their groceries and even add some for our gasoline. Mom said that Aunt Phoebe hasn't been feeling well but I think she is going to a doctor in a few days. She called and wanted a car but we both use ours so I told her no, then she says that they don't need a ride; they can get on the local golden age bus, which will take them wherever they want to go. I never heard of it, but I bet they sit at home on their phones all day finding ways to work the system."

"God bless them." Ben was on the edge of his seat, a good listener. "Maybe they will figure out a way to start getting their own groceries. Any chance of that?" Ben was such an optimist.

"All I know is that the roads are clear and dry right now, with no snow in the forecast this week, so they should be safe. Come to think of it, the weather is easier to predict than those two."

"So, how's the new wife? You are a lucky guy, hope you know it."

"She's working on her list of things she worries about with the preacher, mostly to please me. She's been through a lot. Some of it she doesn't share with me and that's okay, but so much has happened so fast, she needs time to think about it. Shoot, even I need time to think about it."

"Jonas, she lost her best friend in a terrible set of circumstances. Her brother was arrested for the murder. Before that he was stealing money from Stella's church and broke into her house in the night to scare her or probably to hurt her. She's bound to have a few things on her mind."

That was the God's honest truth. It was good to be able to talk about it out loud. I decided to tell Ben about my biggest fear.

"You know that Timmy Lee's locked up in a psychiatric hospital a three-hour drive north in Huntington until he is sane enough to stand trial. I still think there's a good chance that he could bluff his way out of that hospital and come to visit. I am suspicious enough of him that I called the hospital and asked if he was a patient and a female voice asked if I was his son. I told her I was his brother-in-law, and I got a long speech about privacy and confidentiality. Finally cut her off by asking, 'Is he there or not?' Her voice could have been a recording; 'I am not authorized to give out that information except to his immediate family.' I hung up on her and called our sheriff, Elmer, and he called and found out that Timmy Lee was still in isolation and that his assessment two weeks ago indicated he was not fit to stand trial. Good news for now, but Timmy Lee is crazy and smart, an evil combination."

"So, what are you doing to be ready? You aren't just sitting and waiting, I know better than that."

"Last time he came to call, he fed Sugar ground beef laced with a sedative. We have another dog now. A big, smart German Shepherd like Riley may be harder to trick. Riley's gotten friendlier and more comfortable in the few days since we got back. Between the warm temperatures and running free, her life has improved from being chained to a barrel in the Arctic.

"You know, I can see a younger me in that dog. Just like her, I was okay up there, but I didn't know what life could be like until I left Barrow with you and came to the Lower 48. Visiting up there last week underlined my happiness here. Now, my life is just about perfect. If we can get through another six weeks, Mom and Phoebe can go home and set up housekeeping at the senior center. Barbara can raise her grandchildren without the distraction and everyday aggravation of Mom."

"Are you avoiding the Timmy Lee question?"

"No, but it's related to the job and I don't want you to think I don't want to be here, because I do. I love working here. I like solving problems and keeping this plant safe; this building is like my other woman." We both laughed. I knew he understood.

"Plus, I like my co-workers. They're full of pranks and fun."

"I 'spec you're well tired of married man jokes by now. You've been a good sport, even at the wedding. The boys love making you blush."

"Yeah, I know, but their times are coming."

I must've grinned 'cause Ben noticed and commented, "Now that's better, your usual look."

I got real serious again. "Ben, leaving Stella alone in our big barny farmhouse every day since she fired shots from upstairs at Timmy Lee is one of the hardest things I've ever done. I asked Joe to leave me on day shift as long as he can because I don't want her to be alone at night yet. Her accounting service has taken up a lot of her time since we got back, and she's visited Anna's girls and her buddies Tisha and Eliza and taken Mom and Phoebe out to eat and to the movies and the library." I shook my head, "My Stella, she's a ball of energy, now."

"Don't worry about night shift. I'll talk to Joe. If there's anything else we can help with at work, let me know. And," he got up and poked my chest, "if there's anything I can do on the mountain for you or Stella or your mom or Aunt, call me."

113

"Thanks man, but get your bony little finger off me." We high-fived like the teenagers we once were and Ben headed on down the hall.

Talking with my best friend lifted me up. I decided to leave work early and stopped to get some flowers and circus peanuts for Stella. I usually got home about four o'clock when I was working this shift and I was right on time. Just like usual, Stella had supper almost ready, all the animals fed and watered, her accounts all updated on the computer, and a report on all the events of her day. Home and married life were running almost too smoothly.

Peterstown ATM. Photo by B. Crabtree.

Chapter 21

Looming Trouble

Stella

It would behoove Jonas to quit worrying about my mental health and worry about Grandma Mary Jo. She and Phoebe are up to something. I don't know what, but it is in the air and I can smell it.

Tisha and Eliza and I were going out to eat on Saturday afternoon and I hoped they had some ideas for me. We met at the ATM machine parking lot and Eliza drove. We were heading to Alderson to Stuart's Barbeque, an interesting place to eat to say the least. Their sign near the road is a giant red pipe in a full-size tan canoe representing a hotdog. Inside the dining area is a wooden crate with a wire grid and a sign that says, "Stand Back, Rattler." The first time I went, I peeked from two feet away and saw the pink baby toy deep inside. Tisha and Eliza howled.

This time, we sat inside away from the karaoke stage and the noise. Tisha and I ordered wine and I shared my perceptions.

"These two little old ladies are less than five feet tall, they are heavy and gray-headed and everybody's idea of sweet grandmas. The part that can't be seen with the naked eye is that they misbehave. Like little brat kids. For so many years that their family members practically applauded when they got on the plane to leave. We've even gotten a couple of thank you notes from Mary Jo's children. Plus, they treat Jonas like the golden boy and wipe their mukluks on me."

Tisha tipped up the lovely pale drink to gulp it down and the glass clinked as she sat it down. "They are leaving in a few weeks. All you have to do is wait them out. Right?" She nodded at Eliza.

"I don't know. Stella usually knows trouble is coming before it gets here." Then, to me, "What makes you think they are cooking up anything?"

I hesitated, "They are too nice." My friends laughed so loud that other people in the restaurant turned to look at our table. "Shhh, really, they were absolute you-know-whats to me in Barrow. They mocked me and said ugly things in Inupiat to my face until Jonas lit into them."

"Can you visit and hang out with them and maybe get a clue what they're thinking?" Eliza was so civilized.

"Lord, no. It would be awkward. I took them to Brooke and Charlene's house, you know, Anna's daughters, and the Golden Girls hit them up for a ride to Pearisburg to the doctor. They knew I would take them but they didn't want to ride with me, I guess, or just wanted to flaunt that they didn't need me."

Our food was served and we dug in without a word. It was pretty thrilling to eat something I hadn't cooked. Tisha stopped to wipe her mouth. "How about a spy in their house?"

"How would I do that? Go to Radio Shack and get some electronic something or other?"

"Are they real neat people? Like, do they keep everything wiped down and the clothes washed and dishes put away?" Tisha's gears were turning.

"Not especially. They put the trash bags out for Jonas once a week. The house is not spotless but it is okay. And they smoke."

"And they have money, right?" She took another bite and chewed as she watched me.

"More money than they even need."

"Well, think on this: they sound like they need a cleaning lady twice a week in the evenings. You have a friend with a son in college and a high school senior who both need money."

"Tisha, who are you talking about? You?" Tisha rolled her eyes at Eliza who choked a little on her food.

"Okay, I get it. You really want to do this?"

"Yep. I'll keep an eye on them and see what they are into. Better let Jonas suggest it though, if there is a better chance of them agreeing. How much do you think they'd pay? Ten dollars an hour?"

The more I considered this idea, the better I liked it. "Maybe twelve dollars. Two or three hours an evening?"

"Sure thing. As long as they want me to clean, I'll stay. You know my middle name is Clorox and I am the queen of nosy. Who better for this job?"

I had to agree. We ordered dessert, coconut bread pudding, and the chatter changed to church happenings. "Preacher Booth may be retiring in the spring," Eliza reported.

"Retiring or being transferred? Methodist pastors are automatically rotated every five years."

"That's such a dumb rule. Freewill Baptist church congregations keep their preachers until they are too feeble to walk up the steps to the pulpit." Tisha understood the Baptists.

"What do you do if you don't like the preacher?" I wondered what I would do if our next preacher wasn't a good match. Rev. Booth had eventually stood with me during the great Timmy Lee debacle, reappointed me as church treasurer since I'd been back, and performed our marriage ceremony. He was talking to me about how to handle the things that bothered me. I would surely hate to see him go.

"You either raise cane or go church shopping." I figured Tisha had done both, but not for herself as much as for her sons. They were her priority and she smoothed their way in whatever ways she could, preachers included.

The sweet smell of coconut arrived just before our waitress set the dessert before us. I closed my eyes and let the aroma fill my senses for a second.

"Girls, taste this," Eliza was digging in. "Delicious."

She was right. Not one word was spoken until our bowls were scraped clean. We sat around awhile sighing, loosening our belts and relaxing until we had to get on home.

As soon as I got home, I talked to Jonas about some cleaning help for Mary Jo and Phoebe. "Sure, I need to stop by there this evening anyway, I'll ask them about it. Do you think they need it?"

"I don't know what your plan is for your house, long-term, and I don't know how much energy those women have to clean. It sure is starting to smell like cigarette smoke." I just threw that in for meanness. Jonas hated the smell of cigarettes.

"Let's take the dogs for a walk before dark," he suggested. "They need to run and we need to burn off some calories. We can walk around the mountain until we can see down to my house. What's that, a mile?"

Chapter 21

And a mile back, I thought but I said, "Yep, about that. Is your back really strong enough now?"

"Let's take it easy and try it out." We held hands and swung our arms as we walked north out the ridge into the wind. We were really too far away to see clearly, but the yellow glow from the windows looked cozy and we knew they were at home. We talked about going down to visit, but we were getting chilled and decided to go on home and take the truck down. With the wind at our back, the walk home was more comfortable. We bumped shoulders and hips every now and then just to touch each other, I guess.

Jonas started the truck when we got back. I begged off from the visit to his mom to put up the chickens and feed the other animals and get supper together. I figured his chances of success were better alone than with me.

He wasn't gone long. "They went for the cleaning lady idea and were ready for her to start tonight," he reported as he took off his outerwear.

"How else did they seem?" I wondered.

"Fine, except for Phoebe's gout. She was wearing warm socks and said that her feet were swollen and achy, but I couldn't tell any difference from before. They giggled around like schoolgirls telling me about TV shows. They may have CNN and some sit-coms confused, but they were definitely happy. Being away from home may be good for them."

I was thinking about that when he remembered something else, "Oh, they are going to the doctor in Pearisburg on Monday. I told them that you could take them but they insisted Charlene had already agreed."

"Did you invite them to go to church with us in the morning?"

"I did, but Phoebe said she just wasn't up to the walking."

Hmmm. Phoebe was getting around just fine.

Maybe my feeling of looming trouble was wrong, or maybe it wasn't from them; maybe it came from an entirely different precinct, but something was stirring in my future and I could not put my finger on exactly what.

Chapter 22

It was Time to Act

Timmy Lee

It has been long enough. My act has worked for nearly two months without a slip-up. Humming tunes with an orderly has saved me from really losing my mind. Watching him out of the corner of my eye as he started to think I was improving cracked me up. I get a kick out of him watching me when he thinks I'm not watching him. I've heard the others call him Jeff and I am pleased by his name and that I know it. On his days off, I am bored.

He must not have ever mentioned my humming because no one else has ever followed up. I keep it low level, only repeating whatever song he was humming. I add some harmony first and then hum a song that we have never done together. It's been my biggest excitement while I waited. He is a stupid oaf, but he keeps my little secret. I am nearly ready to trust him to keep bigger ones.

Jeff has one-sided conversations; he talks to me some about his family and his old car. He agrees to work extra hours when asked and generally seems like a guy who could use some extra money. My plan to escape isn't settled yet, but I am starting to pencil him in.

"Good morning, Mr. Davis," his ringing voice greets me. How I want to answer back with a voice as strong as his, "Good morning, Jeff." I don't even know if my voice works any more, probably need to test it somewhere, somehow.

This morning, he is less jolly than usual. As he came in with his tray of supplies, he is shaking his head. "Man alive,

119

I got troubles, Mr. Davis." Then he looks at me and laughs. "Not as many troubles as you do, though. Guess I should be counting my blessings, shouldn't I?"

I want him to tell me what was bothering him, but the time is not right just yet for me to ask, so I bob my head at him.

"Looks like you want to know, what with your bobble-headed nodding. Or maybe I just want to tell. Well, here goes; my wife got mad at me and took the boys to her mom's farm in Ohio and left me with a credit card bill for three grand for some stupid dining room set." He whistled low and long and sad. "I don't know for sure but I think she is seeing someone else, too." He looked down and continued. "Meanwhile, I got a dining room table with no one to sit at it and nothing to eat off it. I told her it was going back to the furniture store as soon as they would come and get it. That must have been the last straw for her, 'cause she was gone when I got in from work last night."

That bitch. I try for all the world to look like Scooby-Doo with a question so he will keep talking but he changes the subject. "Mr. Davis, you've been walking a lot lately. I think you might be able to stand in the shower this morning. I'll help you get undressed and get you in there and maybe you'll catch on to washing yourself. I asked the charge supervisor and he said it was worth a try."

I don't like it one damn bit, but I let him undress me and I step into the stall when he nudges me. He supports my arm. The warm water feels good. I shake his hand off and spin under the spray. "Why you ole water dog, you. Here, wash yourself," and he rubs the washcloth with the bar of soap and hands it to me. I rub a little bit on my stomach where my hand didn't have to reach far and then wash my face by bending over to my hand. Jeff waits for a bit then takes the cloth away from me and shampoos and washes me gently.

He wraps me in a towel and sit me in the chair, as if I were a child. Does the son-of-a-bitch not know how humiliating this is?

I forgot about the guards at the door. They stand there watching me, watching my shame, one elbowing the other, sniggering. I growl and then my vision clouds until my face burns and all I can see is red. My traitorous body stiffens and I fall from the chair, convulsing. They will pay. I'll find what they love, what they want, and destroy it, soon.

The trauma team comes. I feel the burn of an injection and drift away.

I wake up in leather cuffs, fastened to the bed. Someone peeks in the little window in the door regularly. When they see I am awake, they unfasten me. When I threw fits before, the checks were every 15 minutes, then every half hour when I seemed to be complying, and finally every hour. I hate all the checks. This was America, for God's sake. I have rights. But, if I had to be watched, I want the privacy of checks spaced farther apart. I can remember when I wasn't being looked at so often. Another offense, the camera; I learned by watching that the camera is motion activated. The wall under the camera has to be a blind spot.

Jeff is gone for the next two days, but comes in whistling the morning of the third day. I hadn't taken a shower those days; the guy just wiped me off rough and quick. After Jeff's absence, I realize if Jeff quit or transferred out of my wing, it would set back what I have planned. It is time to act.

This day, after the shower moisture condensed on the stainless steel panel in the wall, I take my finger and write "I'M OK." Jeff sees it and stares at me. I put my finger to my lips, my back to the guards and lay my open hand in the words, erasing them. He nods and keeps on with his banter about the birds singing outside and the sun shining. I draw a dollar sign on the wall and after he sees it, I rub it away. He nods again and just keeps talking. Jeff gathers up his equipment and leaves without a look or a word. Good man. I smirk at the guards but they don't notice.

After he leaves, the room is quieter than ever while I sit and wait. Either a guard or doctor will come in or they won't. I hate that it is all up to Jeff. His help matters but the wait is hell.

The next day Jeff is back at work, talkative as ever. He helps me into the shower and writes a big question mark under the spigot as he adjusts the water temperature. I spread the fingers of one hand on my leg. He does the same with ten fingers using both hands and we stare at each other. I nod. Doesn't matter to me if we negotiate five thousand or ten thousand dollars, I have no money.

He shows me the toilet paper he carried in, pantomimes writing on it and hides it under the towel. Hmm, but what do I write with? Blood? Urine? I should be more patient. Jeff pulls a stub of a pencil out from behind his ear, palms it and gives it to me. This is going to fly.

Chapter 23

Our Nice Shiny Red Car

Golden Girls

"Azaa! You are a bad driver, Mary Jo. We are lucky that those young men stopped and pushed us out of the ditch. And that we finally found this place again." Phoebe kicked off her muddy shoes and fell back on the recliner.

Mary Jo shrugged and peered out the window. "Where is our car?" She pressed her face to the glass and looked in both directions. "It's gone!"

Phoebe joined her at the window. "Mary Jo, we can't see it from here. We parked it down the road behind the big barn that nobody uses. Then we walked home. That's where it is, Mary Jo. Just because you are scared of Jonas finding out."

Mary Jo and Phoebe's shiny red Mustang. Photo by B. Crabtree.

"Humph. I forgot."

"You forget a lot of stuff. Like how to drive."

Mary Jo didn't argue. "We'll go to Bingo Friday night. We'll leave early so it is still daylight, then only one-way trip in the dark. I don't see too good in the dark."

Phoebe rolled her eyes. "You don't see too well in the daytime, either." She flipped the footstool up on the recliner and stretched out. "We need cash to play. Let's go to the ATM machine at the bank first. That's on the way."

Mary Jo drug a pile of papers from a tote bag. "Here's all the legal stuff about the car. How much it cost and contracts and looks like rules."

"How much did it cost?"

"Atchu. I just gave them the bank card."

"Did you read the rules?"

"You know I can't see that tiny print. They'll call us if they need something."

"I wasn't worried about them, MJ, I was worried about us."

"We'll be okay. Don't worry. Life is too short to worry."

"Well, keep those papers. We might need to look up something later."

"Tired, Phoebe."

"Me, too. All I can think about is our nice shiny red car and how we can go anywhere at any time without asking anybody." Her voice faded. Mary Jo was already asleep and Phoebe joined her within five minutes.

Thumping on the door woke Phoebe.

"Wha-at?" Both Phoebe's legs shot upward. She yelled, "Wait, I'm coming," before she was fully awake, struggled to get her balance and toddled over to answer the door.

It was a neat young woman, even her hair looked clean, cut short with blond streaks, a plastic carryall of cleaning supplies in one hand. "Hello, there, I'm Tisha. Jonas said this evening would be a good time to start cleaning for you."

"Come in, come in. I am Phoebe, Jonas' aunt. Maybe he or Stella told you about me." Tisha nodded. "Yes, yes, we like having a cleaning lady, we never have one before. Where do you want to start?"

"How about the kitchen? That is the room that gets used the most at our house." Phoebe showed her the way and Tisha surveyed the mess. Overflowing ashtrays, dirty dishes from several meals stacked up and scattered throughout the room, fast food wrappers and pizza boxes everywhere. Tisha smiled,

"I better get started," sat down her supplies and propped the trash can lid open for easy access.

Phoebe made her way back to the living room and turned on the TV. Mary Jo's snoring didn't miss a beat through the interruptions.

Two hours later, Tisha had finished the kitchen, Mary Jo was awake and the local news was on. "I have enough time to vacuum the living room and the bedrooms and wipe down the bathroom before I go. I can wash your towels and bed linens the next time I come and get the bedrooms straightened up. How does that sound?"

"Sounds real good," said Phoebe, trying to please. "Mary Jo, let's eat in the nice clean kitchen while she vacuums in here."

Mary Jo grunted and got to her feet and shuffled into the kitchen. "Azaa, looks new in here."

Phoebe stood with the freezer door open. The vacuum cleaner was loud but her voice was louder, "What do you want to eat? There's a frozen lasagna but it will take an hour to heat up. There's some chicken pot pies and maybe one turkey one." She shifted boxes around on the shelves. "Some corndogs, too."

Mary Jo yelled back, nodding, "Corndogs. Do we have mustard?"

"Yes, ma'am. Turn on the oven for me and I'll dig us out a few." Tisha turned off the vacuum, moving her operation into Mary Jo's bedroom, so the noise momentarily quieted.

Phoebe whispered, "Do you have any cash? We have to pay this woman."

"I can go get some at the ATM machine."

"No, you are not going out alone in the dark. I might never see you again."

"Let me look in my bag." Mary Jo went and got it and dumped the contents on the kitchen table. Some crumpled bills fell out with an assortment of wrappers and the paperwork from the car and the bank account and other receipts. "Here's some money. How much we need?"

"I'll ask her when she comes out. Smooth out those bills and see how much we have." Mary Jo dug through the papers and gathered up the money and handed it to her sister.

Phoebe counted. "Probably plenty. Here's one hundred and twenty dollars."

Mary Jo smiled. "But not enough for Bingo."

"Shhh. Don't talk about Bingo in front of her, she might tell Stella or Jonas."

Mary Jo nodded and they went about the business of fixing corndogs for supper and retired to the living room with them for evening television.

Tisha stopped in the living room and wiped the sweat off her forehead and neck with a paper towel. "I worked three hours, so that's thirty-six dollars."

Phoebe counted out two twenty-dollar bills. "Keep the change. You plenty-good cleaning lady."

"Why, thank you. How does Wednesday sound for me to come back?"

"Wednesday would be fine and Thursday, but not Friday."

Mary Jo got interested and piped up, "Yeah, don't come Friday. We got other plans."

Tisha gathered up her spray bottles and rags and loaded her carryall. "See y'all then. Thanks," and let herself out the door.

"I like her," Phoebe commented and the old girls went back to sleep in front of the television.

Chapter 24

Things Were Good

Stella

Jonas has just about persuaded me that all really is well in my world, that I should enjoy the peace and quiet I've always cherished.

We went to church together last Sunday and sat in the pew where I've sat most every Sunday for years. It felt right. Anna's daughters, Brooke and Charlene, sat in front of me and to the right, where their dear mother sat as long as I knew her. Rich people pass down their box seats in their college football stadium; the rural middle class inherits the family pew. Quite a few churchgoers congratulated us on our wedding and welcomed Jonas with handshakes and slaps on the back. He howdied and shook hands and grinned before church, during the "greet your neighbor" part of the service, and afterwards. Preacher Booth hugged us both and invited us to Sunday school classes, which wasn't ever going to happen, but it was nice of him to ask.

We ate Sunday dinner at Hometown Restaurant. Jonas liked the buffet and I liked the company. Friends invited us to join their table. We joined a table for eight and I steered Jonas to the chair on the end so he could focus on food more than conversation. It was fun. Some of his work buddies had eaten earlier and spoke as they left. The waitresses were running back and forth with drinks, but they all took time to stop and congratulate us and ask questions about Alaska. "Is it cold up there?" "Do you live in an igloo?" "Is it dark all the time?" Jonas answered them all with good humor.

Chapter 24

"I've been asked those so many times, I thought the whole county would have heard by now," he whispered.

"They just want to have something to say," I whispered back, pleased that he was getting so much attention. We had been private in our long relationship and I was over the moon to finally "come out" with the man I loved.

My accounting service was doing well. The work had gotten behind while I was gone, but it was all caught up and it was easier to concentrate. I guess as a married woman, I was more content. I had even picked up another customer since we got back.

The animals on the farm were all healthy, the mama goats and sheep were expecting in April. I had the stall dividers ready for when the barn was reconfigured as a maternity ward. The farm was far enough up on Peter's Mountain that our dogs, Sugar and now Riley, were able to run free when we were home and sleep in the shed. They had a hundred-foot run when we were gone. They probably barked too much, but we knew when someone pulled into the yard or when four-footed guests darted through the yard at night. They answered the yips of the coyotes, too, which left us all feeling a bit wild. The chicken coop had been cleaned in November and lined with lots of straw. I left the

Sheep in the farmyard. Photo by B. Crabtree.

chicken manure in the straw all winter for added insulation in the floor. Their water trough had a new-fangled electric coil in it so the water didn't freeze except on bitter cold mornings. That saved a lot of water carrying. If I had one in the rain barrel out by the barn, the sheep and goats might have a better source of water in the winter, should look into that.

I'd cut the wood last spring and fall. Some folks say that wood warms you twice, once when you cut it and once when you burn it. They are right; I tried to get wood in on cool days. I also canned green beans, pickles, applesauce, blackberries, corn, beets, and tomatoes from my own garden. My, well, our pantry shelves were colorful and very nearly full. I was proud of my canning.

The tractor and mowers were all winterized; the antifreeze and oil had been checked and the tires were full.

Jonas' work at the Celanese plant across the Virginia state line in Pearisburg was fulfilling. He loved his job and he knew every inch of the building and the mechanical details needed to keep it running. The facility had changed over from electric to natural gas for power a year ago and Jonas had thrived on solving the unforeseen challenges that came with the new system. Ben McDaniel, his longtime friend, worked with him at the Celanese. After hours they took part in the usual mountain pastimes together: fishing, hunting, doctoring cattle, and fixing cars.

Tisha and Eliza remained my best friends. As far as I was concerned, they knew everything. Plus, they knew everybody in Monroe County and their parents and grandparents and who each of them had dated or hated. Wish all they knew could be put in a book or an app so we could just search for information. Until then, they were only a phone call or email away.

Preacher Booth works with me an hour or two a week, helping me face the bumps in my life more graciously. He prays with me after every session and I can feel the load lifting. Jonas was right. I needed to talk to someone.

Timmy Lee was tucked away in a psychiatric hospital. I figured that he'd get restless and come to his senses before long, but he was still there after nearly two months and that was a good feeling. If he ever got out, I might worry, but I thought I had just about had it with being scared.

Sometimes I got bad places on my skin, "Basal cell carcinomas," the doctor said. "We can watch them or cut them off." I always chose cutting them off and getting rid of the fear of them growing or spreading. They grew slowly, but they grew. Timmy Lee was a bad spot, too, and had been spreading

all of my life. I knew I could shoot him, almost did once before. As bad as a shooting is, the pain he caused was worse. I sort of took a shot at him last fall, in fact. If he was close enough to hurt Jonas or me and threatened, I would use my little friend, the Pink Lady, a pistol. She stayed pretty close by, just in case.

Stella's Pink Lady. Photo by B. Crabtree.

The best part of my life was living with Jonas. There were some little changes but my life was better with him. I didn't know the musky smells of a man, his dirty socks and sweaty t-shirts, and hair needing a shampoo. Wearing his jacket or putting my face in his pillow made me shiver; it smelled so much like him. The bathroom was filled with the scent of aftershave in the morning and some other smells later on that are not as nice. I'm getting to know his expressions, like in his sleep and when he wakes and when he was relaxed and when he was tense. It felt like I was reading a book that I loved, I regret the years together we missed waiting for him to be sure he was divorced, but there wasn't much point in looking back now. And the loving. Ye gods and little fishes, we did enjoy each other.

Sometimes I'd see my hand with the gold wedding band on it and it looked new. For a split second I wonder whose hand it was. Then I twirled that shiny gold circle around and round and smiled at the difference a ring made.

All this to say things were good. My only hint of worry was those two old ladies living in Jonas' house and there was really nothing I could hang my hat on there. Tisha had telephoned after the first cleaning, "They are messier that you imagine!" She added, "And if you think they are only smoking outside, you better think again. I 'bout gagged when I first walked in and the cigarette butts overflowed the ashtrays into the kitchen floor. Yuk."

"Do you see any evidence of drinking?"

"Nope, none at all. Pepsi cans and Mountain Dew bottles around, but not a drop of alcohol. I've got a nose for it, too. We didn't raise three boys without getting real good at sniffing the drivers they rode with, or them for that matter."

"How did they treat you?"

"Just fine. Mostly Aunt Phoebe was more awake. Jonas' Mom seemed like she was out of it, she slept most of the time I was there. They had corndogs for supper. Is that even healthy for old people?"

"Greasy fast food is not near the problem I expected to have. Are they really just sitting around watching TV?"

"Yep, and napping on and off. They seem pretty sweet to me. Messy, but sweet."

"We appreciate you, Tisha."

"Stella, there was one weird thing."

"Ha, just one?"

"Mary Jo dumped out her purse or tote or whatever on the kitchen table and there were a lot of legal documents crunched together. Like contracts. They looked kinda like the fine print that comes when you get a job or buy something, maybe like an apartment lease."

"Hmm, they can't be buying anything big. Or getting jobs. I won't say anything to Jonas just yet, but if you happen to see those again, you might need to straighten them up. And take a little peek at them, if you know what I mean."

"I can do that. Grateful for the extra money. Eddie needs insurance. Do you have any idea how much eighteen-year-old boys are charged for insurance? It's highway robbery."

"Glad it is working out. Holler at me later."

"Yep. Bye."

I hung up with a faint stirring of hope that whatever those two were into, I would at least have a head start on them. Couldn't imagine them working or buying anything, though. Maybe it was something printed on scrap paper or something that came in the mail. They were mailbox junkies because they never had home delivery before. All the villages of the North Slope only put mail in post office boxes. Mary Jo and Phoebe watched for the red jeep that delivered the mail six days a week and rushed out to get their daily junk mail. I thought about putting my extra catalogs and advertisements in there on the sly. They read every word of every piece of mail.

Those two had made it through the first six weeks with flying colors. Maybe I could shake this feeling of dread with a winter walk before Jonas gets home from work. I pulled on his wool shirt and a pair of gloves and hollered for the dogs. Their glee was hard to resist. We headed up the steep path under dark skies. A storm looked to be brewing across the mountain.

132

Chapter 25

It Was Time

Timmy Lee

"Where is $10K?" read the first toilet paper kite I got from Jeff. Hell, I did not have any money stashed anywhere, but I knew I needed a believable answer before the next day. I swallowed the TP after I read it.

I knew that a head injury and evidence of internal bleeding was a sure transport to the hospital downtown. Jeff had gotten me what I needed to fake an injury with a lot of blood, my ticket out. I now was the proud owner of an IV bag, tube and needle. He was also arranging a distraction on the street to the hospital and a car with clothes and shoes for me on a side street, keys under the floor mat.

I just had to maintain for a few more days, be convincingly hurt and run like hell when I got the chance. Maybe Jeff would be tapped to ride the ambulance, but the plan could work without him. There were some details that I hadn't figured out, like what to say about the money that would keep Jeff satisfied. He had me memorize his address in Huntington so I could contact him later with it.

My nerves were on edge.

"Bank deposit box in Bluefield." I wrote on a square of toilet paper. "Sister has key. I'll mail." He would buy that, I think, not that I really had a bank lock box in Bluefield or that Stella would have kept a key for me.

His response the next day was, "Cash in person at Welcome Center 6 AM."

"OK." I wrote back. I didn't see any way around it, but it would be hard to come back to this area.

"10 days. If not, U B sorry." Jeff glared at me when he tucked this message in the elastic of my pajama pants.

Sticks and stones can break my bones but words can never hurt me. That old saying ran through my head from grade school recess. I was seeing another side of big happy Jeff. That bastard was threatening me. Now I saw his face was just a happy mask. He was cold and hard and wanted his way. Guess he was on edge, too. So what that he was risking his job and maybe jail time, but that was his choice, his risk, not mine.

I drew some more blood under the covers that night; probably had two cups of blood in the IV bag now, a little blood would go a long way in my plan. Every morning after I drew blood, Jeff would get me an extra carton of orange juice for breakfast and some extra brownies at lunchtime. Might have to go without this time. When I felt weak, I pulled out the needle, licked the drop or two on my skin, sealed the bag and stashed it under the mattress. Could've used some cold juice then, I was woozy and dry.

I would need to get out of town and rob some places soon to pay off Jeff. Or screw Jeff. He's a fool just like the rest of them. Maybe go to Ohio or Kentucky. Wherever the cops didn't have the road blocked is where I'd go. Once I was out of here, everything would work out. I closed my eyes and felt the rush of hurting Stella. Had to rub my arms to keep the shivers away.

I needed to do this soon. It was time.

Something woke me early, around 4 AM, and I saw the shadow of a guard's feet below my door for the hourly check. I was having trouble breathing. Nerves. So, I decided to do it. Right then. I rolled off the bed hard on the side away from the camera, grabbed the IV bag from under the mattress and made a puddle where my head would lie. Then, I squeezed the last blood in the bag in both ears so it looked like they were bleeding. I ripped my scalp with the IV needle for good measure and stashed it all back in the hiding place. I lay in that blood for what seemed like days, almost went back to sleep but my heart was pounding too hard. When the keys rattled and the door creaked open, it was curtains on opening night. I should get a damn Oscar for my portrayal of an injured disabled man.

Everything went the way it was supposed to. They checked vitals and carried me to the ambulance. There was a discussion about restraints and they decided on "soft" restraints, gauze strips that looped my wrists to the gurney rails down by my sides. Wasn't Jeff, it was another orderly. We took off to the hospital with only the orderly, no guard with me. Guard was probably following in a police car. My car was supposed to be at Charleston Avenue and 19th street, about a half mile from Cabell Huntington Hospital, but it felt like we had gone too far. Jeff, you sucker, you better not leave me high and dry now.

The ambulance swerved and metal grated on pavement, we'd blown the front driver's side tire. My man Jeff had come through. The driver got out and the guard in the vehicle following went to inspect the damage. They yelled at the orderly to get his ass out and help. All I needed. I pulled the slipknots on the gauze, unbuckled the straps, slid through the open back doors, walked across the sidewalk and down an alley looking back over my shoulder; then ran like hell. I didn't know which way 19th Street was but I cut right and headed back the way we'd come and crossed 18th. I was close. I stayed one street over from Charleston Avenue.

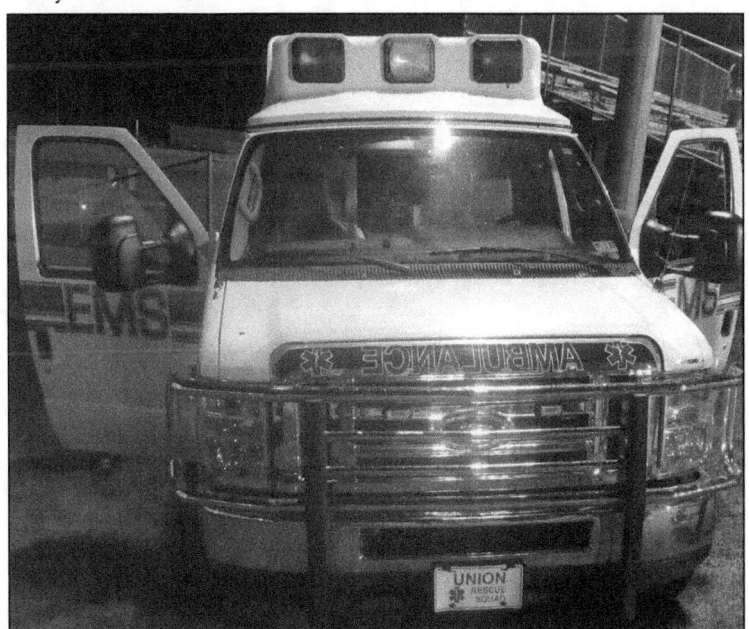

Emergency Medical Services ambulance. Photo by B. Crabtree.

Chapter 25

Good thing it was still dark. A bloody man in paper hospital pajamas, barefooted, wouldn't catch anyone's eye. Shit! Needed clothes and to clean up. I stopped running to catch my breath and looked to the right. There it was. A piece of shit car with West Virginia tags, a beat up grey Cobalt, unlocked and with a pile of clothes in the back seat. Didn't matter if it was the one for me or not. I got in and felt around for the key. Bingo.

It started and I pulled out slowly and looked for bridges to cross into Ohio to get out of this state as fast as possible. I never heard yelling or sirens behind me. It just seemed like a bad dream that I was waking from. I was in Ohio in less than three minutes and hit the back roads. It was still dark when I found a campground closed for the winter. The river water was freezing cold as I cleaned off all the blood with my pajama top. My feet were cold and sore from running and I put on warm clothes and shoes. I got back on the road again, heading south. I would need food and gas, so started looking for places or people to hit. Maybe I would pay Jeff. I drummed on the steering wheel and sang with the radio. My man did well. I was free.

Chapter 26

It's Gonna Be a Hard Time for Stella

Jonas

The call came when I was at work. It was Sheriff Johnson.

"Jonas, we just got word from Huntington that Timothy Lee Davis escaped early this morning. They said that he ran from an ambulance transporting him to the county hospital with a head injury."

"How was he able to run with a head injury? Wait, let me guess, it was fake?"

"Evidently. Get this, armed guards in the car in front of him and behind him, a driver and an orderly with him and none of them saw him escape. It was like he vanished into thin air, they said."

"Great." I was pissed. "What now?"

"They have sealed off his room to go over it with a fine-tooth comb. The hospital is closed as far as programs, even meals, every patient eats in his room. So many staff members are involved in the investigation that they are barely covering the building. Every employee that has had contact with him will be interviewed and the security tapes are being studied now."

"You know he will be coming here, right? He thinks he has a score to settle with Stella." Dead silence on the line. "You still there, Sheriff?"

"Yeah, I'm here. Jonas, we don't have enough deputies to do the minimal service this county needs. State troopers will be on duty with us this evening and that will help, but not all those guys know the county well enough to respond in an emergency. Not sure we can handle extra protection, not with the kind of extended hours that takes."

"Well, who else can you call? We've got an escaped murderer with an axe to grind against his own sister and maybe looking for the preacher, and probably me. He's coming to Monroe County if he's not already here. Looks like you could have a license check or a road block or patrol the back road to the mountain once a day or something. Anything."

"Jonas, we don't know what kind of car he's in, even if he has a car. No cars reported stolen in the past 24 hours in the Huntington area. We're waiting to hear what develops so we know what we are looking for."

"Well, why did you call me, exactly?" I was more than pissed and getting louder. "Did you want me to go looking for him for you?"

"Now, Jonas, I thought you'd want to know. I hoped that you'd tell Stella for us. I don't have one man on the force that wants to be the one to tell her, what with her being in so much danger before, and her being most of the boys' Sunday school teacher at some point in the past. They know her and know that she expects better than this of the system. They would do about anything to help her, but they don't want to be the bearer of bad news."

Silence and then in a little soft voice, "Jonas, she gets awful mad."

I sighed a deep sigh of despair and aggravation. "I suppose I should thank you, Elmer, but it's going to be a hard time for Stella until he is found. Could you let me know when there's any news? Even rumors of news. I know you guys hear things that don't go out in press releases. Call back any time you hear."

"Yes, sir." The sheriff's professional tone returned. "Call us if you need us or if you hear from him. Try to keep an eye on Stella. I better get off here and let Preacher Booth know."

I hung up, thoroughly irritated that Timmy Lee had outsmarted an entire psychiatric hospital staff and was probably on the way here now. Time for me to get on home and break the bad news. When things are on my mind, I can't focus on details, and sure enough, I caught my shirttail in a desk drawer and when I stood up, it jerked the desk and turned over a cup of cold coffee that splashed, just missing my cell phone. I sopped up the mess and blamed Timmy Lee.

On the way to the parking lot, I remembered my phone, still on the desk, and turned around to get it and there was a fire alarm to clear the building. It was a scheduled drill. I knew about it. I had to swim upstream against the flow of employees leaving to get my dang phone. It took me twenty minutes to get to my truck and another twenty to get home, flying low. The clouds were dark, ominous and heavy with snow.

By the time I got there, I wished I had called earlier and told Stella so she could be locked and loaded, but things were fine. She had fogged up all the kitchen windows cooking up an I-talian (as she would say) dinner of homemade ravioli and thick slices of crusty bread.

I took both her hands at the table and told her that Timmy Lee had escaped. She got up and started setting the table without a word. When she was finished, she nodded, "Well, I have had a wire crossed. I've been worrying that something was going on with your mom and Aunt Phoebe. It was Timmy Lee sending messages across the cosmos, wasn't it?"

"Stella, this is more serious than your psychic-ness being right. He could be in the area right now, be armed, hell, just him showing up here any which way, is scary."

"Does the law know which direction he headed?"

"No, he 'just vanished into the air' they reported."

That pushed her over the line. "They did, did they? All the guards, the state troopers, the high-priced doctors, the strait jackets and restraints, the modern brick facility with high-tech security and he still vanished?" She threw pots and pans, an empty milk jug and nearly anything in reach, but nothing breakable, so I guess she was still under some control. I stood back and watched but didn't interfere. She had every right to be aggravated. She kicked the refrigerator once and it must've hurt because she calmed down, took a deep breath and went back to getting supper on the table.

"He is not going to ever bully me again." She placed glasses of ice water at the tip of each knife beside each plate. "I'm wondering how to just avoid him, I mean just get out of his path, but that is letting him control me." She set out the butter. "I believe I would rather shoot him."

"Stella, there's a lot that happens to a person when they take another life. Not just the legal stuff, the thoughts you have, the way you see things. You will absorb a lot of pain and regret and have to deal with guilt later." I thought she was going to say something then, she even opened her mouth and then closed it. I waited until she took the ravioli out of the oven and the smell of garlic and meat sauce overwhelmed me.

She said, all matter-of-fact, "Snow is coming, maybe Timmy Lee stole a car without four-wheel drive and he won't come up the mountain tonight. Let's eat."

My gears didn't change as fast as Stella's, but I ate. Food was delicious. Conversation was a bit slow.

The next morning, deep snow was a pretty surprise because it came so quietly in the night, without the sound of wind or ice pinging off the windows, just a big soft snowflake kind of snow. At home we called it "Whale Snow" because it was like the snow when whales give themselves to the Inupiat people of the North Slope. The snow looked like curtains of white.

After watching it awhile, my boss called to see if I could come in early and leave early. I didn't want to leave Stella, but I was glad to go just to break a trail off the mountain and back. I'd be back before noon. Stella told me if I saw an angry man walking up the road to tell him to go away. The Timmy Lee I knew would be holed up someplace warm right now, so I didn't expect him to be out, but I laughed and said I would.

Stella was feeding the animals when I got ready and I followed her path through the snow and helped her, my subtle way of telling her to get inside. I noticed the handle of her pink pistol sticking out of her jacket pocket when I kissed her goodbye. She would be okay for a few hours. My wife was a spitfire.

Emili, Stella's goat with the sheep in the barnyard. Photo by B. Crabtree.

Chapter 27

Let's Go Play Bingo

Phoebe and Mary Jo

The drive-through ATM machine would not spit out as much money as Mary Jo wanted no matter how she shook her fist or threatened its job. The daily limit policy required by the bank's insurance escaped her. All she could understand was that she was sure that she had more than that in her account and the machine was keeping her money from her. She finally gave up when she had another idea.

"Phoebe, give me your card." Phoebe twisted her shoulder bag around to her lap and searched through it. Phoebe wore it all the time so she could be identified when one of their adventures went wrong. For a long time, Phoebe's fear had been to be dead and unidentified. On the Slope, she thought most people would know her, but here she had to keep her ID on her body or beside her bed at night. She had even updated the information with Jonas' phone number added with a Sharpie. No unmarked grave for Phoebe. She found her card and handed it over.

Mary Jo stuck it in the slot and pulled it out. "Quick, what's the code?"

"It might be 1955, the year I was born." She folded her arms over her bag. Mary Jo turned, "You were not born in 1955. I was born in 1945 and you are three years younger. You're born in 1948." She punched in 1948 into the ATM keyboard. 'Transaction Denied' flashed across the screen. "Give me that card, we've got to start over."

"You've still got the card." Phoebe reminded her primly.

Chapter 27

The card missed the slot this time and Mary Jo dropped it on the pavement. She tried to get out to get it but the car door was too close to the machine. Phoebe panicked and got out on her side to go help, but she couldn't get in the space far enough to reach the card, just far enough to get stuck.

They were screaming at each other when they heard a car door close and a man spoke, "Need some help here?" He was next in line.

Phoebe rolled her eyes and said, "Yes, sir. If you can give me a little pull to get me unstuck and then get it through my sister's head that she needs to move the car, I would appreciate it."

"Nice car. You two young ladies out on the town today?" He offered Phoebe a hand and she took it, shifted her hip and came right out.

"Thank you. Yes, we are going to the doctor," she lied.

Mary Jo had pulled up, parked and was huffing and puffing back to the scene. "Here's the card."

She pointed and their new friend bent down to get it. "Allow me," he said and wiped the card off and glanced at it before handing it to her.

"Come on, Phoebe, we have to go." She turned her back on them and toddled back to the car.

"Thank you again, very much." Phoebe looked back at the man and he was already back to his car, getting in. She hurried around the red Mustang to catch up.

It was quiet in the car. Mary Jo had turned the radio off and was concentrating on finding her way. Finally, she spoke, "You were not born in 1955. You were old enough to go to school in 1955."

"I jokes, you crazy old woman. I know when I was born, but my code is 1955. That is what I told you. Just for some fun."

"Why would you make the code a year you were not born? Of all the years why did you pick 1955?"

Phoebe had had enough and yelled, "Damn it all to hell, Mary Jo! I did not pick the code. It came on a post card from the bank, just like yours. Are you so worried about being older that you cannot let me have a little fun?"

Mary Jo grew quiet again. "I forgot," she said.

Phoebe looked out the window, brooding, then, out of nowhere, yelled, "Pull over MJ, right now. Stop quick at this Quick Stop place." The car swerved over the plowed snow and slush into the parking lot, stopped straddling a yellow parking lot line and Phoebe got out. "Wait right here."

She came back with a heavy grocery bag and got in. "I need a beer. Let's go play bingo," and popped a top as the exclamation mark to the afternoon.

The women found a hilltop park beside a cemetery, which added pause to their impromptu party. They sat, bundled up at a picnic table as the sun went down, consuming three beers each before heading on to bingo. They carefully walked through the snow to deposit the cans, the bag, and the receipt in the trash. Watching Tisha's hard work reminded them that it felt good to be neat. As Mary Jo said, "Now that we have a nice cleaning lady, we can't go around being slobs."

The Bingo Hall in Rich Creek was over the Volunteer Fire Station. The room was warm and full of smoke and when the women entered, they breathed in the familiar smell. They paid their five dollars for six hard cards each plus another two for two dabbers apiece. There were two empty folding chairs side by side. They each claimed a chair and spread out their bingo materials on the old cafeteria table. They arranged the cards and little box of markers between them for easy access. The nearby ashtray was too tempting to ignore, so they both lit up.

"Ah, this is the life," Mary Jo looked around the room, at the lady with the bright unnaturally red hair, the

Bingo Hall above the Fire Department. Photo by B. Crabtree.

143

Chapter 27

three-hundred-pound man in the tight tee-shirt, and the old couple with grandchildren playing under the table with cars. "They are still playing the early bird games, Pheebs, you want some coffee?"

"Ee, sounds good. Here is some money," and she reached a handful of coins to her sister.

Mary Jo returned her money when she brought back a mug of coffee. "Free. Don't know how they make any money giving away coffee."

When the games began in earnest, they fit right in, dabbing and buying paper cards between hard card games and losing most of the time, but winning enough to stay interested. When the door opened and a young man came in with his arms full of flat boxes, the pizza smell overcame the smoke and coffee at least for a few minutes. Soon, it was intermission time and pizza and other snacks went on sale.

The man working concessions was a dapper gentleman with an Atlanta baseball cap and a big grin. He called them over, "You ladies are new here tonight. Welcome." Mary Jo was feeling the beer and kept heading to the bathroom, but Phoebe had it together enough to speak, "Thank you. We like bingo."

"Where y'all from?"

Phoebe didn't know if she should tell since they were sort of hiding their business and their new car from Jonas, but this nice man seemed interested. "We live in Monroe County," she smiled back at him.

"Oh, I see, you are from out-of-state."

Phoebe nodded several times and smiled. "But not from too far out of state."

"I understand. You ladies have a good time tonight." He turned to wait on another customer.

Phoebe watched him work a minute then decided she would get a piece of pizza and a Dr. Pepper so she could talk to him again. She found out that his name was CT and that he worked there every Friday night.

The caller gave a five-minute warning that the games were starting back up and the first one was Triangle. Players rushed to get their dollars to buy paper cards with shaded triangles printed on them. The prize for a bingo within the shaded shape was one hundred dollars and Phoebe was excitedly taping her cards to the table when Mary Jo returned from the bathroom.

"What day is it, Pheebs?"

"Friday, Mary Jo, get some cards for Triangle."

"I think I'll sit one out."

"Okay." Phoebe didn't even look up. She took the lid off her dabber and concentrated on the caller and the light-up board. Then she closed her eyes and mouthed her bingo prayer, "Dear God, if it is your will, let me win, and let me win big." She didn't use it every game, just when she felt good about it and the prize was worth a prayer.

It worked; she bingo-ed first, but it was off the shaded part so the prize was only fifty dollars but she whooped it up anyway.

The night's program moved back to hard card games. Phoebe looked over at Mary Jo's cards and noticed that she was behind. "You missed B-10, MJ, and some more. Here you go." Phoebe placed markers on the missed squares then went back to her cards with the next number called. Mary Jo just watched her, then threw all the markers in her hand on the table and walked out the outside door.

Phoebe left her card, reluctantly, and followed Mary Jo through the parking lot to the car. "Is it the waves?" Mary Jo nodded, tears running down her face.

"Do you hurt anywhere?" Mary Jo shrugged her shoulders then shook her head as if to say no.

"Too much tonight, I expect. Let me get our things. You stay here, right here until I get back and we will go home." Mary Jo was crying openly now, sniffling and wailing.

Phoebe went back in and turned in all their cards. CT came to see what was wrong and she told him that her sister didn't feel well. They needed to go home. "Come back again, I hope your sister feels better soon." He walked her to the door, carrying MJ's parka and tote bag. "Goodbye, Miss Phoebe, y'all be careful, hear?"

Mary Jo had stopped crying and was sitting at the wheel of the car ready to go when Phoebe got in. "I don't know, Mary Jo, if you should drive. Do you remember how?" No response. "Seriously, if you can't drive, we can call Stella or Jonas."

"I will try." Mary Jo started the car and drove carefully through town, back to the main road and all the way to the mountain, slowly and carefully. Phoebe was ready to correct any wrong turns, but she didn't need to and she didn't want to speak and break the spell.

She pulled over the frozen ground behind the old barn near their house and Phoebe patted her leg. "That is the best you

have EVER driven. I mean in your whole life!" Mary Jo smiled
a little, then wrinkled her forehead and studied her sister.
    "And who are you?"

Bingo hall parking lot. Photo by B. Crabtree.

Chapter 28

Something is Wrong

Stella and Phoebe

Phoebe called Stella the minute she got Mary Jo to the house and into bed. "You've got to come. She doesn't even know me. Something is wrong."

It was dark, but not late and Jonas was asleep in front of the news, so she left him a note, took the dogs and her pistol, and went down the mountain to see what was going on. Her car made the first tracks in the driveway, but there were human tracks coming from the field next door as far as she could see in the darkness and she wondered who had been out walking today.

Phoebe met her at the door. "Something is bad wrong. Sister doesn't know me. Me!"

"Where does she hurt?" Stella asked because she didn't know what else to do.

"She didn't hurt. She got mad and frustrated and threw her markers, uh, her chips, and walked out of the door."

"That must be the tracks I saw outside."

"Yeah, yeah, I went after her and brought her back. And she didn't know who I was." She started sobbing. "My only sister. She forgot me. I thought she could not forget me." Phoebe buried her head in Stella's chest, crying.

"Hey, I need you to help me, we will figure this out together." Stella hugged her and held her. "What kinda game were you playing?"

Phoebe gulped. "Cards, yeah, cards. We like to play cards."

"Was it cutthroat? I mean, was she driven hard to win? Enough that she might have felt stressed?"

"No, she was liking the game until she threw her chips and left."

"Something upset her? Did you say something? What had she eaten today, was it a bellyache or the back door trots? Sometimes they hit us all."

"No, Miss Stella, I never said a word. She ate same ole stuff. Pizza for supper."

"How do you know she didn't know you? Sometimes Mary Jo plays tricks."

"No, I could tell from her eyes. The lights were not on in her eyes. She was trying to see me to make sense and remember me, but nothing came to her eyes. She could talk and she came home with me and got into bed. That is different, too, because she likes to sleep in the recliner."

"Phoebe, I don't know. She is sleeping normally now, though. When she wakes up, see if she is okay, if she knows you and is normal. Then call me. I plan to be home all day. We will get her to the hospital if she needs to go."

"Okay. I will watch her and be sure she is sleeping."

"Phoebe, you look like you need some sleep. Maybe Mary Jo's age is just catching up with her. Try not to worry. There's nothing we can do tonight."

Stella slipped her boots on and dressed to go outside. "Call me or Jonas anytime that you need us. I'll tell him and he might come down later."

"Okay." Phoebe wrapped her arms around her in a fierce hug. "You a good woman, Stella Akpik."

Stella squeezed her back. "Thank you for that," she murmured and stomped out to the Subaru and got in. A man sat up in the back seat and she screamed.

"That is just how easy Timmy Lee could have found you, Stella. I walked down when I found your note. I thought it may have been a set-up and you were walking into a trap."

"Shame on you for scaring me, Jonas. Shame on you." She started the car and backed up, jerking the wheel back and forth as if to slam Jonas around in the back seat.

"Maybe you need to be scared enough to realize you are in danger," he shouted. "Slow down, the slush is slick." Instead, Stella gunned the car, fishtailing and sliding from one side of the narrow road to the other. "Have it your way, but we are going to be together every minute until they pick up your brother, as long as it takes." She eased off the gas and drove sensibly until they reached the top of the mountain and turned down their lane.

"You nearly scared me to death, Jonas. I had a gun and my hand went to it. You might want to move slower around me until this is over." Then she gritted her teeth to keep from crying. "Phoebe thinks something is wrong with your mother because she asked her who she was. It was so sad."

"How did she seem to you?"

"She was asleep and I didn't wake her up."

"What was she doing when it happened?"

"Playing cards and winning, according to Phoebe."

"I don't remember them ever playing cards, but I can't think that would have set Mom off. So, where did you leave it?"

"They are to call us if they need us, and we'll check on your mom early tomorrow."

"Do I need to go back down there tonight?"

"No, but you might call Phoebe and calm her down. She was pretty riled up."

"Okay, guess you could finish the drive home or are we going to camp out in the car tonight?"

West Virginia Law Enforcement vehicle. Photo by B. Crabtree

Chapter 28

Stella put the car in gear and eased home, watching the shadows beyond the bright beams of headlights for movement or new footprints in the snow.

Jonas didn't have to remind her. She knew that Timmy Lee was out there somewhere.

Chapter 29

The Police Are Searching

Jonas

My phone rang early Saturday morning and I answered it, expecting Phoebe to be reporting in, but it wasn't, it was the sheriff.

"Mornin' Elmer, do you want to speak with Stella?" I knew he didn't, just getting a jab in. She threw back the covers to scurry to the bathroom. The view distracted me for a split-second.

"Calling to see how the roads are up your way. Have you been in or out yet?

"Yes, sir, both. It melted a lot yesterday and may have been warm enough to keep melting through the night. You planning on patrolling our road today?"

"Jonas, I thought I'd come up and report what we know about your brother-in-law. There is more information."

"Come on up anytime, Elmer, we'll either be here or down at my old house where Mom and my aunt are staying."

"Be there within the hour. Thanks." He hung up but I kept the phone next to my ear a few more seconds listening while I thought about the call.

Stella crawled back in bed, her feet cold from the tile in the bathroom and rubbed them against my warm legs until I fluffed the covers at her. She hates that and will do about anything to avoid a second fluffing. "Is your mom okay? Who was on the phone?"

"Elmer Johnson."

Chapter 29

She sat up in the bed. "Oh, my Lord. Have they found Timmy Lee? Is he dead?"

"Naw, nothing like that. He just has some new information, he said. Coming within the hour."

"We better be up and running, then." She threw back the covers and started getting dressed. I sat up slowly, not because my back hurt but because I expected it to hurt.

I was helping Stella fill the bird feeders when the sheriff's car pulled in slowly. Both dogs ran to greet him. Riley took her cue from Sugar, if Sugar was happy, so was she. If Sugar barked, Riley added her voice to the outrage. Sugar liked Elmer so they were both wiggling to get a pat on the head.

"C'mon in, Sheriff, we've got some toast and cocoa if you want a bite to eat."

Stella joined us tromping into the kitchen; the smell of warmed bread and chocolate seemed stifling after the crispness of the morning air.

"Pull up a chair, Elmer," I motioned to the table, kinda felt like I needed to keep the conversation flowing. Stella hadn't spoken. "Let me take your hat." He was reluctant but gave in, trying hard to be agreeable. I hung it on the coat rack in the foyer.

"Morning, Stella." Elmer nodded at her and she returned the nod.

"I'm here because we got some more information about your brother's escape." He pulled two folded papers out of his inside pocket, put on his reading glasses and read.

"Police are searching for an escaped prisoner from Mildred Mitchell-Bateman Hospital in Huntington, WV. The prisoner, Timothy L. Davis, a white man who stands 6-foot-1 and weighs 201 pounds, has blue eyes and short brown hair. Davis escaped in the early morning hours of January 23 while en route to Cabell Huntington Hospital for treatment of a head injury.

"Davis, 59, is facing a murder charge in Monroe County for the death of an elderly woman in her home late last summer.

"The Logan Detachment of the West Virginia State Police, the WVDHHR, and the Huntington City Police Department are continuing the investigation of the escape. The WV State Police are directing the search for Davis.

"Residents of Huntington and the surrounding area, specifically S. 18th and Norway Ave, are advised if they come home to find evidence their house may have been entered (cut window screen, damaged door, etc.), DO NOT ENTER. Instead, call 911 immediately. With the search underway for escaped inmate, Timothy Davis, 59, it is possible he may have taken shelter at an unoccupied home in the area. Law enforcement will respond and will make sure there is no one currently inside," Huntington's Police Chief Marvin Harvey said.

"Doesn't sound like they know much." Stella was opening up a little.

"I've got another list here, unofficially." He looked at both of us to be sure we understood it was **unofficial**.

Stella and I both shook our heads and he went on, "The hospital search found an IV bag, tubing and needle under his mattress. In reviewing the security tapes, he could be seen moving under the sheets at night, apparently drawing his own blood to use in his faked injury."

"He had to have had help to get that. Somebody in the hospital must have slipped it to him. Has anybody confessed?" Stella was all over that IV bag.

"You know him best, Stella, would he have been able to draw blood from his own body?"

"Yes, yes, yes, he would do anything to get his way. Chew his own leg off like a wolf in a trap, if he needed to."

The sheriff went on, "I figured that myself. Another point of interest is that the IV bag had been disposed of. It wasn't missing from any inventory. It was used and may have been used by a patient with a blood-borne disease."

"Serves him good and proper," Stella cut her brother no slack.

"What else?"

"There are three orderlies who had regular contact. They had done background checks on everybody, of course, but these three are of particular interest. The flat tire on the ambulance was rigged. It had been messed with earlier. Timmy Lee couldn't have done that. He never once left his cell in the seven or so weeks he was there. So, Stella, your theory holds up; he did have help, or incredible good luck. Also, when they went door to door near the location that the ambulance pulled over, one man getting ready to go to work at the bakery saw a bloody man running down the sidewalk across from his apartment building. He described Timmy Lee and the paper pajamas he was wearing. That was about 5:45 AM.

"Marshall University was shut down for the day. Public schools were cancelled and in addition to door-to-door searches, search teams are in place at bus stations, the train station, the airport, the turnpike tollbooths, four entrance ramps to Route 64, and the bridges across the Ohio River. The State Police Air Wing has been deployed to search from the sky, and bloodhounds are being used to track his path on the ground." He took a breath. "Wanted posters with a picture have been distributed, a felony escape warrant has been issued, under-cover escapee recovery teams are in place. The number and frequency of police patrols have been increased. The only stolen car reported in the past few days was found with the owner's ex-girlfriend driving."

He took off his glasses and closed them up. "Folks, I don't know what else we can do that is not being done. Timmy Lee has plumb vanished."

I remembered my phone call a week or two ago. "How about his son, Adam? When I called up there to the hospital, they asked if I was his son. Probably ought to check that out."

Elmer wrote that down. "My guess is they are contacting anyone who has tried to contact him in the hospital and the next of kin. But, I'll report it. Last name Davis?"

Stella answered, "Yes. He sang at our church less than a year ago with the Voice of Glory gospel singers. You might find him through them."

"Now Stella, I know that you did not part with Timmy Lee on good terms."

Stella interrupted, "No kidding, he tried to kill me twice, once here and once at the courthouse. Guess you could say I was not on real good terms with him."

"He may come to this area looking for you and I want you to take no chances. If you see him or have any reason to suspect he is nearby, please call me. Here is my mobile phone number, my home number, and the office number, or if you have a sighting, call 911." He handed us both a card. "I wish I could spare a man and a vehicle to sit up here all day and night, but I can't. Listen to me, now, especially you, Stella. Always be alert to your surroundings. Leave the dogs out at night. Keep a gun handy. If you have people to visit, leave here for a few days. He can't stay hidden much longer."

"Sheriff, Jonas' mom and aunt are living temporarily in his house. Shouldn't they be warned? We hate to trouble them about this, but Timmy Lee hasn't any love for Jonas either. He may look there, too."

"That's my next stop. Jonas, you wanna go with me, maybe smooth the way?"

Snowy Wilson Mill Road near Lindside, West Virginia. Photo by B. Crabtree

"Sure thing, Elmer. Glad to go with you. Stella, maybe you could come and check on Mom this morning?"

After we grabbed coats and hats, I locked the house, something we didn't usually do. Our two-vehicle convoy crawled off the icy hill to the valley below and went to see the women that Stella calls the Golden Girls. Phoebe met us at the door, looking worried. Mom was sitting up, drinking coffee. She seemed fine.

Turns out Phoebe was worried about the sheriff visiting. Mom knew us and other than being pretty tired for this hour of the day, she looked okay to me.

They behaved very well as the sheriff explained the situation and agreed to be alert. After he left, Phoebe asked me, "Does he want us to catch this Timmy Lee?"

"No, no, Aunty Phoebe, he wants you to stay away from this man, he is trouble. Call me or call 911 if you see him anywhere."

"Oh, Jonas, there were footprints up to our living room windows this morning. Might have been him. Come and look."

Stella laughed, "Tell them, Jonas, where those tracks came from."

I was embarrassed. "I was checking on Stella last night when she was visiting. We knew last night that Timmy Lee had escaped."

"And you didn't come in and see us. Tsk, tsk, tsk. That's not being a good nephew, Jonas."

"I know, I know. I didn't want to disturb your privacy."

Mary Jo yelled from the living room. "Don't fuss at him, privacy is a good thing."

Phoebe was thoughtful. "We need a picture of this man. Stella, do you have one?"

"Not with me, but I'll hunt one and bring it to you. Hey, it might be on the TV news, check that out tonight."

We said our goodbyes, hugged both old women, kissed their soft cheeks and told them to lock the door behind us. It was nearly lunchtime the day after his escape and Timmy Lee was nowhere to be found.

Chapter 30

I Was Ready

Stella

I called Eliza and Tisha on Saturday afternoon and told them that Timmy Lee was on the prowl. Eliza offered us her guest room indefinitely and Tisha volunteered to come and sit with a loaded gun, "like a stake-out," she said. I declined but it was nice that they were thinking of solutions.

Tisha also had some news from her cleaning job. "Those papers I mentioned the other night. I took a look at them. Somehow, they have the contract from Newberry Ford for a lease on a new Mustang."

"Must be scrap paper or belongs to somebody else. Has to be."

"I don't know, Stella, could they have leased a car for somebody else? Oh, and I found four bingo dabbers and a trash can full of rippies."

"What? What's a rippie?"

"Pull–tabs, little cards that cost money with tabs that hide prizes that people pull off. Stella, they've been gambling."

"Nope, not possible, they haven't been anywhere except the doctor and with me."

"I'm just telling you what I found." I heard the little explosion of a pop can being opened and a big slurp and swallow. "They are being a lot neater, though."

"Thanks, Tisha. Appreciate your detective work. Later."

She giggled. "Denial, denial, Stella. You are da queen of denial. Bye."

Chapter 30

Then, I called and cancelled my counseling appointment with Preacher Booth later today. Hard to deal with past problems in the middle of a current crisis. I think he was glad, too. He sounded nervous.

Jonas was playing with a new snow blower, making paths through the yard to the truck, to the car, to the shed and the chicken coop. He'd traded a chipper for it at work last summer when no one else was very interested in blowing snow. I liked it because it kept him busy and happy in the yard for two hours straight.

I wish I had something to occupy me for two hours so I didn't relive every moment of life with Timmy Lee. A book or a movie, maybe? A new recipe? Nope, my way was to face things head on.

If he wasn't caught, Timmy Lee would come after me and Jonas. It was personal and he would make us pay. Story of his life, blame anyone else for his problems and hurt them. It was my fault in high school when he didn't have money, and he pinched and twisted me until I was covered with bruises. When his girlfriend left him it was because I said something wrong to her, and he beat me with a belt. It was his method of operation since childhood. When Jonas talked about the guilt of hurting another person, Timmy Lee didn't count. If I ended up shooting him and even killing him, I think I could live with it. It would be better than living with the fear of being hurt, or Jonas being hurt, or the shame afterwards when he hurt me and I hadn't done anything about it.

It was time to be ready. I was armed physically and strong mentally and at peace. It really wasn't complicated. Worry wasn't part of it, being prepared was.

I'd stay home. My 22 rifle was upstairs, the shotgun downstairs, and my little friend, the Pink Lady, in my shoulder holster. I'd wear it under a vest all my waking hours and carry my cell phone in my pocket. The drapes were good ones, light darkening, from JC Penney and I'd keep them pulled until he was found. The windows and doors would stay locked and the dogs would run free. I'd keep within sight of Jonas when he was home and be aware of everything around me. That's all I could do. My brother could bring it on. I was ready. As ready as I knew how to be.

Chapter 31

It's Him

Mary Jo and Phoebe

It was nearly time for the evening news. Phoebe asked question after question about Mary Jo not knowing her the night before. "Didn't you remember anything when you saw me? What did it feel like to not know your only sister?"

"Phoebe, I don't even remember not remembering you. But, if you don't quit bothering me about it, I am going to try to forget you again."

"Tell me one more thing. Did it hurt anywhere?"

"I don't think so, I don't remember. Azaa, read a book about it or something."

"But the people who write the books don't have Alzheimer's, right?"

"Probably not, right."

"The only ones who can tell what it feels like to have Alzheimer's are people who have Alzheimer's before they get it so bad that they forget, right?

"Probably."

"Well, Mary Jo Akpik, that is you and that is why I am asking you questions. To figure out how it feels. I might get it, too. I want to know what to expect. For you and for me. So talk to me?"

"Okay, okay. Ask me whatever you want, but just until the news comes on."

Phoebe leaned forward on the couch and twisted the corner of the fleece blanket that she used for a throw. "Tell me how it feels when you don't know stuff that you used to know."

Chapter 31

Mary Jo scratched her head. "I can see fine with my eyes, but my mind, the wires hooked to my memory, are foggy, like on the river early in the morning. Something is there and I know it is there, but I can't trust it. It pisses me off when I want to do something that I have always done and I have to think about it. Like tie my shoes. Azaa, it takes me ten minutes."

"How do you want me to treat you when you get foggy?"

She was starting to get angry just thinking about it. "Don't yell at me. Don't change anything. Just wait, wait for me, will you?"

"Sure, Mary Jo, you know I will." She leaned closer to her sister, lip trembling, as if she could hug her with her eyes.

"I am not going to get any better, Pheebs, just worse. Better get used to the idea. Nobody gets cured from Alzheimer's."

"How do you know? You don't know everything."

"Mr. Google found it." She spoke with absolute confidence.

"But maybe there will be a cure."

"Naumi, too late for me, and probably too late for you. We gotta live fast. Real fast and do everything we want to do."

"Like what, Mary Jo?"

"Shh, here comes the news. Azaa, they are talking about someone we know. Stella's brother, Timmy Lee, and there's his picture."

Phoebe moved closer to the television. "Oh, my God." Phoebe grabbed Mary Jo's arm with one hand and pointed at the screen with the other. "It's him. It's that guy!"

"What guy?"

"The guy at the ATM machine. When I was stuck. He picked up my debit card. He SAW MY NAME on the card."

"I never saw that man before in my life, Phoebe, you are worse off than I am."

"We have to call Jonas and Stella and tell them. He's close by."

"Azaa, we are not telling anybody anything. We were driving our hot little car and we can't tell about that or Jonas will make us take it back. Besides I don't think I ever saw his face. Are you sure it was him?"

"On hundred percent sure. That was him. He might be trying to hurt Stella or Jonas and we are just going to let him? We can tell Jonas that we saw him from the Golden Age bus," Phoebe reasoned.

"Lying is worse than saying nothing. Besides, I didn't see him."

The television newscaster's voice was the only sound in the room. The furniture didn't creak and the women didn't move. The wind didn't blow and there was no rain or ice or snow beating against the windows. Cows were not mooing and coyotes were not yipping. One of them listened to the news, all the other one heard was the screaming of her guilty conscience.

After the evening news, Phoebe, miffed, announced she was going to bed. Mary Jo yawned. "Maybe we should go out and get some of those pull-tabs again. The VFW in Pearisburg sells them. They're open on Saturday night."

"You need to rest, Mary Jo. Remember last night? I'm not sure we should go back out again. Besides, Stella's brother is somewhere near here and he might be up to no good."

"Ah, he probably doesn't want to hurt two old ladies he doesn't know. Anyway, I was thinking we could go look for him and take him to the police, then it is okay that we didn't tell."

Now, Phoebe was interested. "And everyone will be safe. Good idea. Wait for me to change my shirt and get my boots on."

"Where did I put the car keys? I had to hide them from Stella and from the cleaning lady, she cleans everywhere."

"Try the freezer, that's where I saw them." Phoebe called from the bedroom.

First National Bank of Petserstown ATM. Photo by B. Crabtree

Chapter 31

Mary Jo hobbled to the kitchen, her legs stiff from sitting so long. "Not here," she mumbled as she moved boxes around in the freezer. "Where? Where? Where?"

"Oh, I remember, in the egg carton. I thought we might hatch up another trip. Heheh." Her body shook as she laughed to herself. She grabbed the keys and went to the foyer to dress for outdoors.

"I'm bringing a flashlight, too; it's dark outside." Phoebe reached under the kitchen sink for Jonas' toolbox and found a big flashlight. They chatted and laughed as they walked across the field to the barn nearby.

"This barn is hella scary. Let's walk around instead of through the opening. It might fall in on us."

"Good place to hide a car, though. Can only see it from the hill behind it."

Mary Jo unlocked it by pressing a button on the key. The beep always made both of them smile and they scurried to get in.

Mary Jo drove slowly trying to stay in the frozen tracks of snow until they reached the gravel road. She sped up a little then. "Phoebe, something is wrong."

"With you or the car?"

"The car. It clicks, listen."

"Maybe there is a chunk of ice stuck in the wheel well. It will fall out when you get on the paved road and go faster."

"It's louder, hear it? Like a hammer hitting metal. The steering wheel is wobbling. Look." She took both hands off the wheel to show Phoebe. "I'm going slow until I get to the highway. The pounding, whop whop whop, sounds like a helicopter."

When they reached US Route 219, Mary Jo pulled out and the car swerved but she got it back on her side of the road and pressed the gas to accelerate. The hammering turned into a roar and the steering wheel jerked out of her grip. She lost control. They felt the jolt of the car dropping to the pavement, then watched the headlight beams spin through snow and highway and the lights of an on-coming truck and then another blow, a thunderous crash complete with shattering glass. The car came to rest in a ditch, embedded in a snow bank. The young girl driving the truck that hit them, ran to the ditch but got no answer from the women's unmoving bodies. Shaking, she dialed 911.

Chapter 32

Under our Noses?

Two Monroe County deputies, Ivan Long and Doug Comer, responded to the wreck only seconds before a siren announced an ambulance approaching. Once the attendants loaded both injured women, the deputies searched the vehicle for IDs. Deputy Long found a shoulder purse in the passenger side floor, opened it and found an Alaskan ID with a local phone number written on it. Deputy Long, waiting in the police car for the tow truck while Deputy Comer interviewed the driver of the second vehicle, first called the number in Alaska but no one answered. He then tried the hand-written local number and was surprised when Jonas Akpik answered.

"Jonas, this is Deputy Long, Ivan Long, and we have a car wreck down here on Rt. 219." He paused to listen. "Yes, sir, a two-vehicle crash near Painter Run Road. One of the passengers has an ID from Alaska, name of Phoebe Akpik. Your number is on her ID. She kin to you?" Again, he waited.

"No sir, I do not think she is at home watching TV. She was the passenger in a car driven by another woman, unidentified at the moment."

"Describe her," was all Jonas said.

"She is about the same age as Ms. Akpik, wearing a green hooded coat and fur mittens."

Jonas whistled, "That may be my mother. Are they hurt?"

"Yes, sir, ambulance is transporting to Carillion in Giles County. They are alive, moaning, but not responding otherwise. They were belted in and air bags were deployed."

"I'll be right there." Jonas hung up and yelled, "Stella, Mom and Phoebe have been in an accident."

"At your house? Doing what?"

"No, in a car on the main road. Good God Almighty. We'll go by the wreck on the way then meet them at the hospital."

"Hospital? How bad is it?"

"Not sure, they are alive and moaning is all Ivan said."

They ran for the truck. Stella forgot her pistol but did remember to lock the door. So much for being prepared.

The wreck site was being cleared by the time Jonas pulled in beside the MoCo Deputy's car. "Ivan, where are you sending the vehicle and what is it, was it?"

"New Mustang, sir, cool car. It'll be locked up at Newberry's storage until the state troopers can inspect it. Looks like to me the front tire fell off and the axle broke. That's not official, though, just me thinking out loud. There'll be an accident reconstruction team working on it."

"Okay, man, we are heading on to the hospital. Thanks for calling me." The officer did a half salute, and Jonas stopped again and rolled his window down. "How about the other driver?"

"Katie Adkins, she's shook up but okay. The crash knocked off part of the grill and bent the bumper of her truck. She threw what got knocked off in the truck bed. Was worried to death about the old ladies. She said that she couldn't miss the Mustang; that it swerved right in front of her. Tough girl, she drove her old Chevy truck on home."

"Thanks, again."

Jonas headed south going as fast as he dared, slowing when he fishtailed on the skiff of snow that had blown across the road. "Where did they get a new Mustang?"

"Jonas, Tisha told me about a lease contract she had seen when she was cleaning and I just didn't take it seriously. I'm so sorry I didn't."

"Lease contract? They leased a Mustang? Good God. Under our noses? Where did they keep it? Where did they go in it?"

"I don't know. I just don't know." She was wringing her hands. She voiced the prayer they had both been offering up silently, "Please God take care of Mary Jo and Phoebe. Heal their wounds and keep them from pain and hold them in your hands. Give the doctors and nurses wisdom and guide them to save these women if it be your will. Amen."

"Amen," Jonas added as he pulled into the emergency room entrance.

"You go, Jonas, I'll park the truck."

He jumped out and ran for the door.

Chapter 33

Hospital

Jonas

I guess I expected both Mom and Aunt Phoebe stretched out in hospital beds hooked to tubes and machines. What I found was two empty emergency room beds where they had been examined. I waited for them to come back from radiology, praying they would be all right, anger that they had endangered themselves bubbling just below the surface. A new red Mustang? Driving after dark? As far as I know, Mom had only ever driven on the gravel roads in Atqasuk and Barrow.

By the time Stella found me, they had given me a clipboard with forms to complete and I swear I just stared at the blanks. "Jonas, where are they?" Stella was speaking softly and I knew the empty beds had shook her up, too.

I looked up. "Nah, they are getting X-rays or scans of some sort."

She paced the small space. "Good."

"Can you do this?" I handed her the clipboard and pen. She scooted a chair from the other side of the second bed and joined me. While she wrote, all kinds of thoughts were flying through my head. How we had never had a dad, Mom raising all six of us on her own. When she smoked on the front stoop to keep us from smelling like sigaaqs. The trouble she caused at school when one of us got in trouble. We finally quit telling her anything about school. How she was an extreme personality, way happy or way mad or way sad. How much I owed her for keeping me clean and fed and in school and letting me go away from her to find my path.

Chapter 33

A nurse interrupted, "You all will have to step out for a few minutes, Ms. Akpik is on the way back down."

"Which one?" Stella whispered, but I knew she didn't expect an answer from me. We waited in the outer waiting room until the nurse came and got us. I held my breath.

The nurse smiled. "I think she'll be glad to see you." The air just whooshed out of me and I hurried back to her cubicle. They'd pulled the curtain around the bed. It was Mom. No tubes, but wired to a heart monitoring machine.

"Jonas, what are you doing here?" She looked so small on the bed. I didn't know whether I was going to cry or yell at her. At least she was coherent and knew me.

My voice cracked when I spoke. "We heard that you had a car wreck, thought we'd stop by. Are you hurting anywhere?"

She seemed to think about it and rubbed her nose and forehead. "No more than the usual." I took her hand and held it. The part of me that was scared just had to touch her to feel that she was warm and soft, that she was alive. I fought back questions about the car. One thing at a time.

The nurse came back and got the clipboard, "The doctor will be here in a few minutes with your test results."

Stella thanked her. I was not able to find any manners at that moment.

Mom and I looked at each other openmouthed when we heard Phoebe's shouts coming down the hall. Then we both got tickled. Evidently, she wanted her purse and she wanted it right now.

The nurse pulled the curtain to the adjoining cubicle back and rolled Aunt Phoebe into the area in a wheelchair. She was alert, saw me and yelled, "Well, thank God! Thank God you are here, Jonas, tell them who I am."

Stella knelt down to talk to her and told her that she had filled out all the papers. "You are Phoebe Tuuluk Akpik and they know it."

"Harrumph. This would not have happened if she had listened to me and stayed home tonight." She looked at the bed where Mom had turned her face into the pillow to keep from crying or screaming or laughing. Who knew?

I didn't know what to do. Thank goodness the doctor came in at that moment. Stella pulled the curtain forward again and stayed with Phoebe while the doctor reviewed the folder of test results. "Good news, Ms. Akpik, nothing broken." I squeezed her hand. He continued, "There does not appear to be any internal damage or bleeding, no lacerations, but there is bruising on your chest.

"Likely from the steering wheel, pretty superficial." He looked directly at Mom. "You are going to be sore from the impact, probably for a week or two. Take Tylenol or Motrin when you need it." He scribbled something on the chart. "She should be supervised through tonight, checked on every two hours or so. If that can be arranged, I can release her." He raised eyebrows at me and I nodded. "Yes, sir, we can do that."

"Good, give us a few minutes for the paperwork. Take care of yourself, Ms. Akpik," and he disappeared through the curtain.

"Mary Jo, I want to see you when I talk to you," Phoebe called out from her side of the curtain.

"Well, come on in, then." Mom had pushed up into a sitting position and I was trying to operate the remote control of the head of the bed to catch up with her.

Phoebe rolled through the curtain calmer, maybe because someone knew who she was, but still with something to say. "Mary Jo, we were too tired to go out last night and I told you we needed to stay in." She turned to me, "Jonas, I am sorry that we hid our car from you and I am sorry that she got us in a wreck and made you and Stella worry." She waited for a second as if daring us to speak. "But we need to tell you and Stella something important." She had my attention.

"What is it, Aunty?" I feared disease or bad news from Alaska.

"Stella's brother, Timothy Lee, was in Peterstown day before last. We saw him at the ATM."

Stella inhaled loudly, "How do you know it was him?"

"We saw his picture on the news this evening. We thought we were going to go find him and keep you kids safe."

"Wait a minute, you were at the ATM? How did you get there, why were you there?"

Mary Jo was glad to contribute to the discussion, "In our hot red car. We had to get money for bingo."

I was starting to see some red myself and Stella sensed it, I guess. She put hands on my back and rubbed a little as she asked the girls to tell yesterday's story from beginning to end.

It was hard for me to stay still and listen to how close he had gotten to them, close enough to hand them the debit card. The number of chances they had taken, leasing a car and hiding it and doing whatever they darn well wanted was almost more than I could stand. Suddenly, I was exhausted. "Aunt Phoebe, what have the doctors told you about your injuries?"

"They said I could go on home. Told me to keep ice on my head for a couple of hours and ointment on my arms." She held out her red, irritated forearms. "Got burned from the powder in the airbag."

Stella got them dressed while I went out to the desk to double check her orders. My trust in those two was at an all-time low, but Phoebe had told the truth. We rolled them in wheelchairs to the front door and I went to get the truck.

We decided to stop by their house and gather up gowns, toothbrushes, and a change of clothes and take them to our house. They could sleep in the guest room where we could keep an eye on them.

After some television time, they went to bed. I had about bitten my tongue off holding back on getting the answers I wanted. "Tomorrow," Stella said, "Tomorrow is another day."

Chapter 34

God Was on my Side

Timmy Lee

Damn, the wind was butt-ass cold on that mountain. The top of the hill behind me should've blocked the wind, but no such luck. It stabbed like a driven nail through my cloth jacket. My aching fingers were in my pockets for what little good that did. I'd hike back to the clunker hidden around the mountain soon, but I wanted to watch Jonas' house a little longer.

Waiting was paying off, two old women left the house and walked across the hayfield to a 2017 Ruby Red GT Fastback Mustang parked behind their neighbor's barn. Weird place to park, but okay. They aren't going far in it tonight. I loosened all five lug nuts on the front passenger tire. I rubbed my hands together. This'll be fun to watch. She pulled out so slow that tire wasn't going anywhere, and it stayed on when she putt-putted up the ridge to the gravel road and they were off, out of sight and no crunch, no crash yet. Damn. That little old lady was stupid lucky. It'll run out, that tire won't stay put too long. If they get killed, no one else will think to get their mail. Might be a fat check in there the first of the month. I'll check tomorrow.

It was my good luck that I pulled in behind that shiny red Mustang at the ATM yesterday. I was hoping for something, anything at that ATM, especially somebody old with a handful of cash, but I hit another kind of pay dirt: a name, Phoebe Akpik, on a debit card. I followed the old biddies down to Rich Creek and waited for them to finish in the fire station

– a party or something – then followed them home, to my slut of a sister's boyfriend's house. And one of them had the same name. A relative or at least someone who married into his family. No other Akpiks in West Virginia. Pure blind luck. God was on my side. I knew He would be once I got out of that hellhole.

Since I ran barefoot down that street right into a car sitting there just for me, things went from good to better. Within two hours I was in Pikeville, Kentucky where things were so quiet that I robbed a gas station with my finger tucked in my pants under my shirt. The look on that clerk's face! Woohoo! She woulda done anything I asked, she was that scared. She gave me the money in the cash register and I remembered to tell her to get the $50s from under the drawer. I told her to lie in the floor and count to one hundred, and I cleared the counter into my shirttail, I ended up with dozens of Slim Jim beef jerky, little packs of Tylenol, ChapSticks, homemade-preacher cookies, and some kid's cancer fund jar of change. Then, I ran to the car. Stealing outright is lame-ass, but what choice did I have?

I hit the Commonwealth of Virginia before I slowed down next, stole some tools: a hatchet (inside my jacket), a crowbar (in my pants leg), a ratchet set (in the back waist band), and bolt cutters (in the other pants leg) from the Lowe's in Richlands. Just walked out the front door with them, no one even chased me down. I pulled out laughing and went to a thrift store and bought some clothes that fit better, jeans and boots, this cheap-ass jacket and some blankets. I was pretty tired so I pulled into a welcome center on US Rt. 81, threw back a bottle of OJ, wondered for a second or two how ole Jeff was doing, smiled to myself that he was counting the days until he wouldn't get paid, then fell asleep.

They'd be looking for me in Monroe County. I needed to keep out of sight. There's a hunting cabin on Peter's Mountain I knew about that was probably empty in February, so I left the car hidden best I could on a back road in some pine trees and hiked up with a grocery bag of food to check it out.

Bingo, it was empty. Home, sweet, home. In an hour, I was bored and walked back out to the car to cruise around.

That's when I saw that sweet red Mustang and two old toads in it. Lovely way to spend a Saturday, free as a bird.

Back to business, then I could feel the temperature dropping with the darkness, my hands and feet were cold as blue-belly

Hideaway cabin on Peters Mountain, offering the peace only Mother Nature can give. Photo by Pentax K-3.

hell as I walked through the woods to my clunker. A short drive to the pine tree thicket and a hike to the cabin and my day was over. Might be the last day for those old ladies. I was excited to find out tomorrow. Tonight, waiting for sleep, I'd plan Stella's last day.

There was a stack of wood near the cabin, but the logs were frozen together, so when I loaded my arms, some of the pieces were really two or three sticks of wood. I figured they'd melt waiting their turn in the fireplace. Nobody would notice a little stream of chimney smoke in the dark and I was determined to be warm.

I sat with a blanket around me as the fire caught up. It got so warm that I finally folded the blanket in the floor in front of the fire to comfort my poor, tired body. At first, the flames were bright enough to read by and shadows danced on the log walls. I meant to think about how to torment Stella, but I went to sleep first.

I woke in the night when the fire had faded to just a glowing pile and I got up to feed it. Something moving on the floor caught my eye. I rubbed my eyes and looked again and it was gone. "Shadows," I said to no one. I slept some more and felt something against my bare arm and swiped at it. A bug or a mouse, maybe. Well, I was too sleepy to care; it could share my warm bed. The next time something brushed against me, I jumped up.

Chapter 34

It was a snake. Best I could tell, the snake was pretty good size, a black snake. He must've been frozen in that damn woodpile. I chased him with my hatchet and hacked up the floor awful bad. I checked my clothes over and over and spent the rest of the night with my ass in the kitchen sink where I could watch for him, but I knew I didn't get him. I hated to touch any more wood and I had to keep the fire going. I sang hymns and begged God to take the snake away and I made some promises that Jesus probably saw right through, but when daylight and reality came, the count was up to two living snakes curled up on the warm hearth. I killed them both. Really got into it and screamed and cheered for myself and chopped them into snake nuggets. Wished somebody was there to see how good I was at killing 'em. Worked so hard I had to take another nap. Slept on the kitchen counter, just in case I missed one.

When I woke up, snow was melting and dripping off the trees. Good. If all the snow melted, my tracks wouldn't be so obvious. Maybe my good luck was back after that night from hell. I needed to find dead wood on the ground today so I didn't have to meet any more creepy crawlers in that woodpile.

I needed a Tracfone today to start checking in on Sister Stella. Just see if she was home, let her know I was thinking of her, things like that. I tended to business outside the cabin and gathered a pot full of snow to bring inside to melt for water. The sun was out. "What a good day to be alive," I teased the dead snakes.

Timmy Lee's guest, a common black snake. Photo by B. Crabtree

Chapter 35

Sunday was Not a Day of Rest

Stella

Sunday was not a day of rest this week. The phone was our alarm to get up that morning. Sheriff Johnson called to let us know what was happening with Timmy Lee. This did not fit in the "no news is good news" category. There was no news except he was still at large. Not good. He got pretty excited when I explained that late last night Jonas' mom and aunt reported they had seen him day before yesterday in Peterstown. He wanted to come up and talk to them. I told him not to let any grass grow under his feet, to get on up here.

Then, after that, the insurance company called about the car. Turns out Mary Jo had checked the box for lease insurance and her payment included the insurance, so the car was insured and would be paid for. I thought that was great, but Jonas was so mad about them having a car and madder still that they didn't tell him, so he couldn't really be happy yet.

Finally, Tisha called to see if the old girls were all right. Jonas gave up on sleep and went to the bathroom. "I guess they really did lease a car," she said. She was bummed that they put one over on her, too. "Wish I had been more careful reading those papers. Maybe we could have stopped this from happening."

"Oh, Tish, they outsmarted all of us. Don't feel one bit bad about any of this. Besides, they had insurance and the car is covered."

"But how are they? Did the air bags burn them up or bruise their faces?"

Chapter 35

"Mary Jo has a bruised chest, the doctor said she'd be sore for a few days. Phoebe's arms have some rug burn on them, but they slept good last night and are still in bed." I thought about that a second. "Tisha, I need to go see with my own eyes that they are in bed, they may be down the road somewhere for all I know."

"Okay, bye, girl, have fun with those two." She giggled before she hung up.

I padded down the hall to crack the guest room door an inch or two and saw that they both were still in bed. Shew-whee, I'd scared myself; it was a relief to find them where they were supposed to be.

Wonder where Timmy Lee was holed up. If he really was near, he'd be in an empty house or in his vehicle. I needed to let Elmer know that's where I would start to look for him.

I followed the enticing smell of bacon to the kitchen and found Jonas. He was cooking for us all, not his usual early morning behavior. I got dressed to go outside and feed and water, but he told me to hold on for a minute and he'd go with me. He actually stood midway between the house and the barn, and I thought that was odd until it dawned on me that he was trying to protect me in the yard and his mom and aunt in the house at the same time. This was getting ridiculous.

The sheriff's car roared up shimmying in the icy spots in the road. He jumped out with a clipboard, trying to get a pen ready, jumpy as a long-tailed cat in a room full of rocking chairs.

"Come on in, Elmer, good to see you." Jonas walked with him, but hollered back at me, "Stella, you 'bout done?" He was a man trying to be in more than one place at the same time.

"Go on, Jonas, I'll be right there." I hollered.

"Elmer, go on into the living room, Mom and Phoebe are still upstairs. Give me a minute with Stella, I don't want her alone out here."

Elmer nodded but stayed with Jonas, shifting his weight from one worn boot to the other, chewing on his thumbnail. One of the sheep was limping and I got a frozen pebble out of its foot. It'd stay sore a few days, but should be okay. That's another reminder of Timmy Lee, I thought, a pebble between my toes. Hurts badly when he is near and still leaves a sore place when he goes away. I finished up with the animals and Elmer and Jonas and I went in together.

174

Jonas offered to fix Elmer eggs and bacon and I went upstairs to rouse the Golden Girls. Phoebe was talking to Mary Jo real quiet-like when I tapped on the door. She looked around quick when she heard me. "Stella, we got a problem here. Mary Jo's got her wires crossed this morning."

I sat down at the foot of the bed and wondered what fresh new hell this was.

It only took a second to find out. Mary Jo went absolutely nuts. She kicked and screamed, "I need to go see where Barbara buried that dead baby. Let me go out behind the coal house." Then she thrashed around on the bed and spit at both of us.

I looked at Phoebe. She shrugged and whispered, "She doesn't know where she is right now. It's hard on her to wake up in a new place."

That didn't bother me as much as what she said. "Phoebe, I guess I have a little concern about a dead baby."

"I don't think there really was a dead baby, she just gets upset and says all kinds of crazy things. Oh, and she doesn't like to be yelled at when she's like this." She watched her sister twist around in the covers. "Just in case you thought it was a good idea to yell back."

I watched for awhile and Phoebe sang softly to her and she quieted down and went back to sleep. It probably wasn't a good time for her to be interviewed by the sheriff.

"Phoebe, are you up to talking to the sheriff?"

She just looked at me with those eyes, those inky black eyes that were so deep it was like looking down a well. "Is it about the car or about Phoebe or about the bingo or about Timothy Lee or about the wreck?"

I had to laugh. "Who knows? Anything could happen around here with you two." She seemed to like that and slipped a sweatshirt and sweatpants on over her pajamas, pulled on socks with gripper feet and followed me downstairs holding tightly to the handrail.

The sheriff was eating but he stopped and stood up when Phoebe entered the room. She shook his hand, "Good morning."

"Ms. Akpik, I'm glad that you came out of that wreck last night as well as you did. The boys told me that the car you were in took a hard lick."

Phoebe nodded and held up her wrists to show him the airbag abrasions.

175

"Those airbags are worth the scrapes a hundred times over. They make it possible to walk away from car wrecks today that would've maimed and killed a few years ago." She nodded again.

He cleared his throat, ready to get down to brass tacks. "I've been told that you think you saw Stella's brother in town. Could you tell me about it?"

"Let me just get a cup of coffee," she said, "and I will tell you all I know." I saw a little smile dance around her lips. Could that girl be stalling for attention? Could be, she was usually in Mary Jo's shadow. Which reminded me, I needed to go check on her. I buzzed up the stairs because I didn't want to miss anything, but she hadn't moved so I hurried back down to the kitchen.

Phoebe was telling the story from the beginning; how they were getting bored because they couldn't go places like they could at home, and they faked a doctor's appointment to get a ride to Pearisburg, and the people at Newberry Ford were so nice and had a red Mustang that was just what they wanted. She explained how they needed money for bingo so they had to stop at the ATM, but there was a daily limit. She stopped to refill her coffee cup. The car was too close to pick up her debit card when Mary Jo dropped it, so she got out and got stuck trying to pick it up and the nice man in the car behind them helped her and got MJ to pull up and got the card.

The sheriff was taking notes now. "How did you know it was Stella's brother? Yyou've never met him, correct?"

"Right, and we didn't know until the Channel Six news came on that night. We saw a picture of him."

He stopped writing and asked, "Did Mary Jo recognize him, too?"

She played with the cuff of her sweatshirt, folding it back and forth like a paper fan. The old Phoebe was back. "No," she finally said. "She said she never saw him before in her life. But, sometimes Mary Jo has trouble remembering." I felt sorry for her having to defend her sister.

The sheriff studied her, and then began writing again. "This happened two days ago. Why did you wait until after the wreck last night to tell?"

She began rolling the cuff. "We couldn't tell because Jonas didn't know we had our own car, so we were going out after the news came on to find that bad Timmy Lee and bring him back to you. We would've called you when we found him," she added quickly.

The sheriff laid down his pencil and sighed. "Mrs. Akpik, do you understand that this is an escaped prisoner?"

Phoebe bowed her head and nodded.

"That he is charged with murder, right here on this mountain?"

She nodded again.

"And he is dangerous?"

She nodded once again very slowly.

"Will you promise to leave Timmy Lee Davis to me and my deputies?"

No response.

"Mrs. Akpik, look at me. You and your sister put yourselves in grave danger." She looked up with tears lining the bottom of those deep dark eyes. They got to Elmer, too. He changed his tone and softly asked, "Will you trust me to get this guy and promise to keep yourself and Mary Jo safe? She needs you now."

We could barely hear her. "Yes," Phoebe spoke but she didn't look at him. I wondered if her fingers were crossed.

"Now then back to business. How long did he have the card, long enough to look at it?"

"Yeah, he looked at it."

"How did he treat you, were you scared?"

"No, he didn't threaten us, he was real nice. He asked where we were going and we told him we were going to the doctor, which was a little bit of a lie." She looked at Jonas who was red-faced and drumming his fingers on the counter, a sure sign that he was about to explode. "We didn't feel like we should tell a strange man all our business." Then she batted her eyelashes and blushed. Really? Flirting with the sheriff? New Phoebe had returned.

"What kind of car was he driving?"

"I don't know but it wasn't near as hot looking as our car."

"Color?"

"Grey or, hmm, green, or maybe black. Low to the ground, two-door. I hate to get in the back seat of a two-door car, don't you? Makes my knees hurt."

"Then where did you go?"

"We went on down to Rich Creek to play bingo."

"Did you see his car later?"

"No."

"Did you see him again?"

"No, but we met a very nice gentleman at bingo named CT. He asked where we were from and wanted us to come back, but Mary Jo needed to leave; she forgot how to play bingo, so we had to leave."

"Did she drive home?"

"Yes, and she did real good, especially since she was having one of those spells. And when we got home, she didn't know who I was. Her own sister."

I didn't notice Jonas leaving until the door banged shut and he was gone.

"And the next morning, she was right as rain." Mary Jo rested her case, so to speak, folded her arms and sat facing the sheriff, still writing.

The next thing I knew there was an awful wailing upstairs and I ran to Mary Jo, who was crying her heart out until she saw me. She pointed at me and calmly said, "There's the one who helped bury the dead baby and now she wants to eat all my Pilot bread. Don't let her get my Pilot bread."

"Mary Jo, I am Stella, I am married to your son, Jonas. We have plenty of Pilot bread, Barbara sent some for you."

I reached for her hand but she jerked it away. "Oh, no, no tricks for me."

Phoebe tried to reason with her but nothing doing. The sheriff rapped on the door casing and waited to be invited in. I answered, "Come on in, Elmer. Got any advice?"

He shook his head. "Something's wrong. I'll call an ambulance. She needs to be checked out. May be a head injury from the wreck last night."

I agreed.

"Phoebe, would you pack up her things in case they want her overnight? I'll sit with her. Elmer, will you find Jonas after you make the call?"

"Sure will. Don't you fret Mary Jo. We are going to get some help for you." He had a real comforting voice and she relaxed a little, but as far as I could tell, she was still out of her mind.

I was able to get the sheriff alone in the hallway for a minute. "Elmer, I don't want to tell you your business, but ..."

"You'd be the only one in this county." His smile warmed me and I went on.

"Timmy Lee worked this county like an old-timey snake oil salesman when he was with the church raising money. Almost everybody here would recognize him."

Elmer nodded. He was such a good listener.

"If he is in the area, he is not at a motel or B & B, and it is too cold for him to be living in a camper or a vehicle. Elmer, I'd bet money that he is in an empty house or a hunting cabin. And he is cold. Timmy Lee is impatient, he will move soon. I know him, Sheriff. We, all of us, are in danger."

"Stella, you know that's a good thought. I don't have enough manpower to search every hunting cabin and empty house, but we can check the ones here on the mountain. Some of them will be hard to reach this time of year, but with snow on the ground, we can see tracks. I will be posting an APB for him in a fifty-mile area around Peterstown. Phoebe seems pretty sure it was him there. Basically, this search hinges on her story."

"She has no reason to make it up." I prayed that was true. This new version of Phoebe might just be embellishing for some attention.

"As soon as the ambulance comes, I'll take off to the office to get these alerts online all over the area." He started to walk away, but I laid a hand on his arm.

"Elmer, call us every night. Please. We want to know what is going on." Not to mention, I thought, to check on us and see if we were still upright.

"Will do, Stella." We headed down the steps together.

Only one of us could ride the ambulance and Jonas was in a real pickle about staying with me, so he agreed to let Phoebe ride with his mother and he would drive the two of us. He asked Elmer to ride by both houses a time or two while we were gone just to see if they were on fire or Timmy Lee was hiding in the bushes, and Elmer agreed. We let the dogs out before we left and then followed the ambulance back to Carillion Hospital in Giles County.

After three hours of waiting and testing, we were told that she had a urinary tract infection that was adding to her mental lapses and a couple of days of antibiotics would clear it up. They wanted to keep her all night. Jonas was reluctant but he agreed. He made some calls, we waited around for another hour until Ben came and then we headed out with Phoebe.

He explained on the way home: Ben would sit with her for four or five hours, then someone would relieve him, then another, and we'd all come back in the morning to get her. We picked up a few groceries and drove up the mountain back to our house to wonder what would happen next.

Winter road on Peters Mountain, Monroe County, West Virginia. Photo by B. Crabtree.

Chapter 36

Good to Control Something

Timmy Lee

The stinking cold robbed me of the happiness of being free. Even the sky was frozen blue and the air was cold enough to hurt when I sucked it into my lungs. Cleansing, maybe. I gathered up firewood. There was plenty of wood: branches and dead trees down. I checked every piece of it for snakes. There was one with a tiny-ass bat stuck inside it that came around enough to show his fangs at me. I left that branch behind. Not what I needed tonight, a rat with wings flitting around in the cabin.

When I was little there was a story, maybe a Bible story, about the pieces of a snake regenerating and every piece growing into a new snake. That story had been on my mind, so I decided to take the hacked-up snake parts lying in the floor way away from the cabin and bury them in the snow. If they came back to life, maybe they would freeze before they got back in the cabin. A blanket under the door would help keep them out, too.

Maybe I could cook the snake and eat it. My belly said no. It also said it was lunchtime so I ate another can of beans and a couple of Slim Jims that I'd ripped off from that Kentucky Go-Mart. I was raised on beans and beef, maybe not as spicy as this stuff, but pretty much the same. I didn't miss the tasteless pureed peaches and mushy cereal I was being fed in Huntington.

I wanted to check and see if those old broads got dead yesterday when their wheel fell off, but I didn't know how to find out. Maybe in the newspaper, but this rinky-dink county only had a weekly. I decided to drive by their house and check their mailbox at the very least. I also needed a disguise and I couldn't be seen shopping here. Too many church people knew me from before. Time for a short road trip to an out-of-town Wally World, maybe in Pulaski, Virginia, or north to Lewisburg. Just far enough away to not get recognized.

After the long walk to the car in the cold, it felt real good to sit down and turn on the heat. Good to be able to control something in my life right now. A parking place closer to the cabin would make life easier. "God, be with me," I prayed out loud then pulled a knit cap way down on my face and headed to Jonas' house. It was midday and the red Mustang was not in sight, no sign of any life. I drove on down and pulled up to the mailbox and emptied it. Didn't want to get caught there, so drove way up to the Bradley Cemetery to go through the envelopes. Not much, but today was only the second of March, some government checks came out on the 4th or 5th. That's when I used to hit up the slow-witted Social Security crowd for church donations, while the money was burning a hole in their pockets.

Went north, right by the Lindside United Methodist Church, my former employer. Good riddance. Pretty damn bad when your own preacher turns you in. Almost as bad as your own sister. God, I hated her. I wanted to go get her right now, but no, I had to be strong and plan it out so it was the best it could be. She'd have maximum pain. No slip ups. Maybe let her live. Maybe not. I was about to spasm with the thought. Drove to Lewisburg, shaking my head about how stupid all the police were. No one stopped me. Shopped there about an hour, enjoyed the colors and textures but most of all the warmth. Bought sunglasses for the glare on the snow, the cheapest Tracfone, a set of lighters, and some more canned beans, canned peaches and jugs of water and orange juice. Then, went to the Goodwill and bought a bunch of different hats, a thicker jacket and an egg crate sleeping mat. Could not resist; kinda like the warnings about buying food when you are hungry, I was buying bed gear when I was sleepy and I wanted it bad. It would feel good on the floor.

Curiosity about the old women was about to kill me, so I pulled on a baseball cap with a Steelers logo and went public. Steelers were okay by me. I liked them just fine. I pulled into a parking place at the tiny Ronceverte Library to get online.

Topix is a site for every little town all over the country that gossips and reports wrecks and stuff like prom dates and who didn't get to play in the game last weekend because the coach has so many relatives on the team. Lindside Topix had three reports about a wreck on 219 the evening before but not a damn word about injuries or fatalities. I was pretty frustrated and it felt like the librarian lady was staring at me. My fingers started rubbing together, like they do when I start getting mad. I thanked the bitch anyway and thought, "Lady, you mess with me and I'll have you begging for mercy." I slammed my open hand on the counter just to make her jump then strolled on out of there feeling better.

Filled up with gas. My money was getting low. Had to cut back or rob somebody. Maybe the church deposit on Sunday night. If it was at Stella's, I could kill two birds with one stone. Bad joke. God, it would be good if I could get in there. Had to grit my teeth and change my thinking or I would lose it. I relaxed and pointed my little car south to home.

Still no one at Jonas'. I parked up the road, out of sight, and tried all the windows. A bedroom window was unlocked. I figured that was a sign, so I climbed in. Two people living here, separate rooms, both women. No sign of Jonas or Stella. Smokers. Full refrigerator. A fat bank envelope of money was in an underwear drawer. Score. If I was sure they were dead, I'd camp out here, but I couldn't take the chance. I did steal some cheddar cheese just because I could taste it just looking at it. Some grocery lists were on the coffee table, handwriting samples if I got lucky with a check later. I folded them up and stuffed them in my pocket. I put a pencil under the window when I left so it wouldn't close all the way. I could get back inside anytime I wanted.

It was getting dark so I headed to the cabin, had to build a fire, had to get my phone working, try out my new sleeping mat. I parked in a new place and stumbled over rough ground through the woods 'til I could just see the cabin through the brush and sat down. My fingers were hurting from carrying all the grocery bags. Maybe it was the cold. I left the OJ and water in a snowdrift, should've made two trips. I'd make a second trip and get this stuff after while. Never like doing that, always try to carry too much and get it all. Pissed myself off having to do a job twice.

Chapter 37

Maybe This is the Day

Jonas

This juggling act was starting to wear me down. The ham sandwich I was chewing might have been tasty but I didn't have enough brain cells left to tell. Keeping Mom safe at the hospital, keeping Phoebe and Stella safe here and watching both houses was stretching me and I knew it. Work wasn't even an option. I was close to losing focus and dropping something. The helplessness and frustration were getting to me.

That scum of the earth was not worth all this. I was ready to get my own posse together and go get him. Timmy Lee had better turn up soon.

Just when I felt my fists starting to clench, the phone in my pants pocket buzzed. I prayed to God that it was good news.

It was Elmer. "Evening, Jonas. Y'all okay?"

"Yes, sir. We are fine. What's up at your end?"

"Well, I have some news." My heart raced.

"Do you have HIM yet, Elmer?"

"No, nothing like that, but some progress. Stella may have told you that I was putting out an APB for the surrounding area?"

"Yep." Just keep talking Elmer.

"We got a hit this afternoon. A photo ID software program that Wal-Mart has installed identified Timmy Lee coming in and out of their Lewisburg store this afternoon. We have his sales receipt. He paid cash and bought a phone, food, sunglasses, and lighters, by the way. We are waiting for a video from an independent security service to get the images of

Chapter 37

West Virginia winter. Photo by B. Crabtree.

him in the parking lot. If that works, we may have his car description."

"That's a start, Elmer. Good work." *He's still out there, though.*

"Plus, we have a report from the Mildred Bateman-Mitchell State Hospital in Huntington that two orderlies that had contact with Mr. Davis both resigned. One of them failed a drug test and was allowed to resign. In the continuing police investigation, it was learned that the other man had worked at two other facilities and has an exemplary record for more than ten years. Name's Jeffrey, Jeffrey Gregory. He was at work until this morning. Submitted his letter of resignation, which cited his wife's health problems. Probably nothing there."

"Glad to know any tidbit, gives me something to think about."

"One more thing, Jonas, and it's not official. That red Mustang is down at Newberry's waiting for an inspection but one of the body guys, my wife, Tonya's nephew, called. He said that the wheel that fell off had a big piece of metal missing. It took out a lug nut hole and the surrounding area."

"So what? What does that mean?"

"It may mean that the lug nuts were loosened and one didn't rattle off, it got ripped off. Jonas, someone was trying to hurt whoever rode in that car."

"Timmy Lee?

"Could be. Something else to think about. I won't tell you to sleep tight, because you won't, but rest up all you can."

"Thanks, Elmer. Is there anything at all I can do besides sit here and worry?"

"If you happen to be awake, make a list of all the empty places on the mountain within walking distance of your and Stella's places. It would be a starting place once this infernal cold eases up."

When I pushed the "off" button on my cell, I had to sit down and fight the feeling that I could feel the evil nearby. I wanted to move us all into the stairwell of the house on mattresses and stay out of range of sight and of bullets, but that would scare Phoebe. Not Stella. She wasn't scared and seemed to be gaining courage every day. Her fight was different from mine, one that she'd battled for years, to simply be normal and not let the bastard change our lives.

Stella and Phoebe came into the kitchen chattering over a cookbook, of all things. They had decided to bake a cake. A coconut pound cake, to be exact. They rummaged around getting all the stuff ready to mix and turned on the oven. If I could relax, this would be rare entertainment, Phoebe bossing Stella in her own kitchen.

I didn't want to leave them, but their voices irritated me. I moved into the next room where I could still see them and make my list of possible hideouts for the sheriff. I took a shotgun with me, on the sly, I hoped, and put it in the corner. I knew Stella had moved her pistol to the back waistband of her pants. I went through the house, pulled the drapes at every window and checked all the locks. Some kind of life: hunkered down and armed in our own home.

Ben and the other engineers from my department taking turns sitting with Mom each called during the night as they arrived and left. She'd slept until the sedative wore off and then was disoriented again and they sedated her lightly again. After pound cake sampling and Stella and Phoebe went up to bed, I spent the night on the couch, trying to make a list and answering the phone. The floor was cold when I got up before daybreak. I hoped that Timmy Lee was cold, too, wherever he was.

Elmer called early. "Didn't wake ya, did I?"

"You are an optimist. Tell me something that will let me go back to bed."

"We got the make and model of the car he is using and now have an APB on the car. Should be just a matter of time now. It's silver Cobalt, 2010, little car and two-door just like your Aunt Phoebe said. Beat up and rusted."

"Is it stolen?"

"If it is, it wasn't reported. How is that list coming along?"

"I got fourteen places within three miles."

"Call them out to me and I'll cross reference with our list. We've got help coming from the state today. Since we can say definitively that he is in our district, they are sending a team of experienced troopers."

"Great. Okay, here's the places I know about." I told him about hunting cabins and houses where I thought the owners or renters were gone, probably to someplace warm. He had all but four on his list already; the staff in his office was pretty knowledgeable about the county. He also had three I didn't know about, so there were 17 places to check.

"Good luck today. Maybe this is the day."

Stella's sheep near her barn. Photo by B. Crabtree.

"You be careful, Jonas. Is Mary Jo going to be released?"

"We're waiting for the doctor to make her rounds this morning, then someone will call. Oh, and Tisha Butler will be cleaning down at my house sometime this evening, so don't arrest her." We both laughed.

He said, "I'd rather tackle Timmy Lee anytime than get Tisha riled up. She is so little that you don't give her a second thought, but you cross her and there will no doubt be pay back."

I thought Stella ought to hear the encouraging news, so I snuggled in behind her, not easy since she took the whole bed. I nudged her over and kissed on her neck.

She moaned, "What do you want?" and I told her that this might be the day Timmy Lee gets caught and why.

She sat up against the headboard and rubbed her eyes and asked me to tell it all again. I did.

"Jonas, we need to talk." She was as serious as I'd ever seen her.

"Timmy Lee is going to tell you something that might seem like a lie, but it's not." She hugged me and held me tight. I figured it was something from their childhood and thought this was a very bad time to worry about kid stuff and told her so.

"Oh, honey, it's about Anna."

"Okay? What about her?"

"About how she died."

"Timmy killed her, didn't he?"

She shook her head; lips pressed together, both hands on her stomach. Whatever she was thinking was making her sick. "He's going to say he didn't do it."

"Of course, that's what we all expect."

"Jonas, he didn't."

"Then who did?" I had a terrible sinking feeling and my vision was edged with clouds. My body became numb as I waited for her to answer.

"Me." She spoke in a tiny voice, but she looked me dead in the eyes. I don't know what I said or did, but I needed air. I grabbed the shotgun as I passed through the living room out the back door.

It was a short walk, just around the yard and up to the barn. I let the sheep and goats out and fed while I was up there and carried some water from the outdoor spigot. The cool air helped clear my head, too.

I stomped back inside, still in my shirtsleeves. My head throbbed as my world spun. I needed some answers.

Chapter 38

I Want You Safe

Stella & Jonas

I stayed in bed a few minutes after Jonas rushed out, wondering why in the world I picked this time of incredible stress to tell. Was I self-destructive? I did not tell him how badly Anna was suffering or that she had begged me to do it. He didn't know that he was the only person who knew. All Timmy Lee knew is that he didn't do it, he found her dead in the bed and then forged her name on a document signing her house over to the church so he could live in it.

What's done was done. This could be Jonas' way out of all the trouble about Timmy Lee. He could move back to his place if he changed his mind about wanting me. Of course, that would end the best three months of my life and break my heart, but I am not sorry I did it. Jonas deserved to know the truth to face what was coming and, to be fair, he needed to know that I could do such a thing. I was dizzy with what I had done; these arguments just hung from fragile threads in my brain, nothing was solid or made much sense.

I listened for him to stomp back inside the kitchen door downstairs but he didn't. Time to drag my sorry self out and face the mess I just made. In a daze, I dressed and checked on Phoebe who was still asleep, then went down the stairs. That's when I remembered that Timmy Lee was in the area and maybe he'd jumped Jonas. I ran from window to window, looking out the curtains to try to see him in the yard. The truck was still here. The dogs were gone, too. Both sights were

191

a relief. Then I saw him and my heart flip-flopped. He was safe, carrying his shotgun and heading back to the house.

I was pretending to make cocoa when he came in, but my hands didn't seem connected to my arms. They were moving without any signals from me. I was well and truly out of my body watching from a distance. His voice brought me back.

"Sit down, Stella. We have some talking to do." His voice was not gentle. His foot hooked a chair leg and scooted it out from under the table with a grating squeal. He laid the shotgun on the table and sat down.

I pulled out the chair facing him and sat down, gritting my teeth not to tremble.

"Why?"

I explained. "She had bone cancer. The insurance had run out and she'd sold all her dead husband's valuables, including the Civil War artifacts, to pay the doctor. There wasn't any medication that would touch the pain. There was no one else. Her girls had their own problems."

I shrugged. "First, she tried to borrow my pistol, said someone was on her porch at night messing around." I shook off my numbness a little bit then, remembering. "It was probably Timmy Lee." He nodded once but his expression didn't change, somewhere between anger and hurt.

"Jonas, she pleaded with me. We planned it out, talked about different ways to do it. It was what a friend would do." Something clicked and I dug in. I wasn't begging him to understand or forgive. I had done it because it was right. It was also horrible. I didn't know if it was worth the rest of my life without Jonas, but that was in the balance. I lifted my head proudly and looked him in the eye. "I am sorry that I didn't tell you sooner and I do care what you think, but I am not sorry that I did it."

He looked away first, drummed his fingers on the table, and asked, "Who knows?"

"You. Only you."

"Not your friends?"

"No."

"Her daughters?"

"No."

"Did you love her that much?"

"Yes. You are not going to want to hear this, but she let me know at the cemetery on Thanksgiving morning that she was okay, that she was happy we did it." My tears were splashing onto the plastic tablecloth.

He stared at me and his face morphed out of anger to something else, to curiosity, maybe. "How did it feel, to watch the spirit of your best friend leave this earth, to know that you caused her to go to the next world before her time?"

"It was awful, but it was peaceful, too." Reliving it before his watching eyes dropped all pretenses. "I think about it every day and sometimes I hear Anna whisper, 'thank you,' and I can go on."

"Why tell me now? My mom is in the hospital and a lunatic is in the area looking for us to hurt us. Why now, Stella?"

"Because all this is my fault, my family coming home to rest on your home and your family. If you want out, to be safe, this is your out. Your wife kept a thing from you to keep you safe. Now, knowing the thing can keep you safe. I want you safe."

He got up. "I need to clean up to go to the hospital, take a shower and shave. Answer my phone if it rings in case they call." He laid the phone on the counter as he left. I nodded, emotions choking off any words.

Jonas

She could of told me weeks ago. She could of told me before she did it and I could of talked her out of it. Maybe. I was scrubbing way too hard in the shower thinking about it. I stood under the showerhead with the water so hot that steam filled the stall. We'd get through this. We would. I'd call Ben and kinda feel him out and see if there was suspicion about Anna's death. Timmy Lee was another problem. I couldn't see any way clear to get him off the hook without getting Stella on it.

As I toweled off, I wondered if I could do that for someone I loved. I wasn't sure that I could. It had to take guts to follow through. That was Stella, she wouldn't talk about it long; she would do it. She followed through. A rare thing in anybody these days.

We needed to talk more but it wasn't on the top of today's list. I dressed to go to the hospital, probably that was next on the list, then get Mom and Phoebe back in the house. I needed to call the sheriff and get whatever update since last night. I knew they were searching empty houses today.

Chapter 38

"Jonas, telephone," Stella called as she ran up the stairs with the phone.

I grabbed it through the t-shirt sleeve as I pulled it over my head.

"Yes, this is Jonas Akpik.

"Mary Jo Akpik's son, yes.

"Yes, ma'am, we'll be there within the hour. How is she?

"Good, if she's fussing, she's getting back to normal. We'll be there as soon as we can get there.

"Stella, would you get Phoebe ready to go? I don't want to leave her here alone."

Stella raised her eyebrows. "I can stay here with her and you can run and get your mom."

"No, I'll need some help with Mom. If she is herself, that is.

"I'm going to leave them both at their house tonight, though, because I think Mom will do better in the more familiar surroundings. I need to read up on Alzheimer's, too."

"Okay." Stella looked at me, waiting what seemed like a full minute before she spoke again. "I 'spected a little more conversation about Anna. Are we done?"

"Not by a long shot. Just not now." I found myself growling as I spoke, partly mad at myself because I hadn't guessed her secret.

"Ten-four, I'll get Phoebe up and ready." She pivoted on the ball of her fleece slipper and sprang into action.

I took advantage of the few minutes it would take her to get ready and called the sheriff to get the latest. He was "in the field" according to his secretary. Good, that meant he was helping with the search.

We were noon getting to the hospital. One of the young engineers at the Celanese stayed until we got there. Good man. Mom was classic Mom, griping about having to ride the wheelchair to the curb and complaining about being waked up every hour as they were checking on her to see if she was asleep.

Everybody was hungry so we stopped and went in the Burger King. Those old women enjoyed ordering a meal more than anyone I ever saw. They clapped as they figured out the fine print on the menu and settled for Whopper meals and milkshakes. They were like little kids unwrapping the food and trading regular fries for sweet potato fries and slurps of chocolate milkshake for vanilla. My heart swelled with love for them and how in the middle of this mess they could have such simple joys.

I was seated so I could see the door and the window in case Timmy Lee sashayed in. While I was watching, they decided they needed some groceries. We stopped at Jewell's IGA in downtown Lindside to load up. That took another hour. First they visited with a man they called CT, said they met him at bingo in Rich Creek. Phoebe was glowing. Good Lord. Then, between arguing over what they needed and what brand was better, it took so long that my feet hurt before we got back to the truck. I think they were tired, too. They got quiet during the final leg of the trip.

I told them all to wait in the truck until I checked their house. Stella did, but those two climbed down on their own, carried their groceries and toddled into the house before I was even done. They pooh-poohed my caution and then twisted it around and tried to talk me into getting them a gun.

I laughed, "No way, you two might use it to rob a bank." They giggled and turned on the TV. "Seriously, you stay in this house. Just so you know, Timmy Lee may have loosened the lug nuts on the car you wrecked. If so, he tried to hurt you." I didn't want to scare them too much, but I wanted their attention.

"Keep the phone handy. I will be calling every hour until midnight, because I know you stay up that late. No bingo, no cruising through town. Stay here. Got it?"

"Yes, Son."

"Yes, Jonas."

They stood with hands folded, the very picture of pious old women. I wasn't fooled. "You will stay in this house. You will not let anyone in except Stella or me."

"How about the cleaning lady?" Mom had me.

"Yes, Tisha is probably coming this evening. You can let her in. Keep the doors locked. All the time. Questions?"

Mom spoke softly. "We may need something to help us sleep." Phoebe cracked up, then Mom's fat rolls jiggled she laughed so hard. I didn't know what private joke they were sharing but it was clear that they did not need anything at all and that Mom, for the moment at least, was functioning fine.

"I love you both and I want you safe."

They hugged me and I hugged them and I twisted the bar on the doorknob to the locked position from the inside as I left.

Chapter 39

Where are You, God?

Timmy Lee

Couldn't believe that I made it back to the cabin with no drama. It was like nobody cared that I was out or maybe the past two months were all a bad dream. I built a fire. The dry bark I used for kindling caught up real fast. Nothing to it. I fed the fire with branches and remembered to go back for the OJ and water. Everything was under control. It was dark by then and it took awhile to find the drinks. The half-gallon jugs would keep cool enough sitting inside in the windowsill. Orange juice gave me a boost and I took a swig from the jug every time I felt dry.

I couldn't see the fine print on the directions for the phone by firelight so I lit an oil lamp I found in a cupboard. I could make it out clearer with the oil lamp, but I wished I had bought a pair of reading glasses. Got the phone up and running but couldn't find Stella's number.

No more posts about the old ladies in the Mustang on Topix, so I posted a question. "What happened to the people in the red Mustang that wrecked on 219? They okay?" Nobody responded. They would. Small town low-lifes needed a place to gossip. I signed it "Concerned Citizen" and smiled. The only thing I was concerned about was if they survived.

I unrolled the egg carton foam and stretched out on it, wearing my coat and covered with blankets. I thought I could still smell the blood of the snakes I killed, metal-like and salty. Sleep came and went. I got up a couple of times to throw wood on the fire.

Chapter 39

Then, I woke with a gurgle in my gut. Cramping bad. I barely got out of the house and dropped my pants before I exploded. Burning bowel movement that seemed to never end. When the shit stopped, the gas began. The stink was disgusting. I stood up to try to clean myself with a DQ napkin I found in my pocket. Then something in the black woods screamed. Blood-curdling loud. Close by. I booked it to the cabin with my pants around my ankles, tripped on a stump and fell face first onto a ridge of limestone. Last thing I remember was falling in the dark. Musta knocked me out. Woke up bloody and with my ass so cold, it crunched. My fingers and toes were numb, too.

I decided right then that this was my last night in the frickin' woods. I had to go again so I pushed myself up to a squat and dumped a pile onto my pants leg. All over my leg, too. Reeked of shit. I slid my sock feet out of the pants and made my way back. Socks were soaked, too. I left shitty footprints across the floor and threw socks on the coals as fast as I could peel them off. The cabin felt warm, but the fire was almost out and the wood stack left was just crumbs of bark and twigs. According to my phone it was 5:21 AM. I rubbed my ass until I could feel it again and then it burned so bad I wanted to sit in the snow. My fingers and toes ached. The place on my forehead had stopped bleeding, there was a pump knot and I could feel the blood pulling at my skin as it dried. And it hurt. And my stench was in the air. Damn it all to hell. I was bugging out. Going where there was heat. And a toilet. And a bed. The state hospital was better than this. Hell, jail was better than this. I screamed, "Where are you, God?" and beat my fists on the log wall.

I had another pair of underwear Jeff had left, and one more pair of pants I bought at Goodwill. It hurt when I pulled the briefs and jeans over my ass. I packed plastic grocery bags with what I could carry, stuffed my new phone in my pocket, stepped into boots without socks and without tying them, and used a lighter to find the path back to my car. Even the car would be better than this. I forgot about the earlier scream until I heard it again. Then I ran. Briers and thorns tore my hands. I stumbled and fell and crawled to the foot of a tree and listened to my heart pounding, hoping whatever was screaming wouldn't notice. Then I ran like hell again and somehow, in the blackness, I found the pine thicket and my car. The flop into the front seat hurt like hell. I wasn't sure I could sit long enough to drive. So, I rolled up on the side of one hip, twisted my foot to fit the gas pedal, and fired that sucker up.

I drove the back road until I got to Jonas' house, where the old ladies had lived. No sign of anyone. I parked a good ways off, just off the road, and hobbled up the valley to the house, pushed open the bedroom window where I'd left a pencil and fell over it with my last bit of strength. I didn't give a shit if they were home, if I was walking into a trap, if Elmer Johnson hisself was sitting under that window. None of it mattered. I was done with Mother Nature, that cold-hearted bitch.

I walked through the house. Nothing had changed since I'd been there before. I washed my hands and legs and scrubbed under my nails with a pink bath brush to quit smelling the stench before I crawled into the first bed I came to, belly down. I closed my eyes. I was safe. The old skanks were not home. Probably dead. That was my last thought before daylight streamed in around the cheap too-small shade. I got up to find the bathroom and sat for a long time with my head in my hands. The past hours were fuzzy and I was tired. The unfairness of the world bubbled up, of my being born too poor, and of Stella ruining everything. The flames of anger started to lick my backbone and made me move again.

I felt empty in spite of all I needed to do. I needed to check Topix but no Internet signal made it into this valley deep between the mountains. My stomach was still sore but I was hungry and stood in front of the refrigerator with the door open. Nothing looked good to me. There were some Town House crackers in a cupboard and I ate a handful of them and washed them down with water. I needed to think, so I smoothed the cracker crumbs off the table, then straightened up my bed. Keeping things around me in order helped me think.

A car door slammed outside. "NO!" I screamed inside my head and peeked out from behind the drapes of the front window. The two old women had crawled down out of a pick-up truck and Jonas was leading the way. He was bigger than I remembered.

The key rattled and the door lock clicked. "I told you to stay in the truck," he told the women. "Phoebe, stay with her until I check the house."

I just had time to grab my coat and ease into the closet floor, closing the door from inside. I covered myself with blankets and dirty clothes from the closet floor and made a new deal with God. If he would get me through this mess, I would pray to him every day. I squeezed my eyes shut tight and willed my body to be as still as it was in the hospital. All I could see was the lake of burning fire and brimstone promised to all liars by revival evangelists. Sometimes I wished I hadn't been a gospel singer and listened to all that rot. Right now, for instance.

Jonas moved through the house fairly quietly, but I still heard his big feet step onto the bedroom carpet and listened for him to move again forever through the pause when the mattress crackled. He must've been looking under the bed. I felt the rush of cool air as he threw open the closet door and pushed the few hanging clothes aside. He pushed the door closed and left. I rubbed my nose and held my butt cheeks together tight. Flexing my ass hurt but I didn't know what might come out if I relaxed.

There were people talking but I couldn't understand what they were saying. I might have heard Stella, too, but wasn't for sure. How had those two old women survived the wreck? Both of them on foot, too. Damn, damn, damn.

The front door closed and I heard the TV come on. Good, they wouldn't be in here. Maybe I could just slip out the bedroom window and be gone. No, as bad as this was it was better than camping out. I had nowhere else to go.

It was 2:30 according to the phone in my coat pocket. I'd wait them out until they went to bed, then I'd see what I would see. Maybe just walk out the door, but maybe hold them hostages and trade for Stella, or maybe tie them up and scare them, or maybe kill them both. Killing them really didn't pay Stella back enough, though. Anyway, I had options. Meantime, I was warm and pretty comfortable. I could stay in here for hours but I'd need to change position off my butt. Frostbite pain was settling in and I prayed that my guts were empty. I moved to my knees and then lowered myself face first to get the weight off my ass. Much better. I fumbled for a pack of Advil in my coat and snagged one. I'd taken one of them before, I pushed the other one out of the little pack and swallowed it. A Percocet would have been a better match for the pain.

Chapter 40

He Has Been Real Close, Folks

Stella

When the truck slowed to a stop in the driveway, Jonas took the keys out of the ignition and turned to me. "Why didn't you tell me beforehand?" His black eyes were piercing.

I was ready for the answer to this one, because I'd tossed and turned all night several times figuring it out for myself. "Because if I got in trouble, I didn't want you to have to testify. This way, you truly didn't know and could be honest if you were questioned by the police."

He rested his head on the steering wheel.

"I wanted to tell you Jonas, I really did. I trusted you and I needed you, but I had to do it and there was nothing you could say to change my mind. I didn't want to put you in that position."

He put the truck keys in his Carhartt jacket pocket and opened the door, then turned back to me. "In the future, I want to know if you are planning to kill somebody. In advance. I want a shot at convincing you not to. Just a shot, Stella, could you promise me that?"

I couldn't answer because I was bawling. This meant it was going to somehow be okay, that he wasn't going to leave me.

He pulled the door shut again. "Oh, come here."

I slid over to him and he held me and kissed my neck. I think he cried, too; his face was wet, but he would never admit it. "Promise me," he held me at arm's length after a few minutes and waited.

Chapter 40

"Yes, oh, yes." I choked out the answer he wanted. It was the truth.

"Gettin' cold out here. I need to make some phone calls." We hurried to the house. The world felt light and airy again, the sky felt huge, and our old farmhouse stood as tall and proud as a cathedral reaching toward the sun, and my heart was plumb full of love. The dogs danced over to greet us, prancing and whining happily. I dodged and jumped back at them, rare joy. My world was healing.

Except for the shadow of Timmy Lee. Where was he?

He was in Lewisburg two days ago, too close, but still an hour's drive. Deputies were searching empty cabins and homes near us today. I didn't remember if his car's license number had been reported. That would up the chances of his getting caught. I asked Jonas.

He didn't remember either. "Let me call the sheriff and see what's new today, but first I'm calling Mom. I was not kidding about calling them every hour."

Evidently, Phoebe answered. "Put Mom on," he said.

"You okay?

"Good, Mom. Stay in the house, will ya? Take it easy.

"You do not need another Whopper for supper. Don't even go there.

"Yes, they were good. Once in awhile.

"Okay, I'll be calling back after while."

He looked at the phone. "She hung up on me. Again."

I had to giggle. Mary Jo was a hoot, especially when she felt good. Seemed like the urinary tract infection was clearing up. I'd remind Jonas to remind her to take her medicine later.

The dogs started barking, not the baying yelps for intruders, but their "someone we like is here" yaps. Sheriff Johnson knocked on the door, alternately patting Sugar and Riley while I unlocked the storm door.

"How old is the Shepherd?"

Jonas had appeared. "Maybe fifteen months, I think, why?"

"She's alert, calm, smart enough to remember me from the other day. Might be a good candidate for K-9 dog training. I don't know exactly what age they start training. She may be too old."

"Just as well, she has a job right here on the farm," I added my two cents worth to the conversation.

"I was just getting ready to call you." Jonas opened a drawer to get his note pad and pencil. "Things are happening so fast, I need to keep notes. Riley isn't the only one getting older."

I offered the living room, but the men were comfortable in the kitchen, so they sat down around the table while I bustled around getting warm drinks, tea and cocoa, and butter cookies we'd just bought at the store.

"Elmer, I didn't get the license number of the car Timmy Lee is using, could I get it now?"

"Certainly." The sheriff dug in his inside jacket pocket for his tiny notebook and flipped page after page until he put his finger on a line and read off, "West Virginia UVA-640."

Jonas wrote it down and pushed the pad aside. "Well, what has happened today?"

"We've gotten ourselves a break. Ivan and Doug found where Mr. Davis has been staying." He looked at us both. "It wasn't pretty, folks." He referred to his notes. "At the Kelly cabin about three miles due south of here, there was evidence that it had been recently inhabited. There were Slim Jim wrappers, packaging from a Tracfone, empty tin cans of beans, partially emptied milk and orange juice jugs, a sleeping mat, a hatchet and other things."

"That doesn't sound too terrible." I voiced my opinion.

"The boys found a pair of jeans and briefs frozen outside the cabin directly on a pile of feces, a few feet from blood and flesh. They took samples, sent to the lab, by the way. The boys speculated that the resident was eaten by a bear."

I gasped, horribly torn between fear of it being true and quick acceptance of it as a solution to the threat Timmy Lee posed to us all.

Elmer added quickly, "Stella, I don't think it's true. I can't explain what happened, but there is more unexplainable than just that. They found a pair of men's socks partly burned in the fireplace. The wooden floor had been hacked over a hundred times. Blood was present in many of the gouges. If Ivan hadn't found a mound of what appears to be a cut up black snake near the cabin, we would've thought someone had been butchered in there."

"What makes you think it was Timmy Lee?"

"There was a receipt with the trash in the cabin floor. Guess where it was from?"

"The Lewisburg Wal-Mart?" Again, I was torn between wanting it to be true and hoping he was farther away than Peter's Mountain.

"Yes, ma'am, on the date he was in the store on surveillance cameras listing the items we already knew he had purchased."

"Then, it's him. Less than three miles from here," Jonas growled.

"Folks, we are going to assign an officer to patrol Wilson Mill Road and Painter Run Road regularly starting tonight. If we can locate the silver Cobalt, we'll be another step closer. The APB has some teeth in it now with the tag number. He may be long gone and far away. We'll notify you when he is picked up."

He shut his notebook and tucked it away as he stood. "I need to get back to the office and get the rotation assignment posted for the mountain patrol. In the meantime, let us know if anything suspicious happens up here. He has been real close, folks." He paused. "Are you sure that you shouldn't bring your relatives up here with you?"

"Remember how confused she was yesterday?" Elmer nodded. "Doctors think the unfamiliar surroundings trigger episodes of Alzheimer's or dementia. So, I'm calling every hour to check on them and leaving her where she is comfortable. I guess technically, yesterday was the result of an infection, but the Alzheimer's is getting more and more noticeable." That was the first time Jonas had admitted the disease was worsening and I felt sorry for him and sorry for Mary Jo.

I cleared the empty mugs from the table. "The girls are about ten days away from going back to Alaska, so if we can keep them safe and sound for awhile longer, they will have a room in an assisted living center and in a village where everyone knows them and can help keep an eye on their antics."

Jonas showed Elmer out and locked the door.

The sunset that night was bright red and orange and pink brushed across the sky. I got glimpses of it as I checked the windows and pulled the drapes. What was that old saying? "Red sky at night, sailor's delight; red skies at dawning, sailors take warning." That was it. If it held true, the weather would be nice tomorrow. We went together to feed the animals and even the air seemed the same colors as the sunset. It was thawing. Water was dripping from the barn roof and the chicken coop into the gutter that ran to the downspout that ran to the rain barrel that I filled the water trough with. At least I did when it wasn't frozen. Jonas had fixed all the gates so they were self-closing with cables and rocks. The sheep and goats' feeders were at different heights to match the animals that ate there. In the spring, I wanted to put names on the stalls for all the new mothers. I loved our little farm and all the personal touches that we'd added over time. Farming was easier and more fun with another person. So was life. Two people to make a bed, to talk about the news, to do the dishes. I was so happy that I hadn't messed up our marriage. I took off my glove and stuck my hand in Jonas' pocket and held his hand as we walked back to the house.

The dogs suddenly leaped into action and ran barking in a panic through the brush to the woods. "Get inside, Stella, I'll follow them." He pushed me toward the yard and I ran. The lock on the back door was a push button affair, no key required. I punched in the code and fell into a chair, worried sick about Jonas out there alone. I had time to check the windows to see if I could see and run upstairs to watch, before he burst in the door, shaking his head.

"A rabbit, they were chasing a rabbit. Which they are never going to catch in a million years. It bobbed and weaved and zigzagged. Azaa, those poor dogs were not even close, smelling in one brush pile while the rabbit skipped away somewhere else."

My heart was gradually slowing down, false alarm or not, my body had reacted like it was real. I don't know what was more exhausting, being scared or just sitting and waiting. I needed to stay busy so I logged onto the computer with my client's accounts. I needed to post entries to Boggess Hardware's electronic journal and check to see if any other clients had sent me last week's debits and credits yet. I drifted away into the world of cash flow and got one account updated. Jonas was on the phone and I was vaguely aware that he was talking to his mother.

"I don't know why she would be out of breath," he wondered aloud.

"Did you ask her?"

He grunted, "That would be the last place to get the truth, especially on the phone. All I really know is she was in the house at that moment."

"Hmmm, should we go down and check on them?"

"Nah, I want to research Alzheimer's awhile before bedtime and keep calling them until midnight."

Chapter 40

I couldn't sit up with him tonight. When I reached a stopping point, I realized that the range of emotions and physical activities of the day had caught up with me. As I crawled under the quilt, my bedtime prayer was first, that Timmy Lee would get what he deserved and life would get back to normal and second, I thanked God for the man I had married.

Chapter 41

There Was a Rat in There

Mary Jo and Phoebe

Mary Jo whispered, "Come here and listen." She'd pushed out of the recliner and shuffled across the room to investigate tiny sounds coming from her bedroom closet. The bedroom door was opened a few inches and she didn't go in, but put her ear to the opening and motioned for Phoebe to join her. "Come here."

Phoebe listened. "Oh, it's just a lemming rattling around in the closet." She turned to walk away.

"Shhh! Be still. There are no lemmings here. Besides, one thump was too loud for something as uutukuu as a lemming. Something pretty big is in my closet. And it might be dying, do you smell that?"

Phoebe wrinkled her nose. "Could it be a ground squirrel, like the ones at home, or a weasel? Oh, no, what if it's a rat?" Mary Jo waved her away from the door, back into the little kitchen.

"We gotta sneak up on it, Pheebs. We need weapons."

Phoebe disagreed. "What we need to do is call Jonas. He'll come down here and put it out of its misery. He'll shoot it."

"No sense in bothering him. We can handle this. What would our mothers and grandmothers have done? Take care of it themselves, that's what." Mary Jo looked high and low around the room. "I'll take the biggest cast iron skillet I can swing."

"Since when do you live your life the old ways?" Phoebe grumbled. She was not enthusiastic as she grabbed the fly swatter.

"Azaa, that thing won't work, you can't even hit a fly with it, besides it's not strong enough. Keep looking."

Phoebe drug an assortment from under the sink. "How about a mouse trap?"

"No, keep looking."

Phoebe started reading a spray can. "This might work. Wasp and Bee Killer, even works from 20 feet away."

"No, that wouldn't hurt a rat. Bees are little things."

"I think I saw on TV that career women like in offices were keeping this in their desk in case they were attacked when they worked late. Instead of pepper spray. Cheaper, too. I saw it on maybe the Today Show. Matt Lauer would not lie about such a thing."

"Well, shake it and see if it has anything in it."

"Brand new. Let me get the lid off so I am ready."

The two of them tiptoed into the bedroom, shushing each other and holding their noses as they got closer and the smell got worse. The closet was quiet now. Mary Jo held the skillet high with both hands and Phoebe pointed her poison at the door. Mary Jo held up three fingers and counted down, then Phoebe raised her eyebrows and pointed to herself as if to say, "Me? You want me to open that door?" Her sister nodded energetically. So she grasped the doorknob and turned, then yanked the door open and sprayed the intruder full in the face.

It was hard to say which party was more surprised, the man kneeling in the closet with his jeans down to his knees or the two old ladies expecting much smaller vermin. He screamed and clutched his eyes and fell out of the closet. Mary Jo hit him hard in the shoulder with the skillet with a resounding pop from that joint while Phoebe continued to spray his eyes and mouth. She was remarkably accurate with the long spray spout and got closer and closer to his writhing body to be extra sure. This gave Mary Jo time to raise the skillet again and conk him on his behind. He screamed so loud and long that it got on Phoebe's nerves and she quit spraying and begged her sister to hit him in the head to "turn off that awful squawking." So she did. The man lay in a crumpled heap.

"Why, isn't this Stella's mean ole brother?" Phoebe was in full battle mode. "He's a bad man. Hit him again with the skillet for trying to hurt her."

The ice in the Arctic Ocean at midnight in the summertime. Photo by Yvonne
Fonua.

Mary Jo let herself down beside him and took aim, then
lowered the skillet. "Doesn't seem fair to hit an unconscious
man."

"Don't you want him to stay out? Hit him again!"

So she did.

"And this is for trying to get us killed and smashing up our
nice car." Phoebe wasn't done, she sprayed wasp killer in his
mouth and nose.

"Oh, that's enough. We don't want to kill him."

Phoebe swiveled her head around with a look that clearly
questioned Mary Jo's mercy.

"I better call Jonas to come and get him." Mary Jo struggled
to her feet.

"No, he'll be mad at us for letting him in. We need to put
him somewhere else, outside of the house and call the 911. I
always wanted to call the 911."

"Where?"

"Our ancestors would have put him on an island or out on
the ice and let the gods decide."

"Well, the ice around here is melting fast. We will have to
make do with cold mud, I guess."

209

Chapter 41

Mary Jo thought and thought. "We can leave him in the barn. It will be cold but not way cold. He can find peace there – or not."

"Then we better get moving before he comes around. How are we gonna move him? We can't carry him and besides I am getting tired."

Mary Jo shot her a look, "You get yourself together, Sister, because we still have some work to do. Then Stella and Jonas are safe and so are we." She stood, hands on hips. "We need those little plastic ties and something bigger, rope or an extension cord, and that hand cart on the back porch. You get the ties and stuff and I'll go get the hand cart."

Phoebe sat mumbling for awhile longer, then went to the kitchen and rummaged around in the junk drawer. Mary Jo tried to hold the door with one hand and pull the dolly in with the other and bumped around crashing into the storm door and denting the thin metal. By the time Phoebe reached her to help, she was inside with the heavy metal cart.

They parked the cart beside his body horizontally and drug him on it, pausing to pull his pants up and snap them together. Phoebe, who was doing most of the lifting, reported, "I think I know where the smell is coming from, there is a brown stain in his underpants. He anaqqed in his pants."

"Oh, my God, we will have to clean before Tisha gets here, she will be sick." Mary Jo was clearly more worried about the cleaning lady's sensitivities than her own.

"Wait," Phoebe spoke softly as if he could be awakened by the noise. Mary Jo was ready to fasten him to the cart when Phoebe noticed his jacket still in the closet.

She grabbed the coat and searched his pockets. "Ooo, Mary Jo, this is yours." She handed the notes with handwriting on them. She found a bank envelope with cash in it. "Wonder where this came from."

"Let me see." Her eyes got big. "Looks like mine." Her dresser was three steps away and she ran her hands through the underwear drawer without finding her own stash of cash. "That thief!" She turned and kicked him in the crotch.

Phoebe got tickled. "I told you he was bad. He'd steal the butter right off your bread."

"Stealing from poor old defenseless ladies. Shame on him." She shook her finger at him and replaced the cash in her drawer.

Old Barn. Photo by Robmckay.

"No more time for suaktuk-ing, if we don't get him out of here, you will be scolding an angry bad man."

"Okay. Pull his jacket on him." After much fussing, they got his jacket on and zipped it. They fastened his wrists to the bars of the cart with plastic ties, then wrapped a very long orange extension cord around his middle and legs and the cart. He was too long for the cart so his lower legs and feet hung over the edges.

The two women, arguing every step, finally rolled the unconscious Timmy Lee through the yard, across a bumpy hayfield and into the old barn. They maneuvered around boards that had fallen off and rocks and pieces of tin to find a relatively intact corner of a stall, at least out of the wind.

"Now, what? Did the elders have a ceremony or prayer before they left people?" Phoebe was worn out and more irritable than usual.

"I think they left some food and water and a gun," she said thoughtfully. But that wouldn't work here. "You got a prayer?"

Phoebe nodded, "Our heavenly Father, take this man's black soul and show it the light and if he won't see the light, then take him away to be at your side and learn so those of us here will be safe. Be with our loved ones and us and help us to always do the right thing. Thy will be done. Amen."

"Amen." Mary Jo chimed in. "We better hurry back, Jonas might call."

Chapter 41

Sure enough, as they climbed the stairs to the back porch, the phone was ringing. Mary Jo was huffing and puffing, but she answered it and assured Jonas that all was well.

The women rested for a few minutes, then decided they needed to spray Lysol in the closet floor, which smelled less and less like human waste and more like wasp killer than before. They gathered up the unused ties and wasp spray can and lid and started cleaning the closet. That's what they were doing when Tisha arrived.

Phoebe answered the door and hugged Tisha, "We are cleaning now before you come to clean. Just a little bit in the closet. There was a rat in there."

"Eeuuw. I don't do rats."

"Is okay, we almost done."

Tisha watched Mary Jo's butt wiggle as she scrubbed the carpeted closet floor, rest back on her heels, dip her brush in the bucket of water and then start again. "Looks like you got that covered, Mary Jo, I'll start in the kitchen."

Mary Jo grunted.

Phoebe told her, "I'll dump the water when you are finished," turned on the TV and sat down to watch. Mary Jo joined her in a few minutes and they were napping when Jonas called again.

Chapter 42

Time to Bug Out

Stella

In the place between sleep and awake, I heard Jonas' phone ring in the distance and heard his booming, "Hello, Sis." I knew it was Barbara and it put me on edge wondering what was going on. Was someone hurt or dead? Had the assisted living place fallen through? Since when did I look for the negative in everything? But I had to know so I threw the covers back and sat on the side of the bed, waiting for Jonas to tell me.

"Hey, Hon, wake up." He was taking the steps two at a time, the phone in his hand. "It's Barbara. The senior center says the room we are waiting for has opened up sooner than they expected but they can't hold it for us long. Barbara will change the tickets to as soon as there are seats available, but she needs to know when we can leave here to carry them home."

Not what I expected to hear. "Jonas, we can't leave here with Timmy Lee on the loose." I was wide-awake now. "And we can't send those two anywhere alone." I laughed in spite of myself.

"How about if I stay here and you go with?"

"Jonas, I have work to do, bookkeeping; my job, remember?"

"Take the laptop. You can do it on the plane ride. I will stay here and take care of the place. You and Mom and Phoebe will be out of danger."

I nodded slowly, accepting my fate and hoping this would relieve a little bit of my guilt for not telling him about Anna. "Okay. I'll go. When?"

Chapter 42

"Up to you." Then into the phone, "Barbara, you still there? When is the soonest?" He was quiet for a moment. "I'll ask her."

He looked at me, "Time to bug out. When can you get them ready to go? When could you be ready?"

"Really, Jonas, are we talking about leaving tonight? I have to sleep first, that's for sure."

"How about tomorrow night? Can you be ready and get them packed by then?"

"Probably, yes, I think so." I yawned.

"Tomorrow night at the earliest, Barbara. Yeah, let me know when you have them booked and we'll plan from there. I'll be up until midnight here, at least." He listened. "Out of Roanoke, not DC, that will help me get them there faster.

"Love you, too." He pressed the END button with a big grin. He picked me up and danced with me until I started griping.

"Put me down now, Jonas, I need to sleep. Have you checked on the girls?"

"Not yet, but it's about time."

"Remind Mary Jo to take her antibiotic. It would not be fun for her to have an episode on the plane. Maybe remind Phoebe to remind her, too."

He kissed the top of my head and tucked me in. "Rest up, Hon. A lot to do tomorrow."

I heard his boots on the stairs just before I fell asleep.

The next morning, I wasn't sure if I had dreamed the events of the night before or not. I looked around the room. No Jonas, but my rolling carry-on case was out and open, like a mouth ready to be fed. Must have really happened. I must be going back to Alaska today with two elderly delinquents. They make leashes for toddlers; wonder if they make them for senior citizens. That idea went on my mental list of good inventions. When I had time, I was going to apply for a zillion patents.

Jonas carried a tray into the bedroom. "Breakfast in bed," he announced. It was a good spread: eggs and crispy bacon and buttered toast and cold orange juice. I devoured it, knowing the day was going to get hectic and I needed to be getting ready, not lolling about in bed.

"Tisha called and wanted you to call her back."

"Okay."

"I am going down to Mom's in a few minutes to tell them the news. Then, I'll help them pack and you can come back up here and get yourself ready."

214

"When do we leave?" I casually sipped the juice.

He backed up a step and rubbed his arm. Oh, no. He was nervous. "When, Jonas? Tell me."

"The flight is at four o'clock this evening, you need to check in by two and it's a two-hour drive to the airport. So we'll load up at noon."

I looked at the clock: 8:15. In less than four hours, I'd be on the way to Alaska. I closed my eyes and rested my head on the pillow for one more minute of peace and quiet. I could do this.

"How did Barbara collect money so fast to get them back up there?"

I peeked and saw him smile ear-to-ear. "Barbara's not dumb, she collected enough dollars and miles from everybody when they thought all they were buying was a one-way ticket out. She bought round-trip and has just changed the date."

"How is your mom this morning? Did staying at her own house help her?"

"Yes, right as rain this morning. I was worried about them there alone, but they will be safely on the way home before the sun sets again. And it is a beautiful day to travel."

I sat up.

"Times a-wasting, Woman." He popped me on the hip playfully.

"Let me call Tisha first, then I'll get cracking. Oh, when is my return ticket?"

"Don't know. Didn't ask. Give me a couple of hours to let Barbara get up."

"I kinda need to know how many outfits to pack." Then memories of the last trip hit me. "Jonas, I better have a return ticket for real soon."

"Don't worry, I'll find out. Just remembered, she sent the ticket codes, I can look it up there right now without bothering Barbara."

"Go on then, and find out. I'll see what Tisha wants." I returned the swat on his rear and reached for my phone.

Tisha was good. She'd finished at Mary Jo's and Phoebe's after a kitchen and bathroom and living room wipe down. "It was pretty clean, they'd been gone for two nights and I could tell."

"Thanks, Tish. They behaving?"

"Better than usual. Talked to me a little about leaving and how they want to go home but they have had a really good time here."

"Yeah, a drunken airplane trip, bingo on the sly, a car wreck; they have been busy."

"Well, they've had fun and they love you. Who knew it would go this way?"

"I've learned to love them, too. Someday, we'll be that old."

"If we're lucky. They were kinda weird last night, though."

"Spill it." My heart froze. Weird for these two could be very bad.

"Well, they were cleaning out the closet in Mary Jo's bedroom. Scrubbing the carpet on hands and knees. Spraying Lysol everywhere. Worse than me."

"Why in the world?"

"Phoebe said there had been a rat in the closet. She looked pretty shook up."

"Did they catch the rat? Kill it?"

"I don't think so, but they sure have one clean closet. I told them I didn't do rats."

"Huh, that is weird."

"Okay, gotta go, half the baseball team's coming to eat at our house tonight. Looks like the weather is changing for the better."

"Oh, Tisha, I forgot, I am taking the girls back to Alaska tonight. In fact, I better get to packing. And you have one more cleaning job if you want it, to get their house ready to rent after they leave."

"You know I will. Now you be careful, hear?"

I told her goodbye and jumped up to start counting out underpants and socks for the trip.

Jonas yelled from downstairs, "You arrive tomorrow night, two sleeps and back on the plane. So only one full day in Barrow and leave the next day. I'm going to Mom's and tell them. Want to come along?"

"Sure, why not?" I yelled down the stairwell, then washed my face, brushed my teeth, threw on a sweat suit and hustled down the steps.

We looked at the edge of the fields for anything unusual, fed the dogs and sheep and goats, and turned them out into the sunshine. It was a gorgeous day.

The truck splashed through mud and puddles, formerly ice, on the way to the girls. They were expecting us.

There was an awkward feel in the living room as if the girls were waiting for bad news. Jonas explained that their room in the Senior Center was now available and that Barbara had

Springtime at Stella's farm. Photo by B. Crabtree

changed their tickets and they were leaving at noon for the airport. He was clearly happy that the arrangements were in place and did not notice the looks that were passing between the two women. Finally, he announced, "I am here to help you pack."

"Huh." His mother replied. "We want Stella to help. We have clothes to wash and things to do."

"Mom, all you have to do is pack. We'll take care of the house later."

I interrupted, "Jonas, it's okay by me. You get lunch ready for us to eat and pack me three outfits, PJs, and toiletries and I'll be ready. I can get their clothes washed and dried and packed by that time."

He left and the three of us gathered all the dirty clothes and started the washer. The sheets and towels we threw in a pile for later. They pulled the suitcases out from under their respective beds and opened them for the packing. I grabbed zip-lock bags from the kitchen and we bagged all the shampoos and cleansers and make-up to pack. Then, they chose the outfit they wanted to wear on the long flight, comfortable but nice looking. Finally, we started folding it all for the suitcases, adding items as the dryer buzzed for the first load. We were waiting for the second load to dry when Jonas drove up. The door was locked and his mom took some pleasure in making him wait for her to open it. He did not look happy.

"Stella, I need to talk to you."

The old ladies froze in place. They were acting a little weird today.

"Outside, please." I went with him.

"What? Have they found him?" I so hoped they had.

He was upset. Trembled a little when he rubbed his face. "They found his car."

"Where?"

He pointed on down the road. "Just around the curve. In sight of this house and a short hike to ours."

"Was he in it?" I closed my eyes and prayed the answer would be yes.

"No."

I felt the air whoosh out of me like a leaking tire. Timmy Lee, on foot, and close by. "What do we do?"

"We get them," he pointed inside, "to safety. How much more do you have to do to be ready?"

"Let's go in and hurry this along." I led the way. "Jonas wants to take you out to lunch on the way to the airport just as soon as you are ready." They seemed very relieved and went to change into their traveling clothes. I packed the contents of the dryer and the clothes they had taken off. They needed some cash and to be sure their IDs and credit cards were in their purses. We'd stop at the bank.

I squeezed the suitcase lids down and latched them. Jonas carried the bags to the truck and I did the purse inventory with each of them. "Is my carry-on in there?"

"Yep, and your pocketbook."

I looked down at my clothing. "Jonas, I need to change clothes, I can't fly across the country in sweats. I don't even have on a bra. I need to put on some make-up, too."

Mary Jo cracked, "Even an old barn looks better with a new coat of paint." Phoebe shushed her.

"Now you be nice. Stella has helped us get ready and now she needs a minute to get herself ready. You be good, old woman."

I turned away so they didn't see me laugh. I'd play the hurt card for awhile if it would keep them in line.

On the way to the truck, we heard some awful sounds from down the road and Phoebe explained, "Those cows, they bawl and holler all night sometimes. I wonder why they make so much noise. Jonas, do you think they're hungry?"

Jonas told them that the cows got fed every evening but he'd ask the owner, William Bradley, about them tonight. They both seemed satisfied.

We headed back to our house, girls in the back seat under Jonas' supervision. I ran in to change and at least put on lipstick. Good thing. I do not know what he packed for me, but all the make-up I used was still on the bathroom shelf. I dressed in loose fitting khaki pants and a nice warm top and put an extra pair of socks in my bag for the plane. The floor on every plane I'd ridden was cold. I grabbed my laptop, gloves, and a warm parka as I ran out the door.

We made a stop at the ATM to get cash for the three of us going on the plane. It took more time than it should've to insert cards and punch in codes but we got it done. Once we were on the four-lane, US Route 460, I think we all relaxed. Jonas listed all the places we could go to eat and the girls begged for another Whopper burger, so their last meal in our part of the country was at Burger King. They were giddy with delight.

Jonas unloaded us by the curb at the Roanoke airport and parked the car. We got a cart and rolled our luggage to the United Airlines counter to check in. It was a piece of cake. We rode the escalator upstairs and took a seat in the public waiting room because Jonas couldn't follow us to the gate. We sat away from Phoebe and Mary Jo and talked privately.

"You be careful." I was just realizing that Jonas was alone to face Timmy Lee.

"I'll be more focused with you three in the air. Don't worry about me; I'm going to go over to Ben's when I get back this afternoon. May stay overnight there if Timmy Lee hasn't been picked up by then."

He held my head in his hands and kissed me. "I'm going to talk to Mom and Phoebe, then turn and burn it back to the mountain. Call me between flights as often as you can. I want to know where you are every minute."

"Back at you." My voice didn't break but I had to dig deep for the courage to keep it steady.

He stood and reached out to his mother. "Okay, Mom, it's time for me to take off. Give me a hug." She put her arms around him and rocked until he peeled her off. "I'll be back up North to see you in a year or two. We can talk on the phone every few days. Shoot, you get Barbara to teach you and we can see each other on the computer."

219

Chapter 42

"You gonna be all right, Jonas. That Timmy Lee is not going to hurt you."

Phoebe rushed over, "How about a hug for your old Auntie, too?" She hugged and patted him and thanked him for letting them stay in his house. It was time for him to go.

He put his finger in Mary Jo's face and said very sternly, "No drinking, Mom, or Grandma or whatever you want to be called. Why did you get all crazy and want us to call you Grandma anyway?" She blushed like a little girl.

"Because people like their grandmas better than their mothers. They don't know the mistakes their grandmothers made. They like them more."

I was shocked. Mary Jo actually cared about what people thought?

He moved to Phoebe. "No drinking, Aunt Pheebs." She shook her head agreeing.

Then to me, in a fake stern voice, "No drinking, Stella." The women loved it. I threw my arms around his neck and whispered, "I may need a drink." We walked the long hallway to security. I turned back to see if he was gone and he wasn't, he was staring right at me. I was holding an ID, my boarding pass, a purse, and my carry-on, so I waved the only finger free. I sure hated to leave him. He blew me a kiss and I lost sight of him among the people joining the line.

Barrow and the Arctic Ocean from the air. Photo by Olive Nungasuk.

Chapter 43

I Needed to Focus

Jonas

I hated that she was leaving, but the sooner she got Mom and Phoebe home, the sooner that she'd be back. I didn't even wait for the flight to take off. I headed back to Lindside to find Timmy Lee and see that he was locked up tight. Stella was gone and safe and I needed to focus again.

Traffic was moving fast. The road was dry and the sky was blue. Maybe springtime was coming again this year, after all.

I made it home in record time and felt for the pistol under the driver's seat to carry with me into the house. I searched every room, then relaxed and called the sheriff. "Could I speak to Elmer, please?"

The receptionist knew my voice by now. "Yes sir, Mr. Akpik. Just one moment while I connect you."

"Afternoon, Jonas. Did you get your womenfolk on the plane?"

"You know Stella would not like being called womenfolk."

"I wouldn't say that if Stella was around."

"I miss her already. I did get them to the plane, can't help but feel like they are safer in a blasted plane than here on the ground right now. What's happened since this morning?"

"We've impounded the car. Ran the VIN number and the owner lives in Charleston. He says he sold it to a guy about three weeks ago and got paid cash. He just signed the title and gave it to him. So, dead-end there. Our man was still in the hospital at that point, couldn't have been him." My disappointment was beyond words. "We are sending an officer out to get a description of the buyer. It's not much, but it's all we can do at this point."

"Anything of interest in the car?"

"Not much. Some receipts and get this, a donation jar for a kid with cancer. Taken from a Quick Stop in Kentucky. That punk. We've searched the woods and fields near the car, but there aren't any houses nearby so nobody to ask if they've seen him. He's got to pop up somewhere soon, at a house stealing food, hitchhiking, somewhere. You take care, now, don't take any chances."

I hoped it was my house that he popped up in. I wanted to be done with him. There were phones ringing in the background at the sheriff's office and I realized I was taking up time that he could use to catch Timmy Lee. I ended the conversation, "Thanks, Elmer, good luck today."

Ben McDaniel was my next call. This was his day off and I had one burning question that I needed to ask him. He told me to come on over to his house and join him watching March Madness. WVU had barely made the Sweet Sixteen: the final teams involved in college basketball playoffs. Half of Monroe County would be glued to any WVU competition. I went on up to Bob's or Jewell's and bought a bag of chips and a six-pack of Dr. Pepper. Ben would have an extra cold beer if I had the urge.

It was halftime before we talked with any depth. The Mountaineers were far behind and Ben saw the probable outcome might be too much to bear, so he turned the TV off. I knew he'd get curious and turn it back on, but I wanted to get some information first.

"Ben, I need to know something."

"Anything, man, shoot." He was loading up a paper plate with snacks.

"About Anna's death." He brought his plate of chips and dip over beside me and sat down.

"What about it?" The mood swing in the room was tangible.

"Do you think Timmy Lee did it?"

He sat the paper plate on the coffee table and leaned forward. "Jonas, Anna was much loved in this community. None of us wanted to see her in pain for one more day. Cancer was shattering her bones like glass breaking. Any idea how much that hurts? That sweet lady's life had been full of pain even before the cancer."

"What are you saying?"

"I am saying that it was merciful that her life on earth ended." He took a chip, ran it through the dip, and said, "The half of the county that knew Anna agrees with me."

I shook my head. "You're going to have to spell it out for me, Ben."

He put both hands on his knees. "Whoever killed her loved her."

"So what are you telling me?"

He took a deep breath. "I'm saying that her best friend could have killed her. I am proud and thankful that she could and did and probably so is everybody who knew Anna and the circumstances."

"Why do you say that?"

"Her best friend visited her almost every day for thirty years. The only time she didn't was after Anna was dead. For over two weeks."

"Do you think there will be charges?"

"Not a chance. I figure, in general, any sheriff of a small county like ours knows the rumors and all the undercurrents. I would bet my bottom dollar that Elmer is aware of the possibility."

"Okay. Asked and answered. Thanks."

I fell back on the couch, paralyzed that anybody suspected what I had had to be told.

"You okay, Buddy?" Ben was in my face like he was going to ask me how many fingers he held up.

"Yeah, I'm fine. Just getting used to the idea that even the sheriff suspected but not me."

"She's a heller, Jonas. Life is always going to be pretty exciting around Stella."

"I need to think about all this. Plus, I'm beat. Time for me to hit the trail. Hey, why don't you come up my way while Stella is gone? We can have a Saddle-up Saturday marathon of our own. With all the westerns you have on CD and all I have, we can be entertained for hours."

"Sounds good. Meanwhile, you lay low and holler if you need me." He slapped me on the back. "Get some rest, I'll try to keep the cheering down if WVU should happen to score again."

Riley and Sugar met me in the yard and together we put up the other animals. I hit the sack and slept a couple of hours. Barking dogs woke me up and I stood in a darkened door and scanned the horizon. Nothing. The dogs likely were barking at a possum or a skunk. They gave it up in a few minutes and came to me in the door to be patted.

I missed Stella.

The Chukchi Sea coast eat of Barrow (Utqiaġvik), Alaska. Photo by Olive Nungasuk.

Chapter 44

White Wine, Please

Stella

We spent the first ten minutes of the flight mocking Jonas, saying, "No drinking," to one another in deep voices. By the time we landed at Dulles in Washington DC, the joke was old and we sat quietly in the terminal. We boarded the next flight and were seated side by side with me on the aisle and Mary Jo in the middle.

The flight attendant said, "What would you like to drink?"

Mary Jo beamed, "Whiskey on the rocks, please."

Phoebe said, "Me, too."

They both leaned forward to look at me. "Okay, but just one. White wine, please." Both of them giggled and Mary Jo passed her debit card over to me to pay for all three drinks. They whooped it up when she returned with the tray of drinks. We clinked plastic cups together and drank to Jonas and to home and to family. I almost took a selfie of the three of us but decided against it. Even though this foolishness was not a secret, there was no sense in providing proof. I was real sure that one drink was my limit. No more hangovers with these two, somebody had to be alert and in charge.

They had another drink, then a third. I was going to go see the flight attendant about getting them cut off but Mary Jo grabbed my arm and shushed me. She really meant that her voice needed to be quieter. I got it and leaned over to hear her whispered message.

"Don't ever worry about Timmy Lee ever again." She clapped her hands and pretended to cheer.

"Oh, and why is that?"

"Because we put him out on the ice, where bad people get time to find peace."

Phoebe heard part of what Mary Jo was saying and leaned over her sister, clutching her shoulder bag, words slurring and breath reeking of booze, to tell me not to pay any attention to Mary Jo.

Mary Jo looked at Phoebe. "But, we did it, Phoebe." She looked back at me, "We did, we tied him up." She pantomimed wrapping rope around something. "And we put him out on the ice." She clapped again. "He yelled and yelled but nobody comes to help him, the dirty stinking rat."

She was getting pretty loud and I tried to calm her down by listening seriously and holding her hand.

"Phoebe, do you know anything about this?"

She shook her head violently from side to side until I told her to stop, that she was going to be sick. I thought I might be nauseated myself thinking about what Mary Jo was hinting at.

Phoebe got up to go to the bathroom and waved at me to come with her. So I did. We walked back to the bathroom where there was a line waiting, and she told me that the cows were bawling all night and Mary Jo had gotten it into her head that it was Timmy Lee screaming in the woods and in the barn down the road. "She'll be okay, Stella, just go along with her." I left the line and went to my seat.

Mary Jo couldn't wait to get me alone. "He was hiding in my closet, Stella. I hit him with the skillet. WHAP. WHAP." She acted out the skillet whipping. "Then he was out cold and we tied him to the handcart and rolled him out on the ice. He yelled and yelled all night."

"Are you kidding with me?" I held both of her hands. "I need to know the truth, Mary Jo. No more fun, just the truth."

"I tell the truth." She pulled her hand out of my grip and talked behind it into my ear. "Don't let Phoebe know, though, she doesn't want me to tell."

I got up to let Phoebe get back across to her seat. What in the world? Had Mary Jo made this up? Someone else had mentioned closet. Jonas? No, Tisha. Let's see, they had been cleaning the closet. I'd ask Mary Jo about that.

"Mary Jo," I turned on my sweet voice and got her to take off her headphones. "What were you cleaning in the closet floor last night?"

"The stink where Timmy Lee pooped in his pants." She put her headphones back on to watch a movie. Both of them were watching a horror flick and had ordered a fruit tray. Nobody could spend more money on an airplane than Mary Jo and Phoebe.

That answer matched with Tisha's report of Lysol being used to spray the closet, but it was all pretty bizarre. I had a chance to think while they were occupied. On one hand, if they had indeed moved someone, maybe Timmy Lee, out in the cold and left him, he would be in danger. On the other hand, if MJ were making it up, there would be no danger. And if they had harmed Timmy Lee, I didn't want them in trouble. Surely they didn't kill him.

I should've learned that anything was possible with these two women. I decided to call Jonas. Could I even call from the plane? Where were we? I started to hit the call button for the flight attendant and decided that would give it all away to Mary Jo, beside me, and went to the back instead to ask in person.

They suggested I text until we landed in Seattle, within the hour. A call was not likely to get through at this altitude but it would certainly connect upon landing. Before I sent any text, I was going to clear this up one last time. "Mary Jo, where is Timmy Lee right now?"

She didn't look away from the movie, just said, "Barn."

Phoebe must have super hearing or some psychic sense about what was going on. She made the circular sign with her finger as if Mary Jo was crazy as I was waiting for an answer. She had a point, but it wasn't worth the chance if ignoring her would harm someone.

My text to Jonas got through, all right. I wrote Jonas, "Check the barn near your old house for Timmy Lee. The girls may have heard him yelling in there."

An answer came right back, "Why? I thought it was the cows."

"Just do it. Look for a body, just in case."

"What have those two told you?"

"Jonas, just do it. I'll call from Seattle in about an hour. Please go look."

I decided to have another glass of wine while I waited through the longest hour of my life.

Barrow (Utqiaġvik),the "Northernmost American City," and the hub of the North Slope of Alaska. Photo by Daisy Edwardson.

Chapter 45

Probably Nothing

Jonas

I stood in the hallway with my phone lit up rereading Stella's texts.

I decided to call Ben, "Hey man, you still awake?"

He moaned, "Yeah, sorta."

"I just got crazy messages from Stella. Listen to this." I read them to him.

He didn't hesitate. "Damn, man. Let's go."

"Should we call the sheriff? I am still a pretty big target for this crazy man who is somewhere close."

"Well, if someone is lying in that barn and not dead yet, we better get moving."

"Meet me there, give me ten minutes and wait for me before you go in." Ben was right, but I wanted extra manpower, just in case, so I called Elmer's home phone. His wife answered. "Call his cell, Jonas, he is up there with his men searching for that no-good Timmy Lee Davis."

I thanked her and dialed his cell number. He answered with a weary voice. "Johnson here."

"Elmer, any news tonight? This is Jonas."

"We have searched the woods and the fields around the car, rechecked the empty houses in case he backtracked. Nothing. Not a hair of evidence."

"Did you happen to check the old barn in the curve near my house?"

"I think we did a walk through. Why?"

Chapter 45

"Can you meet me there in ten minutes? Stella just texted me to look there, because of some sounds Mom and them heard last night."

"Yes, sir. I'm on the way home, I can stop by there."

I rounded up a good spotlight and pulled on coveralls and boots and hurried around the narrow mountain road two miles or so to the barn.

Ben was already there. "I bet it's nothing. Your mom has gotten excited on that plane ride and made up some wild story." Ben knew about crazy mothers, he had had one, too.

"She was believable enough to convince Stella. Come to think of it, I heard some noises this morning when I picked them up. Both Mom and Aunt Phoebe explained it away with cows bawling. The noises may have created some imagination-based stories for Mom, too. Shoot, I don't know whether to hope for Timmy Lee to be in there or not."

We saw headlights coming around the curve down by the creek and gathered lights and guns and got out of the truck. The sheriff's car pulled in behind us and the other police car pulled in behind him.

"What say, boys?" Elmer looked plumb wore out.

"Not much, Sheriff. Appreciate you meeting us. Not sure what we're gonna find, if anything. Stella says the old girls heard noises out here last night and had some idea that it was Timmy Lee."

He hung his head and I jumped in, kinda embarrassed, "I know, probably nothing, but if there's a chance, we want to rule it out, right?"

"Yes, sir. Let's go. Ivan, I'll take lead, you stay to my right. Jonas, you and Ben follow and cover us."

So we crunched through the crusty mud, newly frozen, to the dark hole of the barn entrance. Beams of flashlights streaked in every direction like a spook house light show. I stumbled over a fallen roof board and three guns pointed at me. We were on edge.

An owl flew and his wings made a muffled sound. I stood still until it was quiet again. Ivan shattered the silence when he bellowed, "I got something! Sheriff, over here, in the corner stall."

I stepped back and turned to go with the others toward his voice but something held me back. I studied the shadows in the corners and overhead in the loft. Nothing moved but I memorized the dark hulking shapes around me.

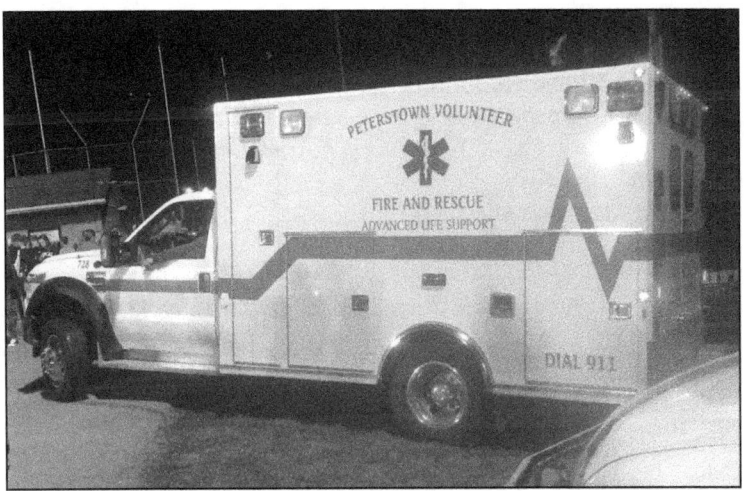

Ambulance. Photo by B. Crabtree.

There was a rustle overhead. Maybe a mouse. Maybe not. A whiff of manure. Odd, no animals in this barn for several years. It wasn't even sturdy enough to store hay. Was it evil I smelled?

Then an electronic beep and the sheriff's voice, clear and strong, "Sheriff to dispatch, we got an 11-41 here, send ambulance to the old barn west of Jonas Akpik's house on Painter Run Road."

"10-4 Sheriff." Her voice was a welcome connection to the world from the darkness.

"Jonas, come and take a look." The sheriff shined his light in front of me, giving me a path to him. I moved forward on unwilling feet and first saw the handle of my wheeled yellow dolly on the stall floor. My eyes traveled the human form on it, tied with an extension cord that could be mine, too. It was a white man, blue around his lips, with a gash on his head. I couldn't tell if he was breathing. I moved around the dolly so I could see his face. Dear God in heaven, it was not Timmy Lee.

"Do you know him?" I felt every man's eyes on me.

"No, sir, I've never seen this man in my life." I felt my way back to the doorway and leaned on a post, then bent over to relieve the tightness in my chest.

I could see flashes as Deputy Long took photos and heard them unwrapping the extension cord and rubbing his bare flesh.

231

Chapter 45

Ben said he had a blanket in the truck and he went to get it. I went with him, just needed some space, but then I was okay. I helped until the ambulance got there.

No clothes, no ID, none of us knew him.

From below, I searched every corner of the loft with my spotlight.

Timmy Lee was still out there.

Chapter 46

I Can't Prove It

Jonas

Ben asked if I wanted to come home with him and sit up awhile until we heard back from the mystery man's condition. I declined, but I wasn't sure what I needed to do. I waited until every vehicle was gone then headed out slowly. On a whim, I swerved into my old driveway to have a look.

Everything looked fine; the motion sensitive lights came on as I approached the house as usual. The lock was undamaged so I pressed in the code and went inside and flipped on the light. The living room was neat as a pin. I was starting to feel ridiculous. Kitchen was a little bit messy, but they might have grabbed a bite as they packed. Bathroom had a pile of towels in the floor. Other than that, it was neater than usual. Probably the way they left it. Big pile of sheets on the floor in Phoebe's room. Mom's room was last. I felt cool air when I opened the door and knew he had been in here since morning. The window was left open. When I finally tore my eyes off it, I noticed a pair of strange boots and a wallet on the bare mattress.

I slipped on the gloves in my pocket and opened the wallet. The first cards were some gift cards for Wal-Mart and Cracker Barrel and a loadable Visa card. Then, bingo, in the back a WV State Hospital ID card for James Jeffrey Gregory. No cash. Stuff had been removed, the wallet had been stretched out bigger than the current load. I sat on the bed to think.

What role did Mom and Phoebe play in this? It was clear that two other people were involved. I needed to get Stella to ask some questions of the women.

She should've called by now. Oh, I forgot, no service here. I carefully put the boots and wallet in a garbage bag, then closed the window and locked it. I hurried up the mountain where I could get a phone call.

Ben called first. The John Doe didn't make it. Stella called while I was on the line with him. I told her there was a body but it wasn't Timmy Lee. She may have snapped because she didn't speak for a very long time and didn't ask any questions. Evidently the girls were not in any shape to shed any light on the situation. They had two more flights to Barrow and getting them on the plane was her immediate problem. We agreed to talk after they all slept.

I texted the sheriff that I had found boots and a wallet. Didn't tell him where. He texted back that they would wait until morning unless I had a name. I sent the name. He thanked me and I sat up in the dark with a pistol all night waiting for Timmy Lee.

At dawn, I tried to wash off the evil that had touched me. I showered and showered and felt better. Elmer came for the boots and wallet. I met him on the deck. He was clean shaven and smelled like Old Spice. Bet he had to wash the evil off often in his job.

He tipped his hat. "I'm gonna need to talk to your mother and aunt, Jonas."

"Figured so. Might want to wait a few more hours. They'll sleep awhile."

"Just a technicality, really, but I want to get their statement." He looked at the mountain for a few seconds and asked, "What do you think? Timmy Lee behind this?"

"I think so. I feel it but I can't prove it."

The dead man had contact with him in the hospital. They may have been in cahoots and the deal went bad.

"I don't know, Elmer. I wish we knew where Timmy Lee was."

"I expect he's long gone, Jonas. Can't prove that either, but my gut says so." He took the garbage bag and drove off into the sunrise.

Chapter 47

Inconclusive

Sheriff Elmer Johnson

The statement by Mary Jo Akpik was inconclusive. The one from Phoebe Akpik confirmed that Timmy Lee Davis had hidden in a bedroom closet at their residence, had been discovered and force was used to subdue him. He was transported to the barn later that same evening by the two women. No charges were filed.

Timmy Lee's fingerprints were present on Mr. Gregory's boots and wallet. So were Mr. Gregory's but no one else's. We got the information back on Gregory's car and put out an APB. Got a hit in Panama City, Florida. A preacher said he had bought it from a lay speaker. The lay speaker has not been located.

Jonas

Timmy Lee is still out there, but seems like I can forget about him from time to time. Spring is turning into summer. Baby lambs are everywhere. Stella is planting a garden. She talks to Josie from time to time and is scheming up a visit from her, but they don't think I know. Tisha's baby boy graduates from high school next week. Eliza and Stella are planning the party.

I talk to Mom once a week. Some weeks are better than others for both of us.

Chapter 47

Stella

All I could remember from the phone call with Jonas was, "There is a body in the barn, but it's not Timmy Lee." I gasped even remembering it.

My sessions with Preacher Booth probably need to be twice a week or maybe every day until I can find some peace and quiet in spite of Timmy Lee being on the prowl.

The girls are safe, living in the Senior Center in Barrow. Away from daily family interactions, they are behaving somewhat better. The sheriff took telephone statements; Mary Jo's so disjointed and spattered with Inupiat words, he couldn't make sense of much of it. They are not in any legal trouble.

I cried when I left them and Phoebe told me not to worry, she would take care of Mary Jo. Mary Jo said, "Worry plenty, there's men here." She jerked her head sideways at her sister.

Mary Jo

Azaa, I know good and well that was Timmy Lee in the closet and Timmy Lee that I whacked with a skillet and Timmy Lee that we left in that barn. I tell you one thing: that skinny old white man comes up here to my hometown, I will make arrangements to leave him on the ocean ice. For real.

Phoebe

I knew Mary Jo would tell. Crazy old woman. I hope she forgets it all soon before her big mouth gets us in trouble with the law. I like our room at the Senior Center and I am talking to an old man in the cafeteria at lunchtime. Aarigaa!

Timmy Lee

I'd never been so glad to see anybody as I was to see my old nurse, Jeff. He'd put a tracking chip in the old car and followed it to find me. Turns out he was a pro at tracking people that owed him money. Lucky for me, because when he found me, I really needed a hand. My body was stiff from the cold. My nose and eyes were still raw and burning from the bug spray. When I told him I had his money in my inside pocket, he cut me loose and unwound a hundred feet of extension cord, so cold it stayed in a coil. I really thought I had a thousand dollars in my jacket and I was more surprised than he was when it was gone. Those damned mean old ladies; they must've stolen their money back.

When there was no moola, he got all mad and wanted to fight. His knife swiped me because I was too slow to jump out of the way in time. I warmed up enough to pick up a board and cold-cock him in the head, then I pounded him with it and tried to ram the sharp end through his gut. But, I didn't hit him in the face. His face was kind to me and I remembered that. I regret throwing his knife in the loft, but I did. His car keys were in his front pocket and his wallet was in his hip pocket. I took them and his boots and drug him up on the dolly and wrapped the extension cord around him, not that he was going anywhere soon. He was still breathing, though. I checked.

After I took his driver's license and insurance card from his wallet, I left it and the boots on the bed at the old ladies' house. Maybe the country bumpkin sheriff would pin this on them.

I still owed Stella and Jonas. Those old Eskimo women just might be in trouble, but I think I was square with Jeff. Ole Jeffo. If he wasn't dead, I bet he damn sure wished he was. Yee Haa.

I was going to quit making deals with God. I told him that if I got out of that closet alive, I'd straighten up, maybe even spread the gospel again, but I got out of it on my own, complete with Jeff's car and papers, so I don't figure on changing a damn thing. Except maybe location. Where was God those two nights I was in that cold cabin? Sending snakes and demons in the night, not helping me. I figure I'll look for God down south in the sunshine.

Southern sunshine at Myrtle Beach, South Carolina. Photo by Refocus Photography.

If you enjoyed *Hung Over with Grandma*, you won't want to miss Becky Hatcher Crabtree's next novel featuring Stella and Jonas and their life together.

Look for *Hung Over with Grandma* at beckycrabtree.com.

Meanwhile, for a first taste of their future, turn the page and catch up with Stella and Jonas and Timmy Lee a year or so later.

If you liked this story and haven't read the prequel, *Drunk on Peace and Quiet,* check it out at beckycrabtree.com.

Drunk on Peace and Quiet received an Eric Hoffer Book Award honorable mention in 2016 in the E-Book Fiction Category.

Samples Sections from Upcoming Book

People living on Peters Mountain keep up with the phases of the moon and enjoy the quiet that is only interrupted by Mother Nature: rolling thunder, whistling wind, yipping coyotes and the like.

If Stella and Jonas never needed to step off the mountain, they would be completely content. The advantages were countless. Their dogs could run free, rich soil grew whatever they planted, and the natural bounty of their little slice of heaven sustained them physically and spiritually.

On the other hand, Stella was studying on one of the minor disadvantages as she did spring yard work. She had picked up bone after bone, all part of a deer carcass the dogs had dragged in out of the woods. She was tired of seeing the bloody, hairy bones and tripping over them and throwing them into the high grass where the dogs found them and dragged them back into the yard. She was finally gathering them up and disposing of them by tossing them into a sinkhole in the nearby barnyard.

It was a huge sinkhole, eighteen feet across and sometimes ten feet deep, divided into a pond and a running stream by a bridge made with silt deposited by the same flow of water that had eroded the underlying limestone. This sinkhole came and went over the years, emptying and refilling as the underground water changed direction. Grass grew on the silt making the mud look solid. The wet places teemed with life: snapping turtles, snakes, and tadpoles. Birds nested nearby and deer and raccoons got close enough to drink from the edges. Sheep and goats drank there and skirted safely around the danger of getting stuck. The silt acted just like quicksand so animals were cautious. She heaved all the bones, even the antlered skull, into the sinkhole, admired the pile of pick-up-sticks made of bones for a moment as they sunk a little in the soft silt, and went in to wash her hands and start supper.

Jonas noticed when he came home from work. "Nice to walk through the yard without looking at the earthly remains of Bambi." He chuckled and Stella got that he was making fun of her fondness for animals.

"Oh, quit. Those bones had been in the yard so long, I felt like I knew that deer."

"What became of the head? Those antlers might be worth something to Bill, that artist over at Ballard. I'd like to give 'em to him."

Stella rolled her eyes, "Well, the head is in the sinkhole, too, but if you treat me real nice, I might get a long stick and dig it out for you." She turned from the stove where she was making gravy and he caught her in his arms.

"Real nice, huh? I think I can arrange that." They kissed until the gravy bubbled dangerously close to sticking to the bottom of the black skillet, then she pushed him away and they sat down to supper.

The next morning Stella returned to the sinkhole with a long branch to fish out the skull for Jonas' artist friend. The sky was dark and she knew rain was on the way but she was determined to retrieve the skull. One antler was sticking out of the silt and reflecting in the muddy water. She tip-toed near the edge and tested her weight on the lower end of the silt bridge. Nothing doing, she thought, so she backed off and tried the ten-foot-long branch to dig under the skull to flip it out of the mud. Success! Then she tried to drag it nearer to her and inched forward to reach it. She took one step too many and with a sucking sound from the mud, her leg sunk up to her knee.

This will be funny someday, Stella told herself, but not quite yet. She reached the skull and tossed it onto safe ground before she tried to pull her leg out with her hands. No luck. It was early morning. Jonas had left for work, the dogs; Riley and Sugar, were nearby. Birds were chirping faintly. The sky was darkening. She sat with one leg and hip safely behind her on the edge of the hole singing a little bit of the Beatles "Oh-blah dee, Oh-blah dah, life goes on ..."

Her voice warmed up, she yelled "Help! Help! Help!" but no one answered. She figured no one was within a mile, but it was worth a try. Finally she remembered the cell phone in her hip pocket. She stared at the numbers. Too embarrassed to call Jonas at work, she called Eliza, her friend, secretary at the Lindside School.

"Lindside School, can I help you?"

"You most certainly can. This is Stella and I am stuck in a sinkhole and I need a little help to get out."

Eliza laughed. "Good one. Kinda busy here, what do you really want?"

242

"I am not kidding! Please call somebody who can get me out of here. One leg has sunk all the way to my, well, upper thigh."

"Are you hurt?"

"No, just stuck."

"Where are you?"

"At the edge of the sinkhole." Stella had spoken calmly but then shrieked. "There's a snake in the water. I see it wiggling away. Keep talking to me, Eliza."

"If it's going the other way, that's a good thing. Where is the sinkhole?"

"Behind the house in the barnyard we use for the ram. He is still in with the ewes this spring, so that is one less worry, I guess."

"Listen, I have to get off the phone to call somebody to help. I'll call you right back. Be brave, Honey."

The phone clicked. Stella was alone again.

Her stuck leg was getting cold and starting to cramp. She hummed the song from Jeopardy because she knew it lasted a minute then hummed it again before the phone rang.

"Hello, are they coming?" Stella's voice was pitiful.

Eliza was a pillar of strength. Dealing with school emergencies for years had given her a calm, no-nonsense demeanor in the face of fire, flood, wet pants, teacher tantrums, just about anything. Her tone was curt and professional. "I called 911 and gave them directions, you know how these new addresses have messed up things. They are on the way but it will be a while before the boys get to the firehouse, get the truck and then get on the mountain. I can talk a minute, but I have a late bus and lunch count to do. Hang on a few minutes; I'll call you back."

"I am okay. If I see another snake, I'm calling back for you to talk me through it." Stella's voice was firmer. She knew what she could and could not take.

* * * * *

The white-haired man shaded his eyes watching the angry Atlantic waves curl up and fall over, crash, and spread out in a soft fan of water. "Just like my life," he thought. "Anger, fight, get over it. Anger, fight, get over it." The pattern never varied and he seldom tired of watching it.

His life was currently in the "get-over-it" stage after a particularly nasty family event, a murder, in fact. He was accused and charged. That was the anger phase followed by his brief wintertime trip seeking revenge. He had completely lost control and that fight had ended badly. The main injustice, he felt, was that some guilty folks got off scot-free.

The man shrugged. All he could do was done. He knew he was getting over it, had been for a year or so. It helped to have a new name and a new life in a warm climate.

Even though it was early morning, the sun was warm on his shoulders. He sat on the sand dune partly hidden by sea grass until the sun was well above the ocean, reflecting off the water like a glaring light. It was nearly eight on Sunday morning, time for him to go. He stood and dusted sand off the seat of his linen pants. His congregation would be soon be arriving.

Preacher Jonathan Wesley walked three blocks inland to the little block building that he'd painted pure white, paused under the steeple and cross that he'd built and unlocked the door. He pulled open one side of the double door and felt the air cooled by air conditioning whoosh out into the heat. His flock would be arriving soon. Mostly people with rough pasts, but he knew just what to say to them.

They didn't have Sunday school, just preaching. He could only handle one sermon a week. Besides, he needed the one classroom for a home, or for what passed for one. A bed, a chair, a TV and a shelf for books and papers were all he needed. He'd used an insulated cooler as a refrigerator for months until he found a dorm fridge on the curb after a big party during spring break. Tourists and college kids threw out a lot of valuable stuff. He'd lived on the proceeds for months, sleeping under empty houses and funding food by gathering and selling items that were put out for the trash truck. He felt like it was a penance for his part in harming a nurse who had helped him back in West Virginia. He'd sung gospel music on weekends and a church friend had encouraged him to preach. She was an evangelist and helped get his ministry started, even paid the rent for the first few months so he could fix up the small Freedom Chapel formerly known as "Myrtle's Tees."

Myrtle Beach and Freedom Chapel were feeling more and more like home to Preacher Wesley. He prayed at the homemade altar, asking for forgiveness as he did every Sunday morning and for God to give him strength to fight off the feelings of unrest and discontent that were creeping back, the same feelings that had gotten him in trouble so many times before. He wanted to keep the "get-over-it" phase of his life in place as long as he could.

The first members of his congregation were entering the church and he rose to greet them, a smile plastered on his face.